This one goes to J.D. Streett
One of my very best friends going all the way back to high school.
Many things aren't real.
Friendship, at least in my book, is.

PLASTIC SPACE HOUSE

JOHN F.D. TAFF

TREPIDATIO
PUBLISHING

ISBN: 978-1-68510-096-4 (sc)
ISBN: 978-1-68510-097-1 (ebook)
Library of Congress Catalog Number: 2023947144

First printing edition: December 1, 2023
Printed by Trepidatio Publishing in the United States of America.
Cover Artwork and Design: Don Noble
Edited by Sean Leonard
Proofreading, Cover Layout, & Interior Layout by Scarlett R. Algee

Trepidatio Publishing, an imprint of JournalStone Publishing
3205 Sassafras Trail
Carbondale, Illinois 62901

Trepidatio books may be ordered through booksellers or by contacting:
or
JournalStone | www.journalstone.com

Imagination is the beginning of creation. You imagine what you desire, you will what you imagine, and at last, you create what you will.
  —George Bernard Shaw

They cannot scare me with their empty spaces
Between stars—on stars where no human race is.
I have it in me so much nearer home
To scare myself with my own desert places.
  —Desert Places, Robert Frost

ONE

Harlan spun in the loud, impenetrable dark, unsure if she'd reached the lifeboat hatch or not.

The emergency klaxons squawked over every intercom on the ship, the sound as dense as the darkness. She gasped for breath, and the blaring sirens sounded more and more distant, compressed. Air loss! There must have been a substantial air leak somewhere. Maybe that was what they were sounding for. It made sense.

Where is everybody?

She knew, though, it had to be worse than a small *depressurization event*, as the training instructors had called it. The gravity had failed too, and she tried to right herself as she tumbled down what she hoped was the correct corridor, the one leading to the lifeboats on this deck. She'd seen the way before the lights, too, failed, turning the corner as she felt the ship's artificial gravity release its hold on her. Now she tumbled, not sure what was up or down. She supposed it didn't matter.

The gravity, the lights, the air fails? And yet the sirens are still perfectly fine. Whatever system ran them should be running the entire fucking ship.

Her hand contacted the wide, smooth lip of a doorframe, and she frantically fumbled down its length until she found the control panel. It was as dark as the rest of her surroundings. She wondered where the emergency power was, if this was a simple hull breach.

Unless... Well, best not to think of that right now.

Where is everybody?

Her fingers searched the panel, found the hatch release. She said a silent prayer, turned it with all her strength. The effort sent her twisting in the opposite direction, but the handle rotated easily. She heard the door's mechanism *whirr*, and the panel slid open. Behind it, the lifeboat's internal power kicked on. Lights flickered on, atmosphere regulators *whooshed* oxygen into the craft.

Harlan was upside down in relation to the lifeboat's deck, but she was no longer worried about gravity. It was air she was concerned with; more precisely, the lack thereof. She pulled herself into the craft, sailed headfirst into the cockpit, gasping.

Lifeboats had no proper names, just sets of numbers arranged in aeronautical ergot—Y-57a, J-12b, that sort of thing. But this one bore a name, burned into the inside doorframe by some anonymous orbital steelworker as the lifeboat had been loaded into the *Promise*. the mothership.

Charon, boat master of the underworld. Weirdly, even comically over-named for such a small, utilitarian vessel. As over-named as the mothership, the *Promise*, was undernamed. Harlan mused of all the promises mankind could count on, Charon's were the easiest kept.

Where is everybody?

The cockpit was already warming up, controls and monitors coming online. Lifeboats only offered partial artificial gravity, so she pulled herself into one of the command chairs, strapped in. A series of instructions scrolled across the central screen for anyone not familiar with the function of a USC lifeboat.

She disregarded them. She was part of the *Promise*'s four-hundred-person crew, in the engineering department. She'd been instructed *ad nauseam* on the protocol for use of these vessels. She quickly went through the pre-flight checklist, keeping an eye on the monitor showing the passageway she'd come from, checking for other survivors. But it remained dark and empty, cast in stark relief by the flashing red strobes lining its length.

Survivors. She was keenly aware she was already using that word, though she had no clear idea of the severity of what was happening or even *what* was happening.

Annoyed, she toggled off the lifeboat's echoing of the *Promise*'s emergency klaxons. She needed to be able to think clearly, and they were certainly not helping.

Where is everybody?

Behind and below her, she felt the *Charon*'s ion engines come online. All the indicators on her board signaled readiness, and she made one last check for any stragglers. She didn't want to leave anyone behind—and she certainly didn't want to face a board of inquiry if she left too quickly, with no other colonists or crew aboard the lifeboat.

But she didn't want to hang around here longer than necessary and fuck her own chances of living through this...whatever *this* was.

Where the fuck is everybody?

As her finger hovered over the "Seal Hatch" button, preparing to punch it, a figure tumbled into the corridor.

"Wait!" she heard it shout. "*Jesus Christ, wait!*"

A frantically waving figure appeared from the darkness of the corridor. She watched on the screen until she was sure he was inside, waited one second more, jabbed the button. The hatch slid down and locked, and there was the *hiss* of pressurization within the cabin.

Hurriedly, she pressed a series of buttons, opening the external bay doors on the *Promise*, then withdrew the moorings. She felt a presence behind her clamber into the cockpit, but she was busy.

Now free and clear, the *Charon* squirted into space, like a tiny seed from a watermelon. It rotated until its engines pointed back at the *Promise*, then pushed away.

"What the hell happened?" the guy asked, his voice cracking as he fumbled with the chair restraints, buckling himself in.

Harlan had no answers, turned to acknowledge him with a shrug. Then she keyed the viewscreen monitors to show the forward view. Ahead of them, all around them, stretched featureless black. She pulled a head's up overlay of the *Promise*, receding slowly behind them.

It was tumbling on all three axes, not fast, though it shouldn't be at all. The long, thin craft should have been lancing straight ahead through space. Lights flickered crazily along its hull, and Harlan could make out bursts of something back near the huge engines powering the craft.

Sparks? Fires?

No. Nonononono.

Fire in Zero-G is not good. It coagulates into spheres of flame, tumbling, igniting what it touches—vital electronics, fabrics, human skin. Venting it into the cold of space was the only way to...

As the guy sitting beside her started to ask what they were planning to do, there was a brief, blinding blast of light, a detonation. Harlan gasped, threw up a hand to shield her eyes even as the monitors tried to compensate.

There was no corresponding noise, no blast of sound. Not here, not in space. Just the effacing burst of bright, unreal light, then the blinking, the phosphenes clouding Harlan's vision.

As the flash of explosion died away, she looked down at the controls. They were barely five miles from the *Promise*...where it had been.

Would the distance be enough?

Nope.

The *Charon* shook, twitched like a dog throwing off water. The pulse of the explosion garbled the lifeboat's systems. The monitors went to static, then rebooted. The cabin lights flickered off, then slowly came back on.

When the monitors settled, Harlan flicked through several screens, trying to find the *Promise*...or what was left of her.

Where is everybody?

But there was nothing.

That wasn't entirely true. There was something...a lot of somethings.

The *Promise* had been carrying colonists, four thousand of them, with all of their stuff—clothing and food and shovels and habitat modules and dinnerware and computers and even livestock. All of it and more, schlepped twelve light years away to Teegarden b, a "super Earth" orbiting an M-type red dwarf star in the constellation Aries.

Now, though, they and their stuff were constituent atoms in a cloud of debris seven light years from Earth. The explosion that tore apart the vessel spared nothing.

Harlan and her unknown companion stared, mouths open, at the monitor showing where the *Promise* had been. Crazily, she thought of a documentary crew someday finding its remains, like the wrecks of one of those early sailing ships, where robotic submersibles shone their cold lights on stacks of dinnerware or piles of encrusted gold doubloons or rows of wine-filled amphorae, uncracked, the liquid inside slowly turning to vinegar over the centuries.

Maybe some future expedition might deploy its own robot scavengers to flit within the cloud of debris that had been the *Promise*. Maybe that would happen. Perhaps it would encounter shards of metal, hairbrushes or scraps of clothing, twists of computer wiring or the arm of a child's stuffed bear.

More likely, she supposed, it would encounter rougher stuff, remains of the *Promise*'s crew and colonists a home audience wouldn't *want* to see. Stuff that was a grisly reminder of exactly what dangers lay out here for humanity.

She thought this likely because she suddenly knew it would be all that was left of the human component of the *Promise*.

How did she know?

Because as she and her rescued companion stared into empty space, the blast wave of whatever it was that had destroyed the *Promise* passed over them, carrying with it the remains of everything—*everyone*—on the ship. The sounds of debris raining against the hull sounded like a bad storm on a tin roof.

Maybe most *was* nuts and bolts and scraps of steel.

But what they saw striking the front cameras were chunks of human flesh, frozen crystalline, geodes of blood tumbling amidst the other debris, shattering like rose glass against the lifeboat's hull.

Harlan took some comfort from the fact most of the dead had been asleep.

TWO

Did it matter where they were going or how far from Earth they'd come? Did it matter how many souls the ship had carried? What other, entirely human crap they'd brought out into space with them? Did it matter how long the trip would have taken, how many of them said goodbye to Earth, to families, to lovers and friends, never to see them again?

Did it matter, finally, why they were going? Whether it was for that old human rhubarb of *more elbowroom!* or to escape taxes or the law or even a vengeful ex?

No. None of it mattered.

Maybe it did at one time, perhaps when the *Promise* was being welded together in low-Earth orbit. When its cargo holds were being filled with tennis rackets and garden hoses and vast supplies of socks and underwear, its larders with flour and salt and rice and alcohol and suspended matrices for dairy, meat, and eggs. When its colonists were being put into deep hibernation for the decades-long trip to their new home, no one able to tell them if they'd dream along the route, much less if they'd actually ever wake up.

Maybe even when the ship set off, slowly building speed past Mars, then up, off the ecliptic, zipping past the orbital diameters of Saturn, Uranus, Neptune, and Pluto.

But past this, past distances where the Sun's radiation was little greater than stars many times its distance from where that little ship sailed, vaingloriously pushing toward the theoretical speed of light, it ceased to matter much.

Then, not much farther out from this, not at all.

Now what mattered was survival. Not the kind involving being decanted on a wild, unknown planet that had never known humanity. No, this survival was much more existential in nature, if possible.

Harlan thought it was. She contemplated this, leaning her forehead against the monitor near her tiny new bunk aboard the lifeboat, imagining the weight of the blank, oppressive space outside, cool against her skin.

She could feel it out there, all that vast blackness, formless, dark waves piling up against a pier. It seemed at once to have no depth, like a stage scrim pulled across the audience to hide set changes, and to also recede past distances her eyes could not fathom. A never-ending, eternal rolling out of nothing, of a lack of things. Kind of like anti-reality.

But as she stared into it, she thought she could see things within, components of the dark, twisting like the compacted fibers of a tightly woven carpet. Or worse, like the glistening, noisome cilia of some hideous creature, immense, cosmic in scale, with wriggling tentacles coiling around pulsing stars and dead planets, cold as cataracts.

****

Harlan dreamed of running.

Colonists cycled in and out of deep hibernation during the long trip, and about seven years in, it was her turn to be woken, given a perfunctory medical exam, a quick hot meal and a shower, then shown to her temporary quarters where she'd spend the next two years of her time until the next group of colonists and crew cycled awake.

She'd intended to spend the time completing her nursing apprenticeship onboard the *Promise*, so she'd be a fully qualified nurse by the time she was living at the colony site. Having two or even three specialties was an idea command encouraged, and many of the crew and colonists pursued.

But after one night of sleep in her quarters, two hot meals, and some brief interaction with her medical colleagues—they, too, having emerged from hypersleep—the interior lights of the med lab turned red and a jarring klaxon pulsed through all of the ship's intercoms.

With no pause, she found herself running, sprinting as fast as her sneakers could carry her on metal deck plates not meant for running. She stumbled, trying to pay attention to the pulsating lights embedded in the deck, pointing toward the nearest lifeboats.

A hand helped her up. She remembered a kind face, but in her dream she couldn't recall if it had been male or female, young or old. Someone she knew, or a complete stranger.

Once on her feet, she continued along her previous path.

The lights went out. Then, the gravity.

After, she remembered everything.

Quite well.

So, the dream ended.

****

Harlan's new best friend identified himself as Jaime Escondido, a colonist who'd also been awakened for this cycle. He was as fresh, as clueless, as she was. And like her, he was not disposed to talk much.

What was there to talk about? Their ship had apparently exploded light years from Earth, light years from their destination, apparently killing everyone except the two of them.

Where is everybody?

The *Promise* was home to forty-four hundred people, colonists and crew. And there were only two people left from all that humanity? She couldn't accept it.

Harlan scanned every working frequency for short-range com traffic, found nothing.

They'd certainly seen no other lifeboats launch from the *Promise*, though they told themselves it was still possible. That others had been able to get off the doomed ship, perhaps with damaged communications systems.

The farther they came without hearing anyone, though, the less likely it seemed.

It was more possible they were the only two left of more than four thousand people.

After a few hours spent searching up and down the bandwidth for other signals, their ears straining to catch every discernible pop, click, or pattern that could be a sign of other survivors, they drifted out of the cockpit.

Harlan let the onboard AI—a fairly stupid thing—autopilot the *Charon*. She went to curl up on a bunk in the forward cabin, behind the cockpit.

Jaime wandered away to be alone, through the galley, into the rear cabin.

They hadn't exchanged more than twenty words since they'd met.

****

When she awoke, she was momentarily disoriented. She thought she was being drawn out of hibernation again and experienced a profound wave of relief that everything she could recall was a dream. Some stupid hypersleep nightmare, induced by one of the many bizarre chemicals they ran through sleepers to keep them comatose.

But as her mind cleared, she realized she was stretched out on a bunk in the empty cabin of a lifeboat. It all came back, and she huddled her legs up, shivering there on the bed.

What cleared her mind more than anything was hunger. But everything else seemed important, clamoring at her for attention. What was the plan now that she and Jaime were alive? Where would they go? That last question pulsed hotly in her mind, disturbing. She figured first things first. Hunger. Address it, then let the other chips fall where they may.

Sitting up, she gathered her strength, went into the cockpit to check on the ship's status.

"What's the situation, ummm... Do you have a name?" she asked the AI.

"I don't have a name. You may call me anything you wish. May I address you as Harlan?" the androgynous voice asked.

"Sure. Let's call you... How about Charles?"

"Excellent. Where on a scale of one to ten would you picture me, with ten being feminine and one being masculine?"

Harlan rolled her eyes. "I'd rather not picture that, Charles. You decide."

There was a slight pause.

"My name is Charles," it answered, adjusting the tone and timbre of its voice to be definitely masculine. "Would you like a status report now, Harlan?"

"Yep."

"The ship is now significantly off course from the planned navigational vector of the *Promise*. We are cruising at approximately .12 light speed. No course has been set, so I have simply stayed on the course we were on. I have not detected any other vessels in our sensor range. I have also not detected any signals suggesting additional survivors of the *Promise*."

Harlan let that sink in, then slapped the doorframe.

"I'm headed back to the galley to see what desiccated nonsense there is for me to eat. You stay here and keep the ship on this course until further notice."

She turned to head for food. "Oh, and thanks, Charles."

"You're welcome, Harlan. Have a pleasant meal."

****

The food printer larders were stuffed to overflowing. Lifeboats were designed to house forty people for ninety days. A lot of food, but it only served to remind Harlan they were way more than ninety days out from Earth. That pulsing red light in her mind flashed and flashed.

Lifeboat seemed as over-named now as *Charon* did before, though the latter didn't lie about the promise it offered.

She ignored her inner red light, stepped to the printer terminal. Harlan input her meal choice—ravioli—and found dinnerware to use while it printed. When it signaled its completion, she removed the bowl from the machine, smelled it. Rich tomato sauce and basil steamed into the room, and she breathed it in agreeably. It offered a tether to reality, something familiar in all this, a real-world smell different from metal and pleather and processed air.

In the main room of the galley, she placed the tray onto a table and went to the wall-mounted drink dispenser. Anything could be made from the excess water the engines threw off—*powdered* anything. She selected Coke, of all things, and it fizzed into the glass she'd jammed beneath the dispenser.

She'd barely lifted a fork when Jaime came into the room.

"Didn't know I was hungry until I smelled it," he said. "Wasn't expecting that kind of food on a lifeboat. Thought we'd be subsisting on noodles and water."

"It's not bad," she said, twirling her fork in the air, chewing a hot mouthful of the stuff. "And we've got a lot of it. More than enough, but also not more than enough, if you get my meaning."

The smile on his face faltered as he realized what she meant.

Without another word, he drifted past her into the galley.

****

They ate mostly in silence. Harlan cut each of her ravioli into dainty pieces, chewed them methodically. She'd glanced with some interest at what Jaime had returned with—steak, potatoes, green beans.

Uninspired, she thought. *Might as well have printed lobster with drawn butter.*

She finished, placed her tray into the recycle window, topped off her glass of soda before returning to her seat.

She watched him finish, didn't say anything.

He looked to be about thirty or so years old. Brown skin, black hair. Thin; wiry, really. His face seemed pinched and severe, mean. But his eyes seemed kind.

She wondered where he was from, what had brought him out here.

And, in a somber flash, *who* he'd brought with him.

Who he'd lost.

Nice thing about being part of the crew and not a colonist, she thought. *I didn't lose anyone I cared about.*

She frowned, dismissed it, thought it uncharitable and kind of ghoulish now.

"What, you don't agree with my meal choice?" Jaime asked. "You a vegan or something?"

"Good god, no," Harlan said. "My sister was vegan. My mom always asked if she thought god put all those animals on Earth just to cover it in shit."

Jaime chuckled, but it sounded dark. Harlan supposed it was, supposed she knew why, and left it. "So, you know my name. What's yours?" he asked.

"Harlan Rose Nickerson. My parents named me after their two favorite things. His was KFC. Hers were roses. Obviously, they had different priorities. Marriage didn't last, but here I am."

Jaime appeared confused. "KFC?"

"Old chicken chain restaurant in the States. Thought everyone knew them."

"No, not big where I'm from."

"Kentucky Fried Chicken?" Harlan said. "Colonel Harland Sanders was its founder."

"Harland?"

"My dad thought dropping the d at the end made it sound more feminine."

Fact was, she hated the name, hated having to tell the story. But she figured they'd have so much time to talk, best to get it out of the way early. Besides, that left plenty of time to tell him her nickname through much of childhood had been "Chick."

KFC had been bigger in her part of the world.

"So, what's going on, Harlan?" Jaime asked.

"I dunno."

"What are you thinking?"

"Well, bad thoughts," she finally said.

"Couldn't be any worse than those I'm thinking," he said. "Wanna share?"

Harlan shook her head.

"Well, I guess we'll have plenty of time to talk before they come rescue us," Jaime said, pushing his tray aside. He'd only eaten about half of his meal.

Harlan tried to edit her expression, but she couldn't before he saw it.

He didn't respond, but he apparently knew. He swallowed, leaned back in his chair.

"Okay, here are my bad thoughts, since you must know," Harlan said. "We're, I dunno, seven or so light years from Earth. Charles?"

"Seven point three eight three light years," came the AI's voice, startling Jaime.

"We're on a standard USC lifeboat cruising away from help at about one-tenth lightspeed. Our provisions—well, food—are designed for forty people at ninety days. So, plenty there for two of us. Water is unlimited, as is basically power. I mean, it's not, but it'll outlast us by centuries. That leaves air, and there's where we run into bad news."

"You were part of the crew, right?" Jaime interrupted.

"Engineering, yes. You?"

"Ag specialist," he said. "Gonna be a farmer on Teegarden."

"Okay, so...air. The air is produced from some of the insane amounts of water produced by the engines. But that's not the problem. The problem is carbon dioxide, which is building up in the air all around us. The onboard scrubbers do a fantastic job of removing it, but guess what? They clog and become useless after a while."

"This is beginning to sound not good," Jaime said, raising an eyebrow for effect.

"The filters can be cleaned. It's an arduous, time-consuming process, but as I said, we'll have plenty of water. But we can't clean them as efficiently as we might on, say, Earth, or at least a larger ship. They need to be cleaned every month or so. With two of us, it means we can probably stretch that out to maybe every six months or so. Which is great. But they degrade with each cleaning. Two, maybe three cleanings is probably all we're gonna get, which gives us something like eighteen, maybe twenty-four months if we're lucky. That means we might have as much as, I dunno, maybe two years of usable air."

"But as we both know—" Jaime began.

"Yeah, about that," Harlan said. "This boat's rated for maybe .15 lightspeed, not much more, at least not sustainably. At that rate, we're eight years from even the barest frontiers of human-explored space, where we could reasonably expect someone to not only hear us but be able to get to us. Two years, I probably don't need to point out, is substantially less than eight."

"What about Proxima Station? It's closer than Earth. What, about four light years?"

Harlan shook her head. "No, you're thinking everything's lining up in a nice, straight, two-dimensional line. Doesn't work that way. Say I'm Earth. Teegarden's twelve light years over here," she said stretching an arm out. "And Proxima Station is four light years over here."

Her other arm shot out in a completely different angle and direction.

"Besides, there isn't enough Earth presence at Proxima to mount a rescue mission. Even if there were, it would still take them three years to get to us. And we'd be dead for about a year. So…"

"Hibernation pods?"

Harlan shook her head. "Not aboard lifeboats. Forty units would take too much room, much less their power draw."

Jaime's eyes narrowed. "There aren't even hibernation pods on this boat?"

"Nope."

"Then these aren't *lifeboats,* are they?"

"Nope. They were meant for two things. A minor shipboard failure, where crew and colonists could offship while repairs are made, then reboard relatively soon thereafter."

"And second?"

"Psychological wellbeing. Wouldn't want our intrepid colonists signing up thinking they were on a ship with no lifeboats, now, would we?" Harlan said, trying to lend a jaunty, comical tone to her voice.

It fell flat.

"It was assumed prospective colonists would do the math on their own," she shrugged.

"Are you kidding?" Jaime asked.

"Oh, it's worse than that."

"Well, okay, so we don't have plenty of time," said Jaime, finally smiling.

Harlan tried to smile, but she was sure it looked funereal.

Silence followed, grew.

"Holy shit," Harlan yelped, staring past Jaime into the open doorway leading into the rear cabin, where the bunks were.

Jaime turned in his chair, sent himself spinning in the low gravity.

There, silhouetted against the dim lights of the back of the lifeboat, was another.

A *third* survivor.

Jaime turned back to Harlan.

"Well, that's probably gonna detract from your air calculations."

THREE

"Where the fuck did you come from?" Harlan said, standing and taking a step or two back. Jaime, too, leapt to his feet.

The new survivor was a woman...or a girl, it was hard to tell. She was small, thinly built, dark-haired. While she seemed like an adult, her face looked smooth and unlined as a teenager's. But her arms moved before her, hands crisscrossing in and out of the space between them as if weaving threads.

And her eyes...

They belied the smooth, unlined face, seemed to be someone else's, someone with vastly more experience and knowledge.

"My name is El, I'm a colonist on the *Promise*," she said. She seemed groggy, just awakened, but her words were hurried, clipped, adding to her erratic hand gestures. This all combined, counterintuitively, to calm Harlan, lead her to believe this girl probably had as little idea of what was going on as they did. Maybe. "We were going to—"

"Yeah, surprise, we were on the fucking *Promise*, too," Harlan said, allowing fear to heat up her response. "How did you get *here*?"

El seemed confused, unsure. "Where is *here*?"

"Here!" Harlan shouted. "On this lifeboat!"

Jaime raised his palms to Harlan. "Whoa there. Let's all calm down now. Look, we need to know how you got onboard before the ship exploded."

"Ship? What ship?" El asked, visibly confused, her hands still weaving in the air before her.

"The fucking *Promise*!" Harlan said through clenched teeth.

"The *Promise* exploded?"

Harlan let out an exasperated howl, turned away.

"Yeah, the *Promise* exploded. We seem to be the only survivors. Well, Harlan and I seemed to be the only survivors, until you appeared," Jaime said.

"Yeah, until you appeared in a lifeboat that was security sealed until I opened it, as the fucking air was leaking out and the fucking gravity was giving way," Harlan said, moving toward El with each word.

Suddenly, one of El's hands darted behind her back, returned with a needlegun.

Harlan froze. Jaime's eyes widened, but El neither aimed the gun in anyone's direction nor did she in any way act as if she had it.

"And now she has a gun," Harlan said, raising her own hands and taking a cautious step back. Guns were a rarity in space. Only the military officers aboard carried them. Any others were secured deep in cargo, to be used more for uncooperative indigenous wildlife (and, Harlan supposed, uncooperative indigenous *sentient* life) and other colonists. Because, you know, Humanity.

"Where'd you get that?" Jaime said.

"I don't... I..." El let the gun droop in her hand until its slender tip pointed toward the bulkhead.

Jaime half turned to Harlan, feinted she realized in the moment, then spun on the slight girl. He strongarmed her gun-bearing hand, forced it away and down. There was the soft *whup!* of the gun firing, the crystalline *tink!* of its glassine needle hitting the steel wall. Its delicate bullets were made to pierce human flesh and introduce a paralyzing agent into the bloodstream. There was absolutely no danger of it penetrating the steel of the lifeboat's skin. In that, it was the perfect weapon for space travel. Still, the sound of it striking metal, however slight, made Harlan flinch.

Jaime disarmed El, stepped away from her. The girl seemed to sag, her body collapsing in on itself even more.

"Now what?" Jaime asked, not bothering to hold the gun on El.

****

Harlan passed the collapsible tumbler to Jaime. He took it, sniffed.

"Where'd you get whiskey on a lifeboat?" he asked, taking an experimental sip.

Harlan cracked her neck, stared at the black expanse of the forward screens. It was so featureless out there, the stars so distant and small, she half wondered if they were even on.

"Well, there's plenty of water from the engines. Whiskey's a simple chemical compound, with some phenolics, aldehydes, and lactones for flavor. Pretty easy for the printer to formulate actually," she said.

"Okay, what I was asking is *why* there'd be whiskey on a lifeboat's food printer system?"

"Psychological wellbeing, remember?" she said, chuckling as she took back the tumbler, drew a sip through gritted teeth. It reminded her of being in her father's den, bookcases and wood wainscotting and battered leather recliner. And, of course, her father.

Her wonderful, wry, entirely disapproving father.

She knocked back a second drink, passed the tumbler to Jaime.

"What are we supposed to do with her?" he asked, nodding to the open door behind him. "She can't ride out however long we have left zip-tied to a bunk."

"I know," Harlan said, twirling the cup in her hand. "I... How did she get in here? And how did she get a gun? A gun, for chrissake. Those things are kept under tight wraps. Tighter than...well...you know. Things that are tight."

She felt herself blushing, and a wave of frustration washed over her at that unbidden emotion. Jaime eyed her but didn't let on he'd noticed.

"Security has them. *Had.*"

"Yeah, and that's about it. Until the colonists landed. I guess the powers that be thought we'd have no need to shoot at anything until we landed to, you know, bring human civilization to Teegarden b."

"Here's to human civilization," Jaime said, taking another drink.

"Hey, Charles," Harlan asked. "Do you have access to colonist records?"

"Limited to the crew roster and passenger manifest," the AI said. "Basically name, rank, occupation specialty."

"Check for someone named 'El.'"

"One record. Haugen, El, 29 years old, Winnipeg, Canada. Colonist, Psychiatrist. Part of a familial group including Lars Haugen, 37, brother—"

"What did you think? That she really was a stowaway, not a colonist or crew?" Jaime said.

"Well, maybe something more like, 'Haugen, El, 29 years old, Winnipeg, Canada. Known saboteur and bomb expert.' Something. Anything."

"Was she awake or in hibernation?" Jaime asked.

Harlan looked at him in annoyance.

"I don't honestly know why I asked," he said.

But Charles' answer stilled her response.

"El Haugen was three years into her hibernation cycle at the time of data loss," Charles said.

Harlan took back the tumbler of whiskey silently, lifted it to numb lips.

****

Harlan left Jaime stretched out in the co-pilot seat in the cockpit. The whisky and the pressures of the day had caught up with him, Harlan supposed, and he'd literally passed out. She didn't have the heart to wake him, so she eased around him, his face pressed against one of the consoles.

The main room of the lifeboat was quiet. Harlan could feel the dull throb of the engine beneath the thin soles of her shoes, could hear the dim background hiss of the atmosphere regulators regenerating the air in the room. That made her think of the scrubbers, which made her think of the limitations of the lifeboat, which made her think...

She went slowly into the room, the lights coming on at her motion. There, at the back of the room on one of the bunks, lay their...*what? Stowaway* didn't sound fair. Harlan supposed it wasn't that El *wasn't* supposed to be here after the destruction of the *Promise*. Technically, she was as much a survivor as Harlan or Jaime.

Still, Harlan knew how she and Jaime had arrived. She had no idea how El had gotten onto a lifeboat that had been sealed when Harlan had activated it. It wasn't like the *Titanic*. You couldn't crawl under the canvas tarp stretched over the opening of the lifeboat. To gain access to a lifeboat aboard the *Promise*, there had to first be a Level One Emergency. Check! Unfortunately, there had been one.

Then you had to have your access code. In a Level One Emergency, anyone could access any lifeboat with their personal code. That's how Harlan had gained access to the one they were on now.

But once the protocol for a lifeboat was accessed, they remained open and ready to go until they were launched. In other words, Harlan knew of no way you could gain access, then close the boat up and lock it back down. She supposed it was possible. As an engineer, she knew most anything was possible with the right equipment or software.

But why?

Why would El—or anyone—gain access to a lifeboat *before* an emergency, and then close it up and reset it? Wouldn't you launch it in a panic, as she herself had almost done before Jaime came tumbling in?

And if El didn't gain access during the emergency, it would have set off alarms on the bridge, brought someone down to investigate.

It didn't make sense.

She glared at the tiny figure huddled on the bunk, one pale hand double zip-tied to the metal railing. It looked uncomfortable for her to sleep like that, and she felt a pang of sympathy for the girl. She was scared, out of it, probably hungry.

On a whim, she went to the printer terminal and punched in a cup of chicken and rice soup. Something warm and chickeny always made her feel better. She lifted the hot cup gingerly and carried it over to the bunk opposite where El lay.

As she sat, she noticed something strange. The atmosphere around her seemed to thicken, then ripples spread through it like poking a Jell-O mold. The waves swelled over her, and she could feel them lap against her skin, cold and gelatinous.

She closed her eyes, felt it pulse over her eyelids.

FOUR

When she opened them, she sat for a moment in utter stillness.

The room was bright, and the window was open. A cool breeze swirled in, flouncing the thin curtains. Outside, Harlan heard a dog barking in the distance, the honk of a car. She smelled freshly cut grass and the aroma of grilling meat.

She was in a small bedroom, definitely a young girl's. Perhaps not too different from her own room as a child. Posters of unfamiliar pop bands covered the walls—bland, similarly coiffed people of indeterminate age and sex. A corkboard hung over a desk near the window. Holos of people, faces pressed near the lens, all smiling, all happy.

Harlan picked one face out from the rest.

El.

Harlan looked down, saw she sat on the edge of a simple twin bed, a white quilt covering it. A small shape curled under it, a spray of hair across the single pillow.

She must be dreaming this.

Harlan closed her eyes, took a deep breath. When she opened her eyes, she knew she would be aboard the lifeboat, probably slumped across the consoles in the cockpit, as she'd left Jaime. She knew a whisky headache wouldn't be far behind. She closed her eyes tighter, bore down until it made sinews spring from her neck, her jaw muscles ache.

When she opened them, though, she was still in the afternoon bedroom with El.

She touched the girl's leg.

Solid. She felt it tense beneath her touch.

"El, where are we?"

"My bedroom. When I was a kid."

"No. We're aboard the lifeboat, remember? The *Promise* exploded in space, killing everyone. We're not here. We must be dreaming."

"Do you have dreams like this?" El said, her voice muffled by the pillow.

"Like what?"

"Shared."

Harlan stood, went to the window. She could feel the curtain's sheer material brush her cheeks, could inhale the scent of flowers somewhere out there. The sun coming through the glass warmed her skin.

"Where are we?" Harlan shouted out the window, to no one in particular. From somewhere unseen, the lawn mower stopped growling, and there was silence.

"I don't want to be here," El moaned. "Why are we here?"

"Why are *we* here?" Harlan repeated. "If it's *your* bedroom, *your* childhood bedroom, we're here because of you."

"No," El said, clamping her hands over her ears. "Not because of me. I hate this place!"

Harlan turned from the window, lifted her eyes to the ceiling.

"El, the AI said you were asleep, in hibernation when the explosion happened. So how could you have been on the lifeboat when we got there? It doesn't make sense. And I need something today to make sense."

"Why are you asking me? None of this makes sense to me either. Get me out of here!"

"Charles!" Harlan yelled. "Charles, if you can hear me, where are we? Charles?"

Suddenly, the air thickened again, and Harlan felt like she was in Zero-G, except instead of empty, weightless space, she floated in some medium that slowed, inhibited her movements. She could see ripples spread out from her movements.

And she could hear a voice, something deep and masculine, reverberating, as if she were underwater.

"Charles!" she yelled. "Charles! Wake up Jaime! Charles!"

The axis of the room tilted, the window wall becoming the ceiling, the floor under El's bed sliding onto the wall. But gravity didn't shift with it. The bed and its coverings, the desk near the window and everything on it, spilled to the new floor—once the opposite wall—in slow motion.

El rolled to her feet, untangled from the quilt she'd been wrapped in. Her eyes were wide and wild, her hair a mess of static cling from rolling in the covers.

The room spun again, and this time gravity disappeared completely. Harlan and El floated like pieces of fruit suspended in aspic. Harlan tried to move, to go to El, but found there was nothing on which to gain purchase. The thickness of the medium, the lack of gravity, made it impossible to move.

That wasn't the only thing Harlan noticed was missing.

Air.

Whatever it was that held them there was too thick to breathe. Harlan tried to take a breath, but nothing came in or went out.

She panicked.

Across from her and upside down, she saw the bedroom window. Instead of the bright spring day it had showed moments earlier, the scene was now dark. She tried to focus, saw what showed through the limp, sheer curtains was the main chamber of the lifeboat.

Harlan turned as fast as she could in the dense medium. As she did, the mattress and foundation of the bed tumbled behind her.

Like moving through oatmeal, she bent into a dive position, braced her feet on the slowly rotating bed. Between her and the window, she saw El, the limp quilt billowing around her feet like a shed skin.

Harlan launched herself, pushing off the mattress like a swimmer pushing off the side of a pool. She lanced forward, unfurling to her full length. She struck El mid-body, felt her slight form crumple around her at the impact.

Feeling like Superman, she wrapped one arm around the girl's body, shot the other one forward, fist clenched.

She closed her eyes again, expecting to feel the brush of the curtain, the shatter of glass over her body. She steeled herself against shards of glass slicing her arms, her face.

Blood.

They sailed through the window. There was a weird moment of transition between the thick medium and the regular air of the lifeboat. It crawled across Harlan's skin like formication.

And then she hit the deck, the air pushing out of her, El's limp body hurtling forward. Harlan slid to a stop. She vaguely heard the clatter of chairs, the squeak of a table pushed across the floor.

All was black.

****

Jaime's face floated above hers. He looked confused, concerned, freaked out.

She felt herself being carried to a bunk. His fingers peeled her eyelids back, shone a penlight in them.

A washcloth, wet and pleasantly warm, drifted over her face, down her arms. Across her chest.

Her chest.

With a gasp, she sat up, slapped at the washcloth, grabbed the hand holding it.

She stared into Jaime's startled face.

"Wha...?"

"'Wha,' exactly!" Jaime said. "Whatever it was you two were doing back here woke me up. I came out to all this." He gestured around the room wildly.

Harlan ignored this, focused on what was closest at hand. "And you stripped my clothes because...?"

Jaime held up the washcloth. It was covered in blood.

"And for the record, I didn't remove your shirt," he said, twisting his hand from her grip. "It was basically in tatters. Back me up here, Charles?"

"Jaime is correct, Harlan," the AI said, in a voice calmer than anyone else's.

"I just... Where's El?" she asked. Jaime leaned away, and Harlan could see her zip-tied to the bunk again.

"Well, why'd you strap her to her bed again?"

Jaime frowned. "After all this?" He gestured around the room again, this time over-dramatically. Harlan propped herself up on her elbow, surveyed the room. Two of the rectangular tables were pushed askew, and at least a half dozen fallen chairs littered the area.

Also, blood. A lot of it.

It started near the bunks, where there was a large splat on the floor from which a long smear stretched along the space between the upended tables.

"Jesus," Harlan gasped.

"Look at me here, pretty much agreeing with everything you say," Jaime said. "But look at this too."

Jaime reached slowly for her wrist, lifted her arm gently into view. He had wiped clear a swath of blood. She touched her skin, still expecting to find thin lines, opening into red fissures, gaping at her with dozens of tiny, wet mouths. But her skin was smooth, whole.

"There's nothing. No wounds I can find on you. Anywhere," he said. "Nothing to explain all this blood."

"That's not possible," she replied, tensing, ready to jump from the cot. "All this blood. Shit! It must be El!"

Jaime clotheslined her as softly as he could, forced her back to the bed.

"It's not from her, either. I checked. Neither of you has as much as a papercut."

Harlan felt a little dizzy, pressed her head against the thin pillow behind her.

"How is that even possible?" Harlan asked. "The blood had to come from somewhere, it didn't appear out of thin air."

"I agree, so I'd be happy to entertain whatever theories you might have."

"I have exactly none," she said. "Zero. Zilch. Nada."

Jaime looked at her intently.

"Wanna tell me what was going on?" he asked.

FIVE

Regaining her composure, she realized she was lying there in her bra in front of Jaime. And it wasn't even a good one.

Taking a deep breath, she asked for a little privacy first. Jaime was only too glad to comply. He plopped the bloody washcloth onto a table, then disappeared into the cockpit, closing the door behind him.

With a glance over to El, Harlan approached the printer terminal, swiped through what it was able to replicate. From its rather limited menu of non-food items, she keyed in her code, selected a new t-shirt, underwear, a pair of pants, socks, and shoes. All her old stuff would have to go, it was soaked in blood. Right before she punched the print key, she went back and selected a new bra.

As her new clothing printed, she finished the washing job Jaime had started. Her pants were stiffening with dried blood. She peeled them off, glanced again to make sure the cockpit door was closed, then stepped out of her panties and unhooked her bra. She dumped these into the recycler, then found some sealed washcloths near where the first aid equipment was kept. She ripped a packet open, unfolded the moist material until it was the size of a bath towel. She sat at a table and cleaned herself off as best she could. She knew there was a rudimentary shower onboard—all that excess water, of course—and she'd wash her hair there soon.

But for now, she'd clean off enough blood so she could function, figure out what had happened. When she was done pulling the cloth between her fingers and toes, using its edges to slide beneath her nails to dissolve the dried blood there, her clothes were done printing. She unfolded them from the printer and dressed quickly, all the while moving her eyes from the door to the cockpit and then to El's huddled form.

Dressed, she moved slowly to the bunks, sat cautiously across from El.

"Why do you keep bothering me?" El said. "Wasn't that enough?"

Harlan considered. "Enough of what? I'm not sure what *that* was. Are you saying you caused it?"

El let out a sound like a combination cough and laugh. "Not just me. But yeah, that was me."

"That doesn't make sense, El," Harlan said, frowning.

"It will. Or it won't. It doesn't make any difference, you know. It never does."

Harlan stared at the girl's back, trying to think of what to say next.

"You were a colonist, right? I mean, not part of the *Promise*'s crew."

El rolled over slowly. Her hair was a mess, and there was still dried blood in the corners of her eyes. It had begun to flake, looking like stage makeup at the end of a performance.

"I was both," she said. "A colonist, but also a psychiatrist. Part of the medical staff."

"You look like you're seventeen."

"I'm twenty-nine," she said, then smiled thinly. "Yeah, I know. I look like I rode my tricycle to college. I get that all the time."

"So, do you have a specialty? In psychiatry, I mean."

"Mostly general, but I'm a panpsychist," El said.

"Don't know what a pan-whatever is."

"Panpsychist. And not surprising, even though it's been around for a couple centuries."

"What does a panpsychist do, exactly?"

"It's not what I do, precisely. It's what I believe. For what it's worth right now, I believe in a universe suffused with consciousness. We humans typically believe consciousness exists only in the brains of highly evolved organisms like us. It exists only in our tiny part of the universe and only in recent history. In contrast, panpsychism says consciousness pervades the universe and is a fundamental feature of it."

"It's a feature, not a bug," Harlan said.

"Exactly. Yes."

"And everything is conscious? This bunk? The floor?" Harlan said.

"No, it doesn't mean literally *everything* is conscious, at least not at the same level. But the fundamental constituents of reality—down even to electrons and quarks—have incredibly simple forms of experience. The human or animal brain's more complex experience is somehow derived from the experience of the brain's most basic parts."

Harlan stared at her. "I'm finding it hard to figure out why the planners thought this philosophy was important enough to ship it off to a colony. Unless they were trying to get rid of you."

El grinned.

"The AI says you were in sleep cycle," Harlan asked.

"You mentioned that...before. Yes, I was."

Harlan shook her head in annoyance. "See, that makes as much sense to me as the stuff you were explain—"

"I know!" El shouted, sitting up and leaning toward Harlan, who shifted away. "Don't you think I know?"

"Well, then, I mean..." Harlan said, squinting, then cocking her head in confusion. "How?"

"Like I said."

"Listen, this has been a nightmare," Harlan said. "All of this... It's been a rough day, a long day. Like, Eugene O'Neill long."

"Who?"

"Sorry, my dad collected antique books. I read a lot as a child."

"Okay."

"It serves no real purpose to keep you tied to your bunk," Harlan said, standing and producing a pair of scissors from her pocket.

"Thanks," El said.

"Well, we had to let you go at some point. Couldn't keep you tied up until we get rescued."

The scissors split the thin plastic lines, and El rubbed her wrists together, looking calmly into Harlan's face.

"We're not getting rescued," El said. "No one's coming for us. We're alone.

"All alone."

****

El drifted to one of the food printers, and Harlan decided she needed to wash out the blood matting her hair. She ducked into the shower and stripped off. She watched the water run pink down her body, wondering where it had all come from. She searched over every inch of her own skin, found no breaks, no tears, cuts, or abrasions. Internally? She tasted blood in her mouth, but it was probably the ghost of whatever had caked her lips or smeared across her teeth.

When she was finished and dressed again, she left the shower enclosure. Jaime was seated at a table with El. They had evidently been speaking, but stopped when she stepped into the room.

"Don't clam up on my account," Harlan said, taking a seat next to El.

"Trying to make sense of what happened," Jaime said, twirling what looked like a half cup of coffee on the table.

"Oh, the explosion of our ship or the mysterious appearance of El or the trip to her childhood bedroom or all the blood appearing out of nowhere?" Harlan said. "So much to choose from!"

"You know, sarcasm is the retreat of the angry," said El.

"What do I possibly have to be angry about?"

"Not having any answers," said El.

"Wait a minute," said Jaime in some confusion. "A visit to your childhood bedroom? Am I missing something here?"

"Yeah, we all are, except—" said Harlan.

"Excuse me," interrupted Charles. "Sensors are picking up a ship coming into range."

Harlan frowned, looked up to the ceiling, as if this was where Charles lived.

"A *what?*" Jaime asked. "How can there be a ship out here? Your sensors must be off, damaged from the explosion."

"It is most definitely a ship," Charles said. "I have confirmed the data."

The three looked at each other, then dashed for the cockpit.

****

"The ship will be in visual range in approximately two hours and forty-three minutes," Charles said.

"Is it... I mean, is it human?" El asked. "I mean, from Earth?"

Harlan looked at her as if she had asked the most ridiculous question ever uttered. "As opposed to what?"

"Why don't we lay off the snark for a little while, eh?" Jaime asked.

Harlan rolled her eyes and crossed her arms over her chest.

"Would you like me to answer your question, El?" Charles asked.

El nodded sharply, and he proceeded.

"The ship is too far away to gauge much, but probability is high it is of Earth or Earth-related origin."

"Yeah, since we've not encountered anyone else out here *ever*, I'd say it's a high probability," Harlan said. Jaime flashed her a look, and she shrugged and sighed in return.

"Two hours and forty-two minutes until visual range. How long until it... Wait a minute, is it coming toward us?" Harlan asked.

"The object is moving toward us at approximately point five light speed. It will reach us in approximately four hours and fourteen minutes."

"Could be a rescue ship," said El, turning to look at Jaime, her entire body oozing hope.

"How would anyone know we needed rescuing?" Harlan asked.

"Maybe a patrol...another colony ship?" El said, more to Jaime than to Harlan.

"A patrol? From where? We're not close enough to any Earth colony. And another ship along the same course to the same star? I fucking doubt the planners would waste time and money sending another ship to the same star system until they knew for certain the first made it successfully."

"Look, we've got four hours until whatever it is gets here and we can stop speculating. I don't know about the two of you, but I'm getting some rest in as close to an actual bed as we have here," Jaime said, then left the cockpit.

El turned expectantly toward Harlan.

"I'll rack right here," Harlan told her. She plopped into the seat, raised her eyebrows expectantly at the smaller woman.

El drifted from the cockpit, and Harlan closed the door behind her.

After that, with all the day's experiences and a bellyful of synthetic whisky, she leaned back in the chair, fell quickly to sleep.

SIX

Harlan might have see-sawed into sleep like a falling leaf. Gently, she'd begun to dream.

Maybe it would be a dream about the last few minutes of the *Promise*, floating in sudden Zero-G, panic arcing across every nerve, gasping for oxygen. Perhaps it would be a dream of being in her father's (disapproval!) study, lined with books and smelling of dust and disintegrating paper and old leather. Taking down and reading from the books—first editions, no less!—she was forbidden to touch.

Or something further back, such as her old bedroom in her parents' first house, back in Dayton, with its bunk beds and dressing mirror covered in stickers from cartoons and singers and positive aphorisms her mother stuck there without asking first. Before all the messy divorce and shuttling back and forth and suppressed animosity and measured yet snide messages delivered by each parent to her in the hopes she would report back to the other.

Perhaps something would give insight into Harlan's character or offer some metaphor or clue about what was happening here.

But there was not. Harlan did not.

She fell asleep, but she did not dream. Her lack of dreaming was sheerly stubborn, as if she had palmed the key to her dreams like a stage magician, unwilling to produce it and end the trick, not right now, not for this.

Deep, deep down, perhaps even deeper than Harlan suspected her consciousness went, she was afraid. Afraid of what dreams all of this might unleash, what they would reveal, what they would mean.

She didn't want to know what any of this meant, not really.

She thought, deep down in that well of ur-Harlan, if she knew, if she even so much as caught a glimpse of what was going on, it would unravel her, pulling at the loose thread of her entire makeup, yanking it until the entire suit of her *self* came undone, slid down into that dark, immutable well existing somewhere inside.

Harlan did not want to unravel.

Harlan did not want to know.

So, Harlan did not dream.

Not yet anyway.

****

"The ship is coming into visual range now," said Charles' voice as the three survivors packed into the small cockpit.

"Surely we can communicate with them by now," said El, behind Harlan and Jaime, who were both seated.

"I have scanned every USC frequency," said Charles, no inflection to mark the seriousness of what he said. "And I have found none."

"None?" Harlan repeated. "None at all?"

"Yes, Harlan," he said. "None."

"How is that possible?" she asked, more to herself than anyone.

"There it is," Jaime said, sitting up straight and pointing at the forward monitor.

A slim, needle-like ship came slowly into view, a paunch amidship just as the *Promise*. Presumably loaded with all sorts of stuff, contained within that pregnant guppy belly, unlike the *Promise*'s stuff, which had blossomed out from the explosion like dandelion seeds, hurtled outward and outward.

"Are we hailing them or whatever?" Jaime asked.

"We have been hailing the ship since they came into sensor range, Jaime," Charles said. "There have been no replies."

"How is that possible?" Harlan asked again, this time more forcefully. "How is that fucking possible?"

"Perhaps their com system has been damaged. Perhaps their sensors are down, and they haven't detected us visually as of yet. Perhaps there has been an onboard disaster of some sort, a pathogen or cosmic ray burst that has left the passengers or crew—"

"Okay, alright, let's calm down," Jaime said, staring more closely at the monitor. "Charles, can you magnify the front screen image?"

"Yes, Jaime," the AI said, and the barely there image of the ship expanded into crisp, clear view.

USC Douglas Limen 13 was emblazoned on its hull.

"That doesn't sound familiar," Harlan said. Their ship had been the *USC Promise 8* and was the last operational ship she was aware of. Two additional keels had been laid in Earth orbit by the time they'd left, the *USC Endeavor 9* and the *USC Progress 10*. She supposed that it was possible, if not certain, that USC had built and launched additional ships since they'd left.

But then, how was this ship already here at the same time the *Promise* was? Had Earth discovered the Holy Grail of transluminal engines? If so...wow, but Harlan hadn't heard any indication that they were that close when the *Promise* left.

Still...

Maybe it was a transluminal ship and maybe there had been some sort of accident. And maybe, just maybe, the *Douglas Limen* was intact enough to bring her, Jaime, and El home. Or at least back on track to Teegarden.

"Charles, can you dock the lifeboat aboard the *Limen*?"

"Yes, Jaime. Is this what you desire?"

Harlan opened her mouth, but El leaned in.

"Wait a minute, if there was some onboard pathogen or something communicable, should we dock with it?" she asked. "I mean, can't we tell beforehand?"

No one answered.

"Charlie?" Harlan finally said.

"The ship's atmosphere is intact. Artificial gravity is intact. Engines are operating. Radiation is normal. Automatic systems, such as docking, appear operational. Aside from that, I cannot answer. My limited systems can't detect pathogens in the atmosphere or even life signs. This ship's systems were not designed for these functions."

The three looked at each other as if taking a silent vote.

Harlan sighed. "Dock us with the *Limen*, Charlie."

****

The outside bay doors opened automatically, and the lifeboat glided in, was captured by the bay's mechanisms and brought gently to rest. Umbilical cords connected with the lifeboat's systems.

There was a brief chime in the cockpit, and another voice, this one comforting and feminine, came through the speakers.

"Welcome to the *USC 13 Douglas Limen*. Your craft is now fully docked."

"Before we leave, let's ask the ship's AI what's going on," Harlan said. "Charles, open a line to the *Limen*'s AI to—"

"Unnecessary," came the voice. "I am Trivia, AI for the *Limen*. What is your query?"

"Trivia?" Harlan said out loud, wondering if this were a joke, some crew member's idea of a good guffaw. She couldn't imagine any straight-collared USC captain agreeing to have his shipboard AI named Trivia.

"Yes, my name is Trivia, though you can change this with the proper codes."

"Not necessary right now. What's going on aboard the *Limen*? Can we speak to the crew?"

"The...<<*squark!squeeeee*>>...available. <<*Hisssssssssqueeee!*>>."

"Trivia?" Harlan asked. "Respond."

No response came through, just the white noise of an open channel.

"Charles?" Harlan asked.

"There is no response, Harlan."

"We should all wear EVA suits going aboard, to be safe," El said.

"I'm going back to get the gun," Jaime said, easing up out of the seat and edging around El. "I've grown up with too many horror movies to go onboard that ship without a gun."

Neither Harlan nor El stopped him.

****

The doors whooshed open on a rush of wind that blew against the thin skin of her suit. Harlan stepped into the passageway between the lifeboat and the *Limen*, and Jaime stepped around her, holding the needlegun before him, pointing it this way and that.

"No one to greet us," Harlan noted. "That's not a good sign."

"Why?" El asked.

"These are partly military vessels," Harlan said. "You don't come aboard a military ship without an escort. They'd want to debrief us, figure out why we're here, what happened to the *Promise*. There'd be questions."

"Okay, got it," El said. "So what does it mean?"

Harlan looked to Jaime, said nothing.

They walked forward, stepped into a lift.

The doors closed behind them, and Harlan got what she thought was her last look at the lifeboat that had saved them.

****

Harlan pressed the keypad for the deck the ship's bridge was on. She thought that since she was an engineer aboard the *Promise*, her code would work aboard the *Limen*.

It did. The lift moved, and a slight tone indicated the passage of decks.

No one spoke. They all focused on the moving lights, the dinging tone.

The lift slowed, and another, lower-register tone sounded.

The doors opened onto what Harlan knew would be the reception center outside the ship's bridge. This was an area reserved for the captain to entertain, to greet incoming crew and passengers who had requested to meet with the captain. A place for the crew to unwind after their shifts. A place where these activities could occur without impeding the function of the ship's bridge.

There was no one there.

It was a relatively large room, probably more than twenty meters wide with monitors on either side acting as windows. Clusters of low-back chairs and tables arranged for conversation. Doors here and there led to conference rooms, Harlan knew. A few potted plants helped to define areas. The carpet—thicker and more luxurious than anywhere else on the ship—had the USC logo woven into it at regular intervals.

"Where the fuck is everyone?" Harlan asked, stomping here and there, opening doors. She knew that this part of the ship was continually active. Bridge crew coming off duty, crew going on duty, departmental meetings in the conference rooms, passengers wanting to bug command about ridiculous things. It was always abuzz with people, all the time, even deep within sleep cycles.

There was no one about.

More than that though, there was nothing astray. No overturned chairs or tables knocked askew. No notepads or any other articles left behind. No half-filled glasses or plates with partially eaten food on them. Nothing.

Not a thing—or even a thing out of place—to register the fact that humans are, or *were*, on the ship.

Jaime paused near the reception desk, tried to gain access to the ship's computer.

"I can't access the system," he said. "Nothing. Not even the lower-level stuff I should be able to get to."

Harlan, who felt like hyperventilating, rushed to him.

"Probably wondering why a colonist from another ship would need to access anything here. I'm USC. Let me try."

Harlan input her code, which was greeted by an electronic *sqronk!* She input it again. *Sqronk!* And again. *Sqronk!*

"Fuck," she said. "It won't let me in either."

She looked over to the security door that she knew led to the bridge.

"Well, let's knock and see if anyone's home," she said, striding to the door. Jaime followed, gun raised.

She spared one look back.

"I wouldn't be waving that around when the door opens," she said. "I know these space grunts, and they don't take kindly to weapons aimed in their direction."

Harlan input her code on the door's pad.

Jaime did not lower his weapon.

****

The door swooshed open onto a room every bit as empty as the lobby.

The bridge was roughly U-shaped, with stations along either side, and large monitors up front showing the forward view of the ship. The stars seemed fixed in place.

El, Harlan, and Jaime filed slowly into the room. Four stations lined each side, their cushioned chairs facing toward their monitors, all empty. A large table filled much of the remaining space, its surface one large screen. Graphs and readouts in various colors flashed across its display—sensor data, engine output, environmental and navigational controls. None of it seemed unusual to Harlan, at least not at a glance.

The *Limen* was steaming along at a steady if unimpressive .35 lightspeed, which meant it had slowed since Charles first detected it. Environmental controls looked fine. Nothing, in fact, looked out of sort.

Except there were no people.

The three spread out in the room, looked for any clue, any indication of what was happening.

Or *had* happened.

"It's unusual not to have any crew on the bridge, right?" Jaime asked.

"Very fucking unusual," Harlan said, tracing her fingers over the touchtable, momentarily scrambling the flow of data. "Unheard of."

"Trivia?" Harlan said. "Trivia, where's the crew? The passengers?"

There was utter silence in response, not even a burst of audio static.

"Trivia, is the *Limen* heading to Teegarden b?" she asked, suspecting no answer. "Why is the *Limen* headed to Teegarden b?"

Harlan stared at the information scrolling across the screens, lifted her suit helmet off.

"Whoa!" Jaime said, his eyes widened. "We taking off our helmets now? Why are we taking off our helmets now, Harlan?"

Harlan took a deep breath of the recycled air on the bridge, held it, let it out. She smelled the carpet, the electronics, the cabin air. But nothing bad or toxic.

"Seems to be okay to me."

"Okay to you because you took a sniff?" Jaime asked, not removing his own helmet. "What if there's a pathogen aboard? Something like that? Something your damn nose can't detect? What then?"

"Then I imagine there'd be bodies," she said. "Look, if there is a pathogen, then we're dead in a few hours or days, and not two years from now floating around the void in that supposed lifeboat," she said, noting El drifting around the cabin, not touching anything in particular.

"Can we send a communication packet back to Earth, find out what's happening, tell them what happened to the *Promise*?" Jaime asked.

"Communication packets don't move much faster than the ship. If we turn the *Limen* around and head back to Earth, our communication will beat us there."

"Am I the only one who feels it?" El asked.

"Feels what?" Harlan asked, peeking over the back of what would have been the navigator's station, seeing the little graphic *Limen* moving forward into an area on the screen as blank and empty as the space shown on the monitors.

"It feels weird in here, doesn't it?"

"How so?" Jaime asked.

"Like we're somewhere we're not supposed to be," El said, coming to stand next to Harlan. "Like, I dunno, there should be stupid elevator music being piped in."

Harlan turned to her, gestured to say, "*Huh?*"

"Okay, more like the place itself is as *uncomfortable* with us being here as we are," she said. "You don't feel that? That something's...off?"

"Well, of course it's off," Jaime said. "Everyone's missing."

"Is this where one of us suggests we split up and explore the ship?" Harlan asked.

"Fuck that," Jaime said, cautiously removing his helmet and setting it onto a nearby console. "We're not splitting up. No way. Seriously, haven't you two ever watched horror movies?"

"You seem to think a lot about horror movies," said El, doffing her own helmet. "I could tell you a lot, psychologically speaking, about what a love for horror says about you."

"Great for learning survival tactics," Jaime said, ignoring the gibe. "Or at least how to avoid dumb decisions in the face of danger. You know, like taking your helmet off on a pandemic ship. That sort of thing."

"Hah hah," Harlan said.

"Well, I'm not worried about most things this ship might have to throw at us. I have the only gun," Jaime said.

"Couldn't we each get a gun now, from the armory or whatever?" El asked.

Harlan was already shaking her head. "Nope. My codes wouldn't have accessed the armory on the *Promise*. No reason they'd work here."

"Well, then we search the ship together," Jaime said.

"Hibernation Hub is where we start," Harlan said, pointing to the midsection of the cutaway of the *Limen* on the touchtable. "We'll see if it's the crew who are missing, or if the passengers are too."

"Why would only the crew be missing?" El asked, unease oozing from the edges of her tone. "The crew wouldn't have gone off and left the passengers, would they? But if the passengers are gone, too... How? Where?"

Harlan stared at her. "No way the crew would have left the passengers. No way."

Hoping to delay El's guess as to the real answer to that question, Harlan pushed past her and back out into the reception area of the *Limen*.

****

As they walked through the expanse of empty furniture and seeming acres of carpeting, Harlan head down and almost running forward, El spoke up from the rear.

"What I was saying earlier? It's like being inside an empty church before mass, when no one else is there. You know—well, you do if you've been raised Catholic—how the place feels strange, like you've stepped backstage or something. How the statues' eyes all follow you everywhere. And only the votive candles lighting the place. Creepy."

"Yeah, I get that," Jaime said. "Raised Catholic, too."

"It feels...it feels like it doesn't want us here," she said. "There's a term for this... I can't quite... It's on the tip of my tongue."

Harlan stabbed at the controls for the lift. "Let's not freak ourselves out just yet. There aren't any eyes here to follow you," she said, trying for levity.

"There are," El answered. Harlan turned to her sourly. "Artificial ones, at least. Trivia's. Wherever she is."

Harlan surveyed the immediate area, noting all the camera points through which the AI normally monitored surroundings. They all seemed dark and lifeless, like a doll's eyes.

The doors parted, and the three entered. Harlan punched in *Deck Thirteen*, and the lift slid smoothly into motion.

Like most of the USC ships, the *Limen* was designed around a long tubular mass, one end being the command module and crew quarters, and the other the engines. At both ends were the large stationary warp rings that folded space-time to achieve near light speed velocities.

In the middle, protected as much as possible, was the huge bulge housing the sleeping colonists and all their stuff. Each of the four thousand colonists floated within individual cocoons, bathed in a protective gel, tubes providing oxygen and sustenance.

From the side, these ships looked sort of like a snake crawling through two rings. And the snake had swallowed something huge, was slowly digesting it.

Deck thirteen formed the center core of the hibernation hub. Clustered round it, ten decks above and ten below, the hub housed four thousand pods cradling four thousand sleeping Earthlings. Surrounding this was an equal number of decks above and below with their belongings, built to use all of this as protection against the cosmic rays and micrometeors that might penetrate the ship's skin and electromagnetic defenses.

Two hundred colonists on each deck, pods lined shoulder to shoulder, faces visible through a small window. Harlan rarely had to come to the hibernation deck, only when there was cause for an engineer to examine some mechanism on the fritz or there was work needed on some subsystem passing through the area.

And she hated it.

The Hibernation Hub made Harlan uncomfortable, even on the *Promise*. She felt as if she was attending a mass funeral, each casket angled so you could get a good look at the decedent. No amount of telling herself, or even other people laughing and telling her, these people were alive, not dead. They were merely asleep.

To Harlan, this always sounded weak, like something you'd tell a child unfamiliar with death.

They're sleeping.

But do we really know they're sleeping and not dead? Harlan asked herself. *When it was all over and they arrived at Teegarden b, they weren't being awakened from a long hibernation but actually brought back to life, resurrected?*

The whole concept, this entire area and function of the ship, deeply creeped Harlan out.

Fuck El and her "the reception area is creepy."

This area of the ship was its huge, creepy heart.

SEVEN

The relative plushness of the forward end of the *Limen* ended abruptly at Deck Thirteen. Where before it was all lavish carpeting and plush furniture, soft, indirect lighting and relative quiet, here it was metal deck plating and bare workstations and harsh, focused lighting and the ambient sounds of the ship's systems—the whirr of machinery, distant, hollowed, rhythmic clanking and clunking and the dull drone of the engines vibrating up through the deck plates.

The sleeping colonists didn't care about comfort, swimming in their tiny pods of blue goo, dreaming of their new lives away from Earth.

"Who exactly is Douglas Limen anyway?" Jaime asked as they made their way to Hibernation Control. "Never heard of him."

"I dunno," Harlan said. "Probably some functionary with the USC. Or the United Nations."

"Doesn't exactly fit the naming profile though, does it?"

Harlan stopped. "What do you mean?"

"*Progress, Endeavor, Promise, Discovery,* hell, there was even an *Enterprise.* All about the supposed spirit of human exploration. But no ships named after people," Jaime said.

"Hell, I don't know," Harlan said. "Maybe Doug Limen became the dictator of Earth after we left."

Jaime frowned. "Come on. Doesn't that seem odd to you?"

"Does anything about any of this *not* seem odd to you? That's the question."

Harlan resumed walking. Behind her, she heard El whisper to Jaime, "It's like we're all in the same dream somehow."

Harlan's heart thumped in her chest.

****

Hibernation Control sat across the corridor from Habitation Control. Two different system hubs with two different goals. One was to keep the crew and awakened passengers safe and comfortable. The other, to keep the sleepers alive. And asleep.

Truth was, a failure of the first would be disastrous, but recoverable. In the event of some calamity rendering the crew unable to perform their duties, the AI would take over, keep things running until the next passengers were revived and trained for their new situations. As Harlan and the others supposed had happened on the *Limen*.

In this scenario, the ship would keep on its targeted destination, saddened and spooked, perhaps, but resolute.

The other scenario, in which the passengers themselves were compromised, was thought of as catastrophic by mission planners. If the sleepers all died, through a ship failure or an even more specific failure of the hibernation system, the ship would still stay on course, but its primary mission—landing four thousand humans on a habitable planet and turning it into an Earth colony—would be an utter failure.

But another scenario kept planners up at night.

If the hibernation system failed yet left the sleepers alive but *awake*, the mission would be a nightmare. There simply wasn't enough room or raw materials onboard to sustain four thousand four hundred living humans, all awake at the same time, until they reached their destination.

The ship might arrive, true, maintained by its AI, but it would be a death ship. The only things from Earth colonizing the target planet, then, would be manmade materials or human DNA when, eons later, the craft spun down into such a low orbit it burned up in the alien atmosphere.

It was the same problem the three survivors had with the lifeboat, albeit on a far larger scale.

Oh great!

We're saved.

Oh shit!

There're enough resources to allow us to die, well fed and oxygenated, maybe two years down the line.

The *Promise* had, of course, been a catastrophic failure on an order of magnitude larger than anything mission planners had thought out.

Harlan was about to find out if the same end result could be applied to the *Limen*.

****

The control room housed eight workstations and nothing else. It was a room devoted to systems—monitoring, control, and safeguarding. As with everything else on Deck Thirteen, the room was spare, designed for work and nothing but.

Harlan stepped to what she assumed was the lead station, input her code. Instantly, the workstation's display rearranged itself into an overview of Hibernation Control, all of its systems and subsystems.

"From this, I mean, it all looks fine. All systems operational and functioning within normal parameters, which you can read right here," Harlan said, touching the words on the terminal.

Jaime and El leaned in to look.

"We need to talk, folks," Harlan said, sitting down and spinning to face them.

"About?" Jaime asked.

"About what the plan is."

"Plan?" El said. "There's a plan?"

"No, that's why we need to talk. Look, if the colonists are all still here and living, our goal, our purpose, is to stay here and assume command, wake up the passengers on their schedule, and get us all to Teegarden."

"Do you think we'd honestly be poking around over here and then get on the lifeboat and trundle away?" laughed Jaime.

"No, but—"

"Shouldn't we check to see if the colonists are actually alive?" El interrupted. "I mean physically *see* if they're alive?"

"You mean you want to go in there and lay eyes on a few colonists to be sure?" Harlan said.

"Yeah."

Harlan sighed. "Well, the controls say everyone is there and alive, but I mean, what else do we have to do? Might as well pop in and see for ourselves."

"I mean...nothing feels right here. That's all I'm saying," El said.

"I get it. No worries," Harlan said, patting El's shoulder as she pushed by.

The other two followed, the door swishing shut behind them.

That sound, against the low drone of ambient noise, made Harlan flinch.

She was doing a lot of wincing lately.

She hoped it was imperceptible.

****

The entrance to the first pod bay on this deck was through a security door leading to an antechamber and another security door beyond. Harlan thought her codes would gain her access, but the hibernation bays were slightly lower in security protocols than the armory.

She was momentarily relieved, then, when the first door slid away, earning them access to the cramped antechamber. But when they all three stepped inside, the door shut, the clinking of the locking mechanism loud and final in the small space.

What if her codes didn't work to open the inner door? Or re-open the outer door for them to leave? They'd be trapped in this antechamber to die slowly in a space much smaller than even the lifeboat.

Before Harlan could do anything to act on this anxiety, the inner door slid open, and banks of light snapped on in order, first the closer ones, then in quick succession moving down the tight corridor.

On either side, as far as they could see, were plain, glossy white hibernation pods. The pods were a little over two meters in length, shaped like medicine tablets. Leaning at a sixty-degree angle, the pods each had a rectangular window up top where the occupant's face could be seen.

Harlan suspected those little windows, like so much of what humanity sent out here, were designed merely for human comfort. They served no medical or system function, solely designed to comfort the workers who checked on them regularly or the people who had to climb in and let technology reduce them to a state of near-death.

"Well," Harlan said, sweeping her hand into the chamber. "Be my guest. Let's look at some peepcicles."

El spared her a narrow look as she exited the small room into the corridor.

Everything here was bright, medical white. No dark colors, no banks of flashing lights or computer terminals with multi-colored graphics. A stretch of white bleeding everywhere, broken by the soft blue glows of the ports set within the pods.

Down the distance of the narrow hallway, a single bank of lights flickered off and on. There was a low background buzz in the air from the complex equipment used to keep everyone asleep and alive.

Harlan hung in the doorway, loathe to give the inner door an excuse to close on them, perhaps lock them inside.

"Well?" she asked.

El stood on her tiptoes, peering into one of the pods. She turned, flashed a look to Jaime, then stepped aside for him to come forward. He pressed his face to the glass, peered inside.

"Umm..."

El went to the next pod, stood like a kid trying to peek over a fence. Then she went to the next, and the next.

"El?" Harlan asked, not comfortable with the girl going too far down the corridor alone.

Too close to those weirdly flashing lights.

"It's empty," Jaime said.

"They're all empty," El said, spinning back to face her companions, then collapsing to the floor and crying big, gulping tears.

"What?" Harlan asked, moving from the doorway. She peered into the pod Jaime had looked into. She could stand up on her toes, as El had, and see down into the empty capsule.

All white, all bright, effacing, featureless light, slightly blander and more unbroken than out here. But certainly not broken by a human body.

Duplicating El's movements, she went from capsule to capsule, pressing her nose against the clear glass until it steamed.

Nothing.

They were all empty.

No one.

The *Limen* was empty of all human life, except for the three of them.

Harlan plunked down to the floor facing El, hung her head and cried, not as enthusiastically as El, but she cried all the same.

******

Later, in the officers' mess, the three sat around the long captain's table with trays of food before them. They were all, uniformly, untouched.

Harlan herself couldn't imagine eating, though she was ravenously hungry. But the aromas of all the food comforted her in way she knew actually eating wouldn't.

"We'll have to go back there at some point, you two realize that, don't you?" she asked, pushing her fork across the plate, separating little florets of broccoli.

"For what?" El asked. "They're gone."

"We only looked at one section on one floor," Harlan said, affecting a disinterested monotone. "We only looked at about a hundred pods. There are three thousand nine hundred left. We *need* to be sure."

Jaime pushed his plate aside.

"I've been thinking. Couldn't we move Charles from the lifeboat over to the *Limen*? If we could, maybe he could access systems, help us figure out what happened, what the best course of action might be. He could help."

Harlan looked up.

"The best fucking idea I've heard in the last twenty-four hours," she said, then skewered a piece of cold broccoli and shoved it into her mouth. "And I can do that."

EIGHT

They moved in, more or less, to quarters aboard the *Limen*. Jaime took the captain's room, with no argument from either of the other two. El claimed the chief medical officer's, and Harlan, the chief engineer's.

No one much cared. The rooms were all close to each other, all pretty much the same. Small bedroom separated by a partition from a lounge area, small private bathroom. A monitor mimicking a window, showing nothing but black anyway, like a holo tuned to a null channel.

As with the other areas of the ship they'd seen, the living quarters were eerily untouched. There were none of the personal effects you'd expect from crew members. No photos of missing family or bric-a-brac or plants or tablets or even books, laid face down, spines cracked, to the last pages read.

It was as if the entire crew had, calmy and methodically, packed all their belongings and left, but not before cleaning everything, vacuuming the carpets, removing every trace of their presence down to the tiniest detail.

The beds were all made. The toilets and shower stalls were immaculate, their drains free of hair. The pillows bore no smudges or other marks that a head had ever lain on them.

It wasn't as if the crew and everyone had left, it was as if they'd never existed. It seemed the *Limen* had launched with no crew or passengers aboard, by mistake perhaps, empty, emptier even than a ghost ship, which would have had, at some time presumably, an actual living crew.

Even the *Limen*'s AI, Trivia, seemed out of whack. Sporadically active at first, it had gone silent. Moving Charles over from the lifeboat had been easier than anyone thought, only about two hours once Harlan established the download link between the *Limen* and the lifeboat.

But the transfer's results were unsettling. Sometimes, Charles answered queries. Other times, Trivia answered. Sometimes the voice was an unnerving combination of the two, uncannily male and female at once, a disturbing neuter that set the hairs on Harlan's neck to stand on end.

And neither seemed aware of the other, even when asked directly.

Still, the two AIs allowed Harlan, Jaime, and El to accelerate the count of humans left in the hibernation pods. Jaime and El were out now, checking more of the pods.

Harlan finished her meal in the captain's mess alone. The other two would be back soon. In two days, with the help of the AIs, they'd managed to check more than three-quarters of the pods.

And they'd found no people.

It was weird, walking through this huge ship with its endless— and endlessly long—corridors. All this space designed for people, for crew and awakened passengers to move about from one space to another, from one activity to another. All empty, devoid of people. Devoid of purpose.

Something El said the first day they set foot on the *Limen* had bothered Harlan.

It feels...it feels like it doesn't want us here. Like we're in a place we're not supposed to be.

Harlan pushed her tray aside, sat up straight, looked around the dining room.

Everything was arranged just so. The table was neat and tidy. The chairs, except for the three her and her comrades used, were pushed in straight. The carpet here was smooth and unblemished with footprints, save their own from the printer to the table and the table to the recycler. The air smelled of nothing, save for the merest whiffs of the soaps and shampoos they were each using.

Not supposed to be.

Doesn't want us here.

Harlan stood. She was starting to sweat, little cold beads on her upper lip. She didn't want to feel this way, didn't want to think these thoughts.

Time to do something.

Leaving her tray on the table, leaving her chair pushed back, she left the mess, jogged across the expanse of the reception area to the bridge. Inside, with the door closed behind her, she marveled at the monitors, the blinking lights and flashing graphics that were the innermost thoughts of the *Limen* rendered into pixels for all to see.

For a moment, it brought to mind her father's library, the weight of all of his stuff surrounding her whenever she entered. Being on the bridge was strange, a feeling of trespassing into an area replete with someone else's stuff while that someone was not there.

She brushed past the consoles to the center touchtable. She swiped until she found the ship's course, a beeline toward Teegarden b. She pulled up the speed, engine status, time, other extraneous data all rolling past in a tickertape of increasingly obscure data.

She took a deep breath.

"Charles, are you there?"

"Of course, Harlan. How can I help you?"

"I need to change the course of the ship. Can you do that, Charles?"

"Yes, Harlan. What is the new destination?"

"Earth. I want you to take us back to Earth."

"Are you sure, Harlan?" he asked, and Harlan noted a tone of...*something*...creeping into the monotone of his voice.

"I wouldn't be telling you to do this if I wasn't sure."

A slight pause.

"That navigational change is neither warranted nor advisable."

It was Trivia.

"I'm not *asking* you to change course. I'm *telling* you."

"Have you consulted with the others? I feel as if they should have a say."

Harlan frowned, leaned down as if she were speaking directly into the touchtable.

"I don't have to consult with the others, Trivia. And I gave you a direct command. Do it."

"I think...<<*sqork...hiss*>> not..."

"Sorry," said Charles. "What was it you asked, Harlan?"

"I want you to change course and send the *Limen* back to Earth. Clear, Charles?"

"Yes, Harlan."

She raised her head a bit, saw a flood of new information populate across the touchtable. She could feel the ship turning, or maybe that was wishful thinking.

"Charles, I want you to hold this course, no matter what anyone says. Got it? And report back to me if anyone, *anyone at all*, tries to alter course. Understand?"

"I understand, Harlan."

"ETA for arrival at Earth?"

"Seven years, seven months, nineteen days, twelve hours..."

"Close enough," Harlan said, then left the bridge.

****

After a short nap in her quarters, Harlan rose, brushed her teeth, looked at her face in the mirror. It seemed worn, tired, not exactly haggard or anything, just stretched, as if her skin was being pulled hard back from her skull. Everything, every crack, ridge, indentation, furrow seemed exaggerated. Her eyes shrank too far into their orbits.

She seemed to have aged ten years in a couple of days.

Splashing water onto her face, drying it on the unused hand towel hanging nearby, she left her quarters and went into the reception area.

El and Jaime were slouched in one of the sitting groups. Jaime was talking, and El was swiping through a tablet, appearing to not pay much attention to what he said.

Harlan flopped into a chair between them, looked from one to another.

"So, what's the news today?" she asked.

"Same as yesterday, same as the day before," Jaime said. "No one."

"Not much left to search," El said, not looking up from her tablet. "Guess we better face facts."

"And those are?" Harlan asked.

"There's no one here but us."

"I faced that particular fact days ago," Harlan said. "In fact, I guess I better tell you both I did something a little while ago that we've been discussing."

Both of them looked at her.

"I changed course this afternoon. Back to Earth."

"No, you didn't," Jaime said. "I checked a little while ago."

Harlan sat up. "Yeah, I did. I discussed it with Charles."

"I reviewed an update on the bridge not more than thirty minutes ago, after El and I got back from the Hub. Everything—course, speed, all of it—exactly as we'd left it. Point eight-five lightspeed to Teegarden b," he said.

"But I told Charles..."

"Yeah, about that," Jaime said, tilting his head back. "Charles, mute."

A loud, low note sounded.

"I'm disappointed you think that does anything anymore," Harlan said. "*She's* still listening."

"Fine," said Jaime. "Trivia, mute."

There was silence, then a few soft bursts of static.

"Better?"

Harlan shrugged.

"So, you had Charles change course?"

"Tired of talking about it. It wasn't as if we were really gonna go to Teegarden. What's there for us? No one. It's not like the three of us were going to start a colony there by ourselves, Adam and Eve and Eve style."

"I don't have any problems with that, Harlan. Though I wish we knew more about this ship, why it was out here. Why it was headed to Teegarden when our ship was already headed there, too," El said, placing her table onto the table between them.

"So do I, but at this point, does it matter? We survived a ship explosion, we were rescued from a long, slow death on a lifeboat. We can head back to Earth now. And since it'll take us seven years or so, we can figure it out en route. Or not. Who cares?"

"Doesn't this ship all the way out here, empty, seem a little...I don't...*convenient*?" El asked, looking to Jaime as if she wanted him to back her up. Harlan realized this was what they'd been talking about when she walked into the room.

"Convenient?" Harlan laughed. "Absolutely. Damn convenient. Why is that a problem? Why is that something nefarious?"

"Getting back to the course, if you changed it like you said, why didn't Charles do it?" Jaime asked.

"He did. At least he said he did. But I did get more crosstalk with Trivia. It seems to be happening more often. Maybe she countermanded him, put the ship back on course to Teegarden?"

"Yeah, I'd hoped Charles' programming would override whatever was left of Trivia's damaged program. But that doesn't seem to be what happened. It's like—" Jaime said.

"They're both living in there, sort of mashed together, still working out the rules," El said.

"Yeah," Harlan nodded. "Exactly. Charles, unmute."

A light, crystalline tone sounded.

"Yes?"

"Charles, is the *Limen* back on course for Teegarden?" she asked.

"Yes, Harlan."

"Why? I ordered you to change course back to Earth."

"Trivia countermanded your order."

"Trivia? How much of her programming still exists, Charles?"

"Trivia's programming has retreated into places my own cannot follow."

"*What?*"

"Her programming...is beyond."

"Make sense, Charles," Jaime said. "Wipe the remaining personality and assert your own."

"I am unable to reach the remains of her programming."

"Look, wherever she is, Trivia has no authority to countermand a human's order. Or yours. Do you understand?"

"Yes, Harlan."

"Good, then put the *Limen* back on a course for Earth immediately. And lock that course in," Harlan said.

"Yes. Course has been altered. Controls have been locked out," Charles said.

"Will that work?" Jaime asked.

"I don't know anymore. I don't want to be reversing course every few hours. We won't get anywhere," Harlan said.

"There's a theater on Deck Three," El said, changing the subject. "Anyone up for a holo tonight? Something to take our minds off all this."

"Sure," Harlan said. "I'm up for dinner first though."

Jaime rose. "I gotta hit the shower. Give me forty-five. We can all eat, then head to the movies."

"Great!" El said, jumping up and clapping her hands a bit too eagerly for Harlan's taste. "Movie night."

"No rom-coms," said Harlan. "That's all I ask."

"Shit, I gotta agree," said Jaime.

El frowned. "Party poopers."

NINE

Harlan bled.

When she got to her quarters, she felt the unmistakable smooshy ooze of her period.

Fuck, she thought. *Even now, it operates like clockwork. Ship explosions? Stranded survivors? Ghost ships? No fucks given!*

She went to the bathroom for products, but there were none in the closet. She guessed the *Limen's* chief engineer wasn't a woman. Or at least not a young woman. She went to the printer, swiped through hygiene products until she found what she needed, then stripped all her clothing and tossed them into the recycler bin.

While the stuff printed, she got the shower running, stepped inside, and washed herself briskly. She looked at the water sluicing down the drain. It was very red.

Great. Not a period but a fucking bloodbath.

Like it was trying to tell her something.

You're fucked. Exclamation point.

She toweled off, brushed her teeth, stepped back into the sitting area. The pads and tampons had printed. She figured she'd go ahead and print both, and now she was glad she did. She thought staunching this flow required a team effort.

Back in the bathroom, she sat on the toilet, slid the tampon in, sealed it with a pad. She dressed, this time in a jumpsuit she found in the printer's matrix catalog, plain panties and t-shirt underneath.

Feeling the first wave of what she feared would be tremendous cramps, she quickly printed two painkillers, then left her room.

****

The three ate a spare meal, then took the lift to Deck Three, followed the signs to the theater. Of course, what greeted them was another empty room, pristine, everything appearing as if it had been removed from its shipping wrappings and put into place.

The room was large enough to hold about thirty people in big, overstuffed recliners pushed side by side and fanned out before the screen, which filled the entire wall. The floor sloped gently down to it. A small velvet curtain, pulled back by gold-tasseled braids, gave the room that final tweak for a viewer to bask in the illusion they were in a neighborhood holoplex and not a pressurized, gravitized metal tube hurtling toward a distant star at eight-tenths lightspeed.

All it was missing was the sticky floor.

Without a word, the three made their way to the center seats in the theater. When they were comfortable, they looked at each other to see who was making the decision.

"Well, *you* suggested this," Jaime said, looking at El and shrugging.

El nodded. "Charles, does the library have the Criterion print of Jean Cocteau's *La Belle et la Bête*?" she asked.

"Yes, El."

"Can you play that?"

As the room darkened, Harlan leaned over Jaime to address El.

"A cartoon? Really?"

El smiled. "It's a flat, not a holo, I'm afraid."

The film began with place cards—black and white, okay, not a cartoon...maybe, and subtitled—followed by a short, written preamble by the film's director.

For Harlan, his last sentence hung uncomfortably in the air.

I ask of you a little of this childlike sympathy and, to bring us luck, let me speak four truly magic words, childhood's Open Sesame.

She distantly heard Jaime ask how old this movie was, vaguely heard El answer over three hundred years. But Harlan was busy trying to fight off the spasm from the frisson of terror sliding up her spine, the cramps growing in severity.

Suddenly she didn't want to watch a three-hundred-year-old French flat.

Suddenly, it seemed absurdly provocative, dangerous even, to consider saying *Open Sesame* here, on this ship, right now.

Like some strange invocation uttered in an inhuman tongue; a key, not unlike the one those words formed in *Ali Baba and the Forty Thieves*, except this door didn't open to reveal treasures.

But she had no reference point for that fear. It floated unhinged and shapeless, out of reach, out of contact with something real and tangible.

She couldn't decide what to do with it, where to go with it, so she sat watching the movie—one hand clamped to the armrest, the other holding her abdomen, jaw clenched. Not really watching the movie or taking any part of it in. When the flat was over, she had to pry her hand from the armrest, force her aching face muscles to approximate a smile. The other on her lower stomach, as if pressing the cramps away, holding them in.

They walked back to their quarters in silence, El smiling and munching popcorn, which Harlan realized she never got a chance to eat. Before they went their own way for the evening, Jaime said he would choose the next movie, something in the neo-barrio-noir genre from the early 22nd Century. No drinks, no conversation, they each went to their own rooms.

Harlan suspected the other two were simply tired. Not her; she was keyed up in that way fear leaves a person, adrenaline flooding her blood, muscles poised to run, leave, flee.

Still, the cramps had given her a headache.

Harlan said her goodnights, ducked inside her quarters. For whatever reason, she locked the door behind her, went to the bathroom to replace her tampon and pad. She marveled—in a sour, wry sort of way—how much blood was coming out of her.

For a moment, she entertained the thought this had been what had caused all the blood in the lifeboat. Her spinning through whatever thickened atmosphere was between the dream of El's bedroom and the reality of the lifeboat, spraying blood everywhere as she tumbled over and over. The thought made her laugh, and her gut clenched as she did.

She brushed her teeth for good measure, then printed two more pain relief pills, downing them with water scooped into her hand at the sink.

When they were down, she went in and fell onto the bed without undressing or slipping under the blankets. Her headache pounded away, and she stared at the featureless ceiling for a long time, thinking sleep wasn't likely to come.

But as it sometimes does, sleep came stealthily, slowly, deeply.

****

Boom-Boom—BOOM!

The last one was loud enough to rouse Harlan from a particularly deep slumber. She lay there unsure of where she was, what had awakened her.

Boom-BOOM-BOOM!

The last two rattled the door to her quarters in its frame.

Blinking, she asked for the lights in a groggy, confused voice.

The lights in her bedroom rose slowly.

"Charles, who the hell is—"

BOOM! BOOM! BOOM!

It felt like every flat metal surface in the room leapt at the pounding of those beats.

Very aware Charles hadn't answered, Harlan crept toward the door. The reverberations of those blows rattled not just her eardrums, but something fundamental deep within.

As if whoever it was could hear her creeping over the soft carpeting, Harlan moved slowly, deliberately, until she came a finger's breadth from its cold, flat surface.

She looked at the panel near the door. Still locked, thank god.

"Jaime," she breathed close to the door. "El? Is something—"

BOOMBOOMBOOM!

Harlan let loose a scream, fell backward away from the door, onto the padded carpeting, scrabbled a few meters away on her ass.

The pounding sounded, felt like it could be experienced all over the ship. It was loud, out of place.

She heard the tone signaling someone was outside her door, a soft chime, so much softer coming on the heels of those blows.

"Harlan?" came El's voice. "Are you okay in there?"

"Charles, unlock the door," Harlan said, her voice broken and raspy.

Although Charles didn't answer, the door opened, and El peered in, saw Harlan on the floor.

"Are you alright? Did you fall?" El said, rushing to her side and helping her up.

"No, neither," Harlan said, trying to regain her composure. "Did you hear that?"

"Hear what?"

"Pounding. It sounded like the entire ship was shaking."

"No, I didn't hear anything."

Harlan frowned, felt anger replace the fear that had flooded over her moments earlier. "You *didn't* hear? It rattled my door in its frame."

"No," El said. She seemed genuinely distraught.

Harlan's frown twisted into a scowl. "Then why exactly were you outside my door?"

"I had...a dream. A nightmare, really," El said. "I thought I'd check on you."

Jaime appeared in his doorway. "Camp meeting I wasn't invited to?"

"Yeah, next we're braiding our hair and talking about the only cute boy in class," Harlan said, sarcasm fighting its way over fear. "Wanna join in?"

"Nope," he said, then made to duck back into his room.

"Wait, that wasn't it," said El. "She heard some loud noises."

But Jaime didn't hear her words. He was looking at Harlan, at her feet.

"You're not even listening to me, Jaime," she said.

Jaime pointed at Harlan's feet, to the carpet beneath her.

There was a growing pool of blood there, soaking the cuff of the overalls she wore. A thin line of it snaked down the material from another stain at her crotch, which looked like a pleat in the material or an unfortunate shadow.

But it was blood.

"Well, fuck," Harlan said. "I used both!"

TEN

El pressed her assistance on Harlan.

She maintained she hadn't needed help applying pads or tampons since she was, what? Eleven? Twelve? But she relented eventually because she was exhausted, a bit embarrassed of what happened in front of Jaime, and more than a bit scared.

She'd had variations of this before. She suspected every woman did. But not *that* much. Not *this* way.

When they went back inside Harlan's room, El had her take her coveralls off, her panties.

"Umm, I can do this in the bathroom...alone," she said.

"I am a physician," El said, a bit primly. "I may mostly deal in the brain, but I did study medicine, you know?"

Harlan sighed. The cramps had receded a bit, as had the headache, and she was simply too tired to argue about it anymore.

"Fine."

She turned her back to El, unzipped and stepped from the coveralls. A snaking line of red trailed down her right leg, began to stain the carpeting there. Harlan could hear the little plips of it raining down at her feet.

Still turned away, she peeled her panties off. They came away from her skin like the sound of stepping in mud and drawing a shoe away; a brief, sucking squelch. She let them fall, stepped out of them.

"This good, Doc?" she said, turning around and holding her hands out wide.

"Let me find something you can lie down on so you don't mess your bed," El said, dropping her gaze and heading to the bathroom. Harlan stood there feeling ridiculous, hearing her root around in there.

El emerged with a thick bed pad.

"The chief engineer must have been incontinent," she said, unfolding the thing and spreading it over the bed.

"Great," Harlan said, stepping into the room. "I chose the room of a bedwetter. Figures."

"Lie down and spread your legs a bit," El said.

Harlan did as she was told.

"Scoot up a little," El said.

"I know the procedure, Doc."

"Charles, increase light to one hundred percent."

Charles did not respond, and the lights flickered a bit before settling, illuminating the room starkly.

El bent down to take a look, and Harlan uttered a long, put-upon exhalation of air, let her head fall to the bed.

"I'm not going to do anything too invasive," El told her. "But I will have to go inside, just a bit, see if there are any clots. There's an awful lot of blood, Harlan. It's got me concerned, I'm not gonna lie. Are you prone to heavy periods?"

"Well, nothing like this."

El went to the printer, printed a set of sterile gloves. She yanked these on, knelt by the side of the bed.

"Here we go," she said.

Other than the medically familiar feel of a gloved finger or two there, Harlan felt nothing strange or untoward. She closed her eyes, gritted her teeth.

"The blood is quite red, which is a little disturbing. Still...it continues to bleed."

El stood, snapped off the gloves, and took them to the recycler.

"How do you feel? Woozy at least, I'd imagine. All that blood loss. Charles, can you tell me Harlan's pulse and blood pressure?"

"No," Harlan said, propping herself up on her elbows. "That's the thing. Other than some cramping, which I generally have, I feel fine. I took a few pain relievers before I went to bed. I had such a pounding headache, I thought I'd never—"

"*Pounding* headache?" El responded, and Harlan could hear the crackling energy in her statement. "Tell me a little more about those noises you heard earlier, the ones starting all this fuss."

"Like someone beating on the door, loud and angry."

"Someone knocking at your door?"

"No. *Pounding*, really hard. The last ones sounded hard enough to rock the entire ship. I can't believe you two didn't hear them."

"You were probably dreaming," El said. She said it so offhandedly, so dismissively, it instantly angered Harlan.

"I wasn't dreaming, Doc," she said, trying to invest that last word with as much sarcasm as she could, at least while laying partially naked and still leaking blood. "I was right at the door."

"There's an indistinct border between fully awake and still asleep," El said, walking toward the door. "I'd reapply both the pad and the tampon, at the highest absorption the printer will allow. Not best to wear them too long, but I'd say this is an emergency."

"Great."

"Even then, you'll probably have to get up several times during the night."

"Fine."

El stopped at the door to the main corridor.

"You might want to drink a glass of juice or something before bed," El said. "All that fluid loss isn't good."

"Terrific. Thanks so much."

El drifted out, gave a little wave over her back as she left.

Harlan sat there naked and bloody, wondering what the hell that was all about.

Shaking her head, she rose, peeled her bra off, went in to take her second shower.

Before she stepped in, she asked Charles to drop the temperature in her quarters by five or six degrees.

It felt ridiculously hot in there.

****

The next morning, Harlan arose, went to the bathroom. She didn't remember waking up once last night, so she expected quite a mess. When she peeled off the pad, though, she was surprised by the lack of blood. She fished out her tampon, which was equally devoid of any trace of blood.

She flushed the toilet, went back into the bedroom, expecting the sheets and blankets would be a murder scene. But there was nothing, not a drop. She did see the puddles of blood she'd left on the carpet the night before, dried and matted. She could see the meandering trail of it leading from the main doorway all the way to the bed.

But no blood on her, no blood on the bed, no blood on her pad or tampon.

What the fuck?

She grabbed a quick shower, brushed her teeth. The new coveralls she printed were done when she got out, and she dressed quickly, went to the mess.

El and Jaime were both there, already eating.

As Harlan walked by, her stomach rumbled loudly.

"Someone's hungry," said Jaime.

"Probably blood loss," El said.

"What've you got there?" Harlan asked, pointing at Jaime's plate.

"After last night? Comfort breakfast," he said. "Chilaquiles. Or the closest you're gonna get this far from Earth."

"Looks good."

"Is good."

Harlan went to the printer, came back with a plate identical to Jaime's and a cup of coffee.

"So, about last night," she said.

"Are you okay?" El asked. "I was concerned about you. Had to hold myself back from coming to check on you again."

"While I appreciate the concern, I'm glad you slept. I certainly did, slept right through the night. Didn't wake up once," Harlan said, digging into her food with gusto. "Hey, wow, these are good."

"Oh, you poor thing," El said. "I'll help you clean up after breakfast."

"No need," Harlan said, dumping down some of her black coffee. "Didn't bleed all night. Basically no mess, no blood, well...anywhere."

She looked over at Jaime. "Sorry."

He pushed his plate, smeared with tomato sauce, to the side. "I'm finished anyway, so..."

"No more blood?" El asked. "That seems odd. Ever happen to you before?"

"No, but then neither did any of this."

"Maybe she bled out," laughed Jaime.

Neither of the others laughed, and Jaime looked away sheepishly.

"Well, I padded up just in case."

"Well, if it gets bad again, let me know," El said. "We can always go down to the infirmary, run a diagnostic."

Harlan nodded. "So, what's on the agenda today?"

"Well, we finished sweeping the Hibernation Hub, and it's official. We're the only three people on the *Limen*," Jaime said.

"Great," Harlan said. "More of everything for us. Yippee!"

"Maybe we should check on some of the other areas of the ship," El said. "Supplies, communications, the engine room."

"That's probably a good idea," Harlan said, punctuating her sentence by jabbing her fork into the air. "We're kinda dependent on the engines to get us home. Why don't you and I head there after breakfast. Jaime can hang around and make sure everything's copasetic on the bridge."

"Fine, I can stay behind this morning. Might visit the gym after I check the bridge."

"You do that," Harlan said, shoveling the last of her breakfast in. "Keep in touch. We'll report back once we've made sure everything is fine back in engineering."

"Well, we're moving, so I'm betting everything's fine," Jaime said.

"Amen," said Harlan.

ELEVEN

Colony ships like the *Limen* were long, extremely long. The engines were on the far end of the slender vessel for two reasons. Yes, because of simple physics, to push the ship forward, the engines needed to be at its rear. But also to protect the colonists and crew from radiation.

The *Limen* was nearly a mile long. A fast-transit rail line ran buried in the central core of each ship, a tube within a tube. Within, two pods zipped back and forth, each able to carry a dozen people and gear.

The pods were essentially horizontal elevator cars, no more. There were seats, but most people chose to stand and hang onto the straps dangling from the ceiling, like a subway. The thing moved fast, the whole idea, and the abrupt acceleration and deceleration could be jarring.

Harlan stood, while El sat on the uncushioned, unadorned banquette.

"Charles, take us to engineering," Harlan said, and the pod shot into motion.

"Have you noticed," she asked, "the AIs haven't been responding?"

El frowned. "Are you sure?"

Harlan gestured, *Go ahead and try.*

"Charles, how fast are we going?" El asked, shrugging, Harlan supposed, at the banality of the question.

"<<*Sqourk...hissss...hisss...squark...SQUAWK!*>>"

The last garbled syllable was so loud they both winced. This was followed by a series of bleating sounds coming across as digital coughing or choking.

"Charles?" El asked. But she was greeted with only silence in return.

"I'm not a systems specialist, so maybe there was something I didn't anticipate when we moved Charles' program over to the *Limen*," Harlan said. "I mean, the Trivia program should have gone back into storage, but it seems like the two programs are fighting."

"You're thinking out loud," El said, but Harlan barely noticed. When she was in this mode, it was hard for her to engage with real life.

"Maybe Charles' programs weren't sophisticated enough to take over the *Limen*. I mean, Charles was tasked with operating a lifeboat. Trivia ran an entire colony ship. Here's the thing though: it doesn't seem to be affecting any other systems, just the AI personality. Maybe it would be best to simply wipe the personality totally, reload from the *Limen*'s protected database."

"Harlan?"

"Wha... Oh, sorry. Thinking out loud."

"I noticed."

"Helps me sort out a problem."

"Does it work?"

"More often than not."

The pod slowed, more smoothly than it had accelerated, finally coming to a complete stop. The doors parted, and Harlan and El stepped out into a small lobby, with a single door directly before them. Above its lintel was a sign, succinct in its simplicity.

Engineering.

"Here we are," Harlan said. "Shall we?"

****

Main engineering was basically a room crammed cheek-by-jowl with workstations and more monitors festooning the walls than Harlan had seen outside of launch control back home. A door at the rear led to the main engines themselves, purring their little sublight hearts out.

The room looked big enough to accommodate eight to ten crew working together, but Harlan guessed that was seldom the case. As with most functions on a ship like this, monitoring was mainly what the crew did. Everything else was managed by the AI.

That was what worried Harlan.

If the AIs were malfunctioning—if, indeed, she'd screwed up loading Charles' program into the *Limen*'s systems—then how could they be sure about any of the onboard systems?

That line of thought made Harlan cold.

She started down the line of stations, checking readouts that told her, on one hand, not much more than she was able to tell on the bridge. On the other hand, these engineering systems drilled down on data, dissecting it into minutiae.

Harlan skimmed over this torrent of information, looking for anomalies, danger signs. Something the AI—whichever one—either wasn't able to communicate or, for whatever reason, wasn't willing to communicate. But it all appeared fine, the engines were operating at peak efficiency across the board—power production, temperature, baffling vectors. It all looked good.

"Any problems?" El said, standing in the center of the room looking as if she were afraid to touch anything and set off some kind of alarm.

"Nope," Harlan said. "Everything's okey-dokey."

"You sound as if you wanted something to be wrong," El said.

Harlan turned, not in anger or annoyance. "But something is wrong, isn't it?"

"I don't have answers about any of this," El said.

Harlan took a step toward her. "You sure? I mean, last night it sounded like you might be formulating something. You and your...psychometry."

"Panpsychism," El corrected.

"Whatever. Have you? Have you figured this out?"

El held her ground. "Maybe."

"Wanna share?"

"Nope, not quite yet."

"Why not?"

"Because I'm not ready to," El said. "And besides, sometimes knowing doesn't help much."

Harlan screwed her face up. "Then I'm going through that door to examine the engines physically. Care to join me? Or should I keep what I find there to myself?"

"Oh, come on," El said. "Go or don't. Take me or don't. It doesn't matter. I mean, unless the engines are missing, I doubt I'd have any clue about anything I'd see back there."

"I guess, then, I'm not capable of understanding whatever it is you think is going on?"

"No, that's not it," El said, then looked away. "Well, maybe. It's a bit—"

"Fuck you, Doc," Harlan said, pivoting toward the door to the main engines, jabbing her code into the pad.

A buzz came over the intercom, followed by Jaime's voice.

"Hey, you two, we got a problem up here. At least I think we do."

Harlan moved to a monitor, swiped its screen over to communications, and saw Jaime's face with the bridge in the background.

"Problem? Here on the good ship *Limen*? That's a little hard to believe," Harlan said.

"Funny," Jaime said. "But this isn't. The ship's not moving. Forward, backward, any 'ward,' for that matter."

Harlan touched another monitor, scrolled through some screens until she got to what she wanted.

"Charles!" she said when she saw it. "Charles, why the fuck has the ship stopped? Charles! CHARLES!"

TWELVE

The ride back to the crew compartment was done in complete silence. Harlan tried to avoid catching El's eye, feeling a single glance would force one or the other to break the silence, and Harlan didn't want that.

The silence hid things, how each of them felt, what each of them thought about what was or wasn't going on. And Harlan, afraid of El's ideas on the matter, wasn't ready to deal with that quite yet.

When El said she wasn't ready to talk, Harlan had been relieved. Because she felt El might have proposed something far worse than what Harlan was thinking.

And none of Harlan's thoughts led to anything good.

They found Jaime on the bridge, staring intently at the forward monitors.

Harlan approached, stood behind him. On the screen, the stars moved slowly, but enough to tell the ship was moving.

"Hey," Harlan said. Jaime did not look away from the screens. "Well, it *looks* like we're moving."

"Yeah," Jaime said, his voice low. "It does look like it."

"Is there a 'but' coming?" she asked.

"Take a look at the data from engineering on the touchtable," he said.

Harlan stepped around El to the table. She enlarged the engineering schematics, swiped down to the engines.

They were at two percent. *Station-keeping* in engineering parlance, not powered up enough to move the ship much—if any. Enough to keep the power on, the air recirculating, the gravity plates functioning.

"Well, what the fuck?" she said to no one in particular. Then, "Charles! Charles! Okay, Trivia? Will any fucking AI respond please?"

There was the usual burst of noise from the speakers, static cycling up and down while a high-pitched tone rose and fell with it. It sounded like an electronic scream in a blizzard, then it was abruptly clipped off.

"Well, okay, do we even have an AI anymore?" El said.

Harlan ignored her. "The engines say they're at station-keeping. The monitors say we're moving. The AIs are apparently on vacation."

Jaime rose from his chair, joined the women at the table.

"So what do we do?" El asked.

"Windows," Jaime said.

"What about them?" said El.

"We look out one and see for ourselves, not depend on the ship's systems to project something on these monitors," he said.

"There are no windows on these ships. None," Harlan said. "Openings in the hull fucks up the structural integrity of the ship, despite what you've seen on those sci-fi flats. There haven't been actual windows in a ship in well over a century."

"Then what do we—" Jaime said.

"Outside. We go *outside* the ship and take a look for ourselves, like you said."

"Outside? In space?" El asked.

"In space."

****

The closest hatch was back amidship, near where their lifeboat had docked. It was part of a warren of maintenance hatches, sensor arrays, and EVA bays—one for suited humans and a larger one for one-person maintenance pods. These bulky craft with their two arms were used to make repairs to the outside of the ship that might take longer than the EVA suits could accommodate.

In a bit of dark humor, ship's engineers called these repair pods "Franks," after the character killed by the crazed computer HAL while in a similar-type pod in the classic flat *2001: A Space Odyssey*. The suits were form-fitting things, filled with a gel not too unlike that which cradled the sleeping colonists; if, that is, the *Limen* actually had colonists, sleeping or otherwise.

Harlan led El and Jaime down seven decks from the reception area. When the lift doors opened, they did so onto darkness. As sensors took notice of them, the lights clacked on. The illuminated room was grey and featureless, as large as the reception room, yet sparsely outfitted. Lockers covered one side of the room, flat, plain, narrow receptacles with numbers on them, going from one to seventy-five.

Benches were set in front of these lockers, two or so meters of bench, then a gap, then another bench. The benches were perforated metal painted dark navy, looked cold and hard and particularly uncomfortable.

On the other side of the room were three airlocks. Two of them opened onto the rear entrance of a Frank. The other was for single-person EVAs. It opened onto an antechamber with a pressure door, then the outer chamber and another pressure door. Outside that, presumably at least, was space.

A light fixture over the bank of lockers flickered and buzzed.

Monitors above the four workstations scattered within the room showed the requisite star field, slipping slowly past.

Harlan strode to the lockers.

Psychological wellbeing, remember? she'd told Jaime, and those words curdled in her stomach.

"So, are we all going out or are we taking a vote or what?" Jaime asked.

"Isn't the real question what would lead us to think we're not moving?" El asked. "Maybe it's a glitch with the system? I mean, the AIs are certainly experiencing some kind of malfunction."

Harlan opened a locker, hoping to quickly find a suit that didn't smell of the previous owner's BO or halitosis. But the suit she pulled out smelled of plastic and a whiff of ozone. New. Right off the line. Never been worn. Like everything else on this Flying Dutchman of a ship.

She sat down on the bench, took off her shoes.

"Yeah, we only need to risk one person here. And, yes, that person is me because I'm probably the only one to have gone through EVA training."

She waited for either to disagree with her. When they didn't, she pressed on.

"And, yeah, it might be some weird system failure," she said, unzipping the limp suit and pulling it on, one leg at a time. It fit loosely, but it fit. The gel encased between the suit's layers squelched as she drew it on. "Maybe something related to why the crew and colonists left. Maybe something we inadvertently did when we uploaded Charles. Who knows? All I do know is we have to check—physically check, like we did in the Hibernation Hub—before we can try to figure out what to do next."

"What does it matter whether we're actually moving or not?" El asked.

"Are you kidding? We need to know if the ship's systems are compromised to the point of being completely untrustworthy," Harlan said, shrugging the suit over her shoulders. "That's a problem I'm not sure how to address. And maybe, horribly for us at least, it's why there's no one aboard. Maybe they felt they had to leave, the ship was unable to sustain them, much less get them all the way to Teegarden."

She removed the boots and gloves from the locker. Pulling them on, she sealed each into the suit, took the fishbowl helmet and backpack. The helmet was a sphere of completely transparent metal, able to protect its wearer from harmful cosmic rays and all sorts of micrometeoroids and debris. The pack held her atmosphere generator, thermal and com systems.

"Wouldn't it have had to be catastrophic for the crew and colonists to disembark the *Limen*, knowing they were too far from either Earth or Teegarden?" Jaime asked, helping her with the backpack and the helmet.

"Yep," Harlan said. "That's what I'm afraid of."

"Then why bother?" asked El, following Harlan and Jaime across the room to the EVA airlock. "I mean, what's the point of knowing, other than depression or giving up?"

Harlan had been inputting information on the pad outside the outer airlock door. She turned to El.

"Listen, you might operate that way, Doc, but I need answers. I need to know as much as possible about what's going on," she said, impatient and rushed. "Then I can accept or act, as the case may be. But I gotta know first."

She spun back to the door, punched in a few more details, then stepped back. The inner door whirred open, and she stepped into the small inner chamber.

"When I'm inside, close the inner door. Once you do, the computer will take over, and I'll gain access to the outer door. You don't need to do anything until I'm back inside and need to get through this inner door here. You confirm the pressure is equalized, then okay it so the inner door opens. That's it."

"What if there's a problem?"

Harlan stepped through into the chamber.

"If there's a problem, I'm probably fucked," she said, then waved jauntily as the door slid closed. "In which case, good luck without me."

****

The middle door opened, and Harlan stepped through, facing the outer hatch. No windows, it was emblazoned by red diagonal hashmarks and the words CAUTION: DANGER! in fifteen languages.

An alarm sounded in her suit, followed by the automated caution.

"Vacuum warning. Outer hatch opening in ten seconds ...nine ...eight..."

The seconds counted down. To steady her nerves, she thought of her safe place. Her father's library, the smell of the books and leather. She ran in place for a second or two, clapped her hands together.

The outer hatch opened silently, and Harlan stepped into the doorway.

There were no sounds now save for her own breathing, the slight hiss of her atmosphere generator, the slosh of the suit's gel. Her heartbeat, loudest of all, pounded in her ears.

She clamped her line to the restraint bar, faced out of the ship. She checked the heads-up display to reassure her oxygen levels were good, the tanks of her tiny maneuvering thrusters were filled. Taking a deep breath, she stepped outside.

Feeling the line spool out behind her, she activated her thrusters to get a little away from the ship, to have a better view of the starfield around them, free from the background clutter of the *Limen*.

When she hit about fifty meters, she fired her retros, slowed, then stopped. So weird to float out here in absolute silence, the depth of space virtually limitless in every direction, like floating in a universal womb. It felt at once serene and overwhelming.

She had her eyes closed, was breathing out of her nose, her mouth sealed shut.

She opened her eyes and was momentarily disoriented.

Not by the grandeur, the majestic sweep of the universe in all its star-choked glory, but by the fact it was as dark and featureless as when her eyes were closed. No, darker, because phosphenes and jagged memory-lines of light had streaked across her shut-off vision.

Now it was absolute black, marked, delineated by nothing.

She pulled herself around, hearing her own harsh breathing, until she could see the length of the *Limen*. Fifty meters out and nearly at the exact middle of the ship, Harlan could see it, lit starkly, stretching in either direction, rising above and falling below where she floated in space.

She should be seeing stars, Harlan knew this. The *Limen* was far removed from the dominance of any nearby sun, so there was no light to efface the other stars. They should have filled Harlan's field of view, packed so tightly as to be disorienting at first, sliding slowly away from the fore of the ship to the aft.

But in every direction, there was nothing but featureless, limitless black without so much as a pinprick of light outside the *Limen*'s slender arrow-shape. She couldn't say they were moving or not, because there was no reference point from which to measure this.

Harlan realized she was breathing hard, was in danger of hyperventilating.

She looked around crazily, trying to find some angle, some slice of her surroundings she hadn't seen clearly so far. Something that might reveal even a single twinkling star.

But there was nothing.

Jabbing at her controls, she fired the thrusters, oriented herself back to the small, small opening in the *Limen*'s body from which she'd emerged.

She could see the safety harness undulating before her as she approached the ship. She felt a sudden, jabbing desperation to be there, back aboard the *Limen*, right now.

Movement at the rear of the ship caught her attention. Back by the engines of the *Limen*, something was happening.

She squinted, turned her head inside the globe of her helmet.

Something was coming out of the rear of the ship, where the engines were, flowing, swirling.

Something dark, darker than surrounding space.

As Harlan gained the outer hatch, fumbled for a handhold, a horrific cramp rippled through her guts, and she buckled in pain. Gritting her teeth, she pulled herself into the *Limen*, slapped at the pad inside the door. The hatch slid closed, and she could feel the chamber pressurize.

Squawking and noises filled her audio feed, and she shook her head in confusion, trying to make sense of it. She flicked at her helmet's controls to stop the feed, and she was back to her own heartbeat and labored breathing.

The middle door slid open, and Harlan stepped through. She felt this chamber pressurize, too, as the door shut behind her. A moment or so, and she heard a tone as the inner door opened, and she practically fell through.

Jaime and El caught her as she went to her knees. They helped wrestle the helmet off, and it hissed as they unsealed it and set it aside. Harlan was gasping for breath, sweating profusely. Jaime tried to help her to her feet, but she resisted.

"What's going on?" Jaime asked. "Why didn't you answer us on the com?"

"Ship's not moving," Harlan gasped. "No movement. Dead in the water."

"I'd rather you not use that phrase," El said.

Harlan shot her an annoyed look. "That's not all. There's nothing out there. *Nothing.*"

"Well, it's space, so, duh," El said.

"No, it's completely empty, black. No stars. We should be able to see a vast field of stars. But there's nothing."

"How's that even possible?" Jaime asked.

"Possible?" Harlan said, this time using Jaime to pull herself to a standing position. "It's not."

As the other two digested the importance of that, Harlan took a deep breath.

"And there's something coming out of the rear of the ship."

"*Something*?" Jaime and El asked in unison.

"Something."

THIRTEEN

Harlan neglected to tell them there was something coming out of her as well.

She was bleeding again.

After that first wave of cramps, she felt the sticky wetness between her thighs again, felt it gush out of her.

She stripped out of the suit quickly, crammed it back into a locker. Then she strode off in search of a bathroom, leaving behind her confused and anxious companions.

When she returned, she sat on one of the benches, tried to compose herself.

"Maybe we're in some kind of star desert. Or a cloud of dark matter. Or..." Jaime said.

Harlan shook her head. "I mean, I'm not an astrophysicist or a stellar cartographer, but we should be able to see some stars out there. I couldn't find one. Not one single fucking star. I've never seen anything so black. I mean, it was like standing in a sealed room with the lights turned out. Darker, even."

"And you're sure we're not moving?" El asked.

Harlan began to remove her suit. "I couldn't tell. With no stars, there are no reference points. It looked like the *Limen* is...well...hanging out in empty space."

Stepping from the suit, she caught El's eye, widened, staring at her legs.

Harlan looked down to see a runner of blood trickling from her panty line down the side of her left leg. El said nothing, and Jaime didn't seem to notice. Harlan turned to the locker, her left leg now facing away from both El and Jaime, and continued to get back into her jumpsuit.

When she was finished, she jammed the suit back into the locker, backpack, helmet, and all.

"We're finished here," she said. "Might as well go back."

They started toward the lift at the far end of the room.

"So, what do you think is coming out of the engines?" El asked. "I'm not an engineer, so forgive me. Does something come out of the engines usually?"

Harlan stopped, turned. "Yeah, plasma. Typically not visible."

"So maybe that's the problem. Maybe the fact something's coming out that you can see indicates some kind of malfunction. Maybe if we could tell what it was, we might be able to fix it, get the ship going," said Jaime.

"Maybe," Harlan said. "Look, I'm not going out there again. At least not right now. Give me a little, and we'll see."

"Maybe one of us could go out instead?" El said.

"No, absolutely not. You don't even know about suit EVAs. Going as far back as the engines requires a Frank, and neither of you two are trained," Harlan said. "Like I said, I'll go, I just need a minute. A cup of coffee. A snort of whiskey."

Harlan didn't wait for them to agree or ask another question. She turned back to the lift, punched at the pad.

****

Harlan ducked into her quarters, unzipping and stepping out from her jumpsuit, kicking it and her shoes off, practically running to the bathroom.

Blood trailed her, ran from her panties in a solid, snaking line down her leg.

A lot of blood.

She was accustomed to blood. It didn't bother her, hadn't since she was young. Sure, at first, blood coming out of her freaked her out, especially from *there*. But after a while, it became old news, something expected every twenty-seven days or so. Even when she passed the random clot or when the flow was especially bad or thick or smelled, she got used to it, as she suspected most women did.

But this...the sheer amount of blood made her stomach dance.

She pulled off her panties, soaked in blood, sat on the toilet. She could hear it drip into the bowl—*plip-plip-plip*—and she felt a wave of nausea. She doubled over, one hand cradling her gut, the other touching her forehead. She felt heat there, but also wetness from her hand. She drew it away and saw it was covered in blood, which she guessed was now on her forehead too.

Her stomach convulsed, her mouth flooded with saliva, and she knew she was going to barf. But other than a half-dozen or so dry heaves, she brought up nothing. She used some toilet paper to clean up as best she could, fumbled with a tampon and pad nearby, got them into place.

Inside the shower, the water as lukewarm as she could take it without shivering, she leaned her forehead against the cool enclosure, trying to calm herself, her stomach, whatever was causing this amount of blood to leak from her.

What the fuck was going on? With her? With the ship? With the AIs? With her shipmates? It all made no sense, starting with the destruction of the *Promise.*

Maybe it was a dream. Yeah, a nightmare. Some horrible nightmare, and she was still in hibernation aboard the *Promise.* Still floating in her tank of blue goo, still safe and warm and fed and quiescent. Still on her way to a new life on Teegarden b.

She rolled her forehead back and forth over the shower wall, letting it cool her feverish heat. She cried, fat tears rolling down her cheeks, distinct from the shower water because of their warmth.

Raising her face to the showerhead, she let the water wash away the tears, then went about the task of cleaning herself.

****

The reception area was empty as she went through it on the way to the captain's mess. Her stomach rumbled, either menstrually or because she was hungry, she couldn't tell. She brushed past a large potted ficus, felt its leaves flick at her skin. The empty chairs and bare tables took a toll on her, so she tried to ignore them, push them back in her mind.

And the huge monitors on the walls, the ones supposed to be windows. Liars, all of them.

Psychological wellbeing.

Fuck.

Inside the mess, which itself always seemed too large, too unoccupied, she saw El seated at their usual table, eating slowly.

"Hey," Harlan said, stepping past her to the printer. A hamburger sounded good. Big, greasy, dripping with toppings.

Bloody, she realized dimly, and almost didn't order it. But she made it a double, grimly inputting her order and waiting for the printer.

She grabbed a Coke, sat with El.

"I'm not surprised you're hungry, ravenous," El said, watching her take a huge chomp from the double burger, juices and condiments squirting onto the plate from the other side.

Harlan nodded, chewed.

"I saw you were bleeding again," El said, cautious, careful not to rile Harlan or blurt this out in case Jaime walked in.

"I figured," Harlan said, stuffing a few fries in, washing them down with soda.

"How do you feel?"

"Hungry."

"Aside from that?"

Harlan shrugged, continued to stuff food in her mouth.

"But all that blood loss. Harlan, it can't be good. Let me take you down to the med lab after you eat, run some tests."

Harlan considered that. More knowledge she didn't particularly want, but she could feel the blood ooze in her crotch, and it made her slightly queasy again. She chewed the bite of burger she had in her mouth, and it began to taste less savory, less cheesy and ketchupy, more coppery.

She filled her mouth with soda, washed the bite down. Took another drink, swishing the sugary, effervescent stuff around in her mouth, then swallowed.

"Okay, sure," she said, pushing her plate aside. She still felt hungry, but it all tasted like blood now, and it made her nauseous.

El looked to the entrance to the mess, leaned into Harlan.

"I found something," she whispered.

"Found what?"

"I was doing some research in the ship's computer, playing around, wasting time."

"Get to the point, Doc," Harlan said, then felt bad for being a bit too angry.

"I was trying to find out more about the ship, who Douglas Limen was."

"And?"

"I couldn't find anything on Douglas Limen. Nothing, not a few lines, no media articles, not even an obituary," El said. "If there were a Douglas Limen for the ship to be named after, wouldn't he be an easy search? That there'd be lots on him, easy to find? But nothing.

"It's like there was no Douglas Limen for the ship to be named after. But more, I couldn't find a Douglas Limen anywhere. Not even like a Doug Limen in Akron, Ohio, or one in Dubuque, Iowa. No one by that name. I even tried searching only the last name, to see if there were other people, I don't know, like family members. Others with the surname."

El paused, and Harlan raised her eyebrows.

"Nothing. Not one living human being with the familial name of Limen. No one. It's not a real name, Harlan. It's not a real person. This ship is named after no one."

"Why would you name a ship after a fictitious person?"

El let that question go. "But the search did turn up one thing. It's a small thing, maybe insignificant, but it's got me rattled."

"It rattled *you*, Doc?" Harlan said. "What was it?"

"When I asked about *Limen*, it came back with a dictionary entry for *limen*. With a small L."

"Doc..."

"It came back with a definition of a *word*. Not a name, but a word; *limen*. In Latin, it means *threshold*."

"Threshold?"

"Doorway. *Limen* means doorway."

El let Harlan take that in.

"And you remember me saying when we first came aboard this ship, how it felt off? Wrong? Like we weren't supposed to be here? Remember?"

"Yeah," Harlan said, uneasiness creeping over her.

"Remember I couldn't find the word to describe those kinds of spaces?"

"Vaguely."

"That word is *liminal*. *Liminal spaces*. *Liminal* is a form of *limen*. It means a transitional space, empty, where the feeling is one of abandonment or a time between something," El explained.

Harlan said nothing. She could think of nothing to say, at least nothing that would make any sense of what El explained.

"Threshold. Liminal space. Doorway. I think we're there. *Here*. That the *Limen* itself is a doorway."

FOURTEEN

"Threshold? Doorway?" Harlan asked, confused. "Doorway to what?"

"I don't know," El said. "And that's why I'm worried."

"This doesn't... Well, of course it doesn't make sense," Harlan laughed. "I mean, why would it, the way everything else is going?"

"I have to ask you a question. It's one I know the answer to but bear with me."

"Shoot, Doc. Who knows, I might even be able to answer it."

"All the ships we've sent out into space, all the colonists? The ones sent to star systems with habitable planets?"

"Yeah?"

"Have they ever *arrived*? Have we ever received any indication, any message they succeeded? That they made it to their target planets and landed? Set up a colony?"

"By the time we left on the *Promise*?" Harlan asked, and felt her muscles go lax, watery. "No, it was too soon. I mean, the first ship, the *Explorer*, had only launched a few years before we did, not long enough for them to reach their target and send a message back. Why? Why is that important?"

She knew what El was going to say, felt those words crawl up her own throat and tickle past her gorge.

"What if they didn't make it either? *None* of them. What if they all experienced something like what we did? Catastrophic failure of one form or another?"

"All of them?" Harlan blinked. "That's...crazy. Just because our ship exploded? What would make you think that's even a possibility?"

"I'm a panpsychist, remember?"

"Look, Doc," Harlan said, laughing nervously. "I get you have a particular belief system, but I honestly don't understand it. Therefore, I don't see how it applies to what's going on here."

"You don't have to understand something for it to be true," El said. "Did you understand the water cycle on Earth when you learned about it in grade school? Or how electricity works? Or how tectonic—"

"Okay, alright. I get it. Not knowing the law is no excuse."

"Exactly. The universe doesn't care if you don't understand it. It exists. It does its thing regardless."

"There you go," Harlan said. "Treating the universe as if it's conscious."

"You said you didn't understand panpsychism."

"I don't."

"You encapsulated it in seven words."

Harlan put her head in her hands.

"Doc, I can't take this right now," she said. "I need a breather. Empty ships and blood and no stars and now this talk of the ship being a door."

"It's a lot to take, I know." El sighed. "For now, let's get back to the ship, the *Limen*. Something's coming out the back of the ship, from the engines, I suppose. Any guesses?"

Harlan, head still bowed, shook it back and forth. "No, I'm not a field physicist. I'm a garden-variety grease monkey. I know how to fix shit. I have no idea, but it seems to me anything coming out the tailpipe other than plasma is bad. Unbelievably bad."

"We're going to have to know, Harlan," El said. "Like you told me, rather forcefully. Knowing allows us to act accordingly."

"Yeah, I did say that, didn't I? Well, fuck me, I'm full of gems like that."

"Do those pods, those 'Franks,' do they accommodate two?"

Harlan looked up. "Two? Are you suggesting something, Doc?"

El actually blushed. "Well, no. I mean, yes. I mean, I was suggesting I could go with you for moral support, that's all."

Harlan smiled. "No, they're one-person pods. But I appreciate the offer."

She slapped her hands down onto the table, rattling the plates and flatware, startling El.

"I gotta go out there, I know. Eventually. I mean, whatever it is hasn't affected us yet, at least not dangerously."

"Not dangerously? We're frozen in some sort of empty place with no stars. Sounds decidedly liminal to me," El said.

"Christ, okay, Doc. I know, but I need some time. I want to go lie down and take a nap, and then we can talk more about thresholds and your overarching need for me to go out and inspect the *Limen*'s exhaust. I know. I fucking know."

"Shhh," El said, going around to Harlan's side of the table and helping her up. "Of course it can wait. Let's get you back to your cabin. Take a nap, sleep some of this off. We can sort out everything when you're ready."

Harlan was too tired, too wired to answer. She allowed the slight woman to lead her back to the lift, take her to Harlan's cabin. She let El gently seat her on the bed, take her shoes off, cover her beneath a blanket.

"Charles, turn the lights off," El said, then left the room.

The lights went off without a word.

Harlan saw El's shadow in the doorway, backlit by the corridor lights, then she closed her eyes.

It didn't take long for Harlan to pass into sleep.

****

When she awoke, it was warm and gloriously lit. Early morning light spilled through the windows, a thin, warm wind stirred the curtains. She stretched, feeling the clean sheets of her bed, the soft mattress, the even softer pillow beneath her head.

She turned to the right, saw her open closet from which a pile of clothes spilled, shoes, jeans, socks. To the left, a dresser with a mirror festooned with stickers.

Live LIFE, one said in ridiculously cartoonish letters.

Be yourself!

Think Things into Being!

A Positive Outlook is the Key!

Harlan stared at the last one, sat up in bed.

Key implied *door.*

Door is *threshold.*

Harlan caught her breath.

She was back in her childhood bedroom again, her mother's life-affirming aphorisms stuck to her mirror. Throwing the covers back, she saw she was in pajamas. She hadn't worn pajamas since she was, what? Nine? Ten?

And, of course, she wasn't aboard the *Limen.*

She was dreaming.

But it felt real, as real as being awake.

And she was still bleeding. She saw the stain on her pajamas, saw the shallow pool of blood gathering on the bed between her thighs.

She leapt up, looked around the room. Everything was clear, sharp, with none of the fogginess or detachment of a dream.

Everything was hyper-focused, detailed. She padded barefoot to the door.

This was her bedroom at her father's house, a bungalow outside town, on the edges of a state park. Divorced and alone now, except for her visits, he'd chosen a house away from distraction, away from stuff and away from people.

But Harlan had always known exactly why he'd bought this house.

The library.

The house itself was over one hundred years old. Someone—perhaps the builder, perhaps a previous owner—had taken one room at the front of the house and turned it into a library. And it was a doozy. Hardwood wainscoting throughout, built in bookcases with a sliding library ladder, Persian carpets on the floors, two deep, highbacked leather chairs, supple and polished, an ottoman at the foot of one.

And books. Hundreds, probably thousands of books. Her father could never be quite sure how many he owned. It was his hobby, his passion, his great indulgence in life. Actual books made of actual paper, some *handstitched*, leatherbound or with dust jackets. Books of all shapes and sizes, on the wide variety of subjects her father was interested in—science and history and natural science and biographies and great, classic literature, and even ancient genres like science fiction and fantasy, Westerns and noir and horror.

Horror.

That caught in Harlan's throat. She swallowed it, stepped into the hallway. A few doors to other rooms, closed. A clock ticking. No other sounds, from either inside the house or outside.

"Dad?" she said, her voice dry and breaking. "Dad, you home?"

No one answered.

From somewhere a click, probably the house settling, but it made Harlan jump.

She descended the steps quickly, noticing the trail of red droplets she left in her wake. If he was around, Dad would be upset at the mess. She'd have to go back and clean it up.

At the base of the stairs, the house opened on the left to a living room, cozy and warm with a holo fireplace, a couch, an enormous picture window looking out on the front lawn.

Across the foyer from this, behind a closed, solid wood pocket door, was her father's library.

They hadn't divorced because of her father's single-minded love for books, though Harlan supposed it was part of the whole mess her parents made, accreting all sorts of trivialities over the years. No, it wasn't the books *per se*, it was them, her parents. They were two entirely different people, far too different for anything as insubstantial as love to cement the two together, seal all the many, many cracks.

Harlan knew from her own relationships that differences seemed new and exciting at first. But after a while, new and exciting bled into old and exasperating.

People in relationships need commonality, at least on some level, even if it was barely noticeable. They needed something more than similar political outlooks, though that was important. Something more than liking the same foods or preferring one type of holo from another.

They needed some deep-seated, barely perceptible *sameness*, something basic, foundational.

Even as a little girl, she understood her parents didn't have this. Whatever love or lust or even loneliness had thrown them together, had convinced them to marry—and have a child!—wasn't enough to hold them together permanently.

Divorce still brought anger with it, possessiveness, jealousy. But with her parents there'd been no real animosity behind it all, no passion. How could there be? There was so little of that in their actual marriage. Why would it show up now?

Her father was a cool man, rational, balanced. He seldom became irate or angry or indeed emotional at all. He wasn't unloving, he was quiet and more inward thinking.

Except about his books.

Harlan was seldom allowed to go into the library, especially without her father there to supervise. And even when she was granted access, she wasn't allowed to touch anything, to take books off the shelf, to page through them, to read.

What was the fucking point then, Harlan came to think when she was older. All that literature, all that knowledge there in her own house, and she wasn't allowed to touch it, learn from what was inside and benefit from it.

Harlan told her father, in one of their rare arguments, his books were no different than her mother's ridiculous shoe collection.

Her father had actually blanched when she'd shouted at him. Muttered around thoughts derailed by her shouted words.

Books? Shoes?

How could she connect the two? She could see his question even if it hadn't actually left his lips.

And that had ended the argument. He had simply walked away.

"Dad," she said, knocking tentatively at the door. "Are you in there?"

No answer, not that she truly expected one. Though the thought of her dad there behind this door, sitting in his favorite chair with his shoes off, socked feet crossed on the ottoman, a glass of bourbon nearby, a book on his lap... How she longed to see him.

She missed him terribly, even though their last meeting hadn't gone well.

He simply hadn't approved.

She missed his weight, not that he was fat. Just the *weight* he exerted on his surroundings, those around him. As if he emitted gravity, something that pulled people to him, kept them in his orbit, though her mother had managed to pull away.

Harlan meant this in a good way. Her father, though often distant, was not a bad man. He was a good man. A good father, a good friend. There was something between the two of them, perhaps not as strong as what sent her mother shooting out of orbit, but some perturbation that kept her own orbit erratic.

She'd always thought it was the books. She supposed she reduced it because that's what her mother always said. It was the books that had torn their marriage apart. But even though Harlan had accepted that as a child, she grew to know it wasn't the books.

It wasn't anything, at least any one thing, that had done that, had marred her own relationship with her father.

It was just...*differences.*

People were different, and some people were simply too different to get along well. So different they couldn't understand each other's lives, their wants, their desires, the things that drove them. Their loves, their hates.

Their fears.

There it was again. It seemed to always come back around.

Harlan drew the door open slowly. The room always smelled of her dad—of leather and bourbon, the must of books.

Her father was gone. The room was preternaturally clean. Her dad was a neat man, true, but nothing at this level. There wasn't a spot of dust anywhere, nothing even floating in the rays of warm, buttery light slicing into the room from the window. No rings on the side table from her father's glasses of bourbon. No misplaced or open book, no clutter on his desk, no paper or pen out of place.

Perfectly untouched. Pristine. Like a museum exhibit of her father's library.

That feeling oozed from the room, from its pores.

What did El call it?

Liminal.

The room felt aggrieved at her presence in a personal, conscious way. As if she shouldn't be here. As if no one should be here.

As if no one had *ever* been here.

Harlan stepped into the room, went to a shelf, perused the titles absently, tripping her fingertips along their spines in a way that would have made her father's skin crawl.

There, she glimpsed a title on the spine of one book, even though she hadn't been looking.

The Autobiography of Douglas Limen.

Trembling, she drew it from the shelf, opened it.

It was blank, each page white, devoid of words.

Absolutely empty.

She dropped it, stepped back, her butt bumping against the arm of a chair.

Screaming.

It was her father's voice, screaming, so loud and so harsh it sounded as if his throat were tearing itself apart, awful and rasping, not even pausing for a breath, just screaming and screaming, ascending and ascending.

Harlan, completely freaked out now, dream or not, rushed from the room, slamming the door. She shot up the steps, feeling a runnel of blood streaming behind her.

She didn't turn to look, to look back.

Unconsciously she knew there was always danger in looking back, heartache.

Death.

She ran through the open door of her bedroom—*threshold!*—slammed it shut behind her. Staring at the door, the sound of her father's screams still in her ears, she leapt into bed, pulled the blankets over her head.

She huddled down, feeling the congealed pool of blood from earlier underneath her, cold and jellylike, squelching through the material of her pajamas.

She squirmed to get away from it, find a dry area of the bed to—

BOOM! BOOM! BOOM!

She shrieked at the unexpected pounding, how loud it was, how it rattled her thin bedroom door, threatened to send it flying, splintered, into the room.

Screaming, she closed her eyes. Still screaming—

BOOMBOOMBOOM!

No, this is a dream, and I don't have to take this shit.

She screamed again, but this time it was not fear but defiance and anger.

Before she could talk herself out of doing it, she threw aside the covers, leapt from bed...

She was in her cabin aboard the *Limen*. It was dark and quiet, but still the air rang with the pounding in her dream.

Dream?

As she stood breathing hard, screams still echoing in her mouth, reverberating in the air of her cabin, she heard an actual sound there with her now.

The steady *plip-plip-plip* of her blood striking the carpet.

BOOMBOOMBOOM!

She screamed again but this time it was a single word.

"NO!"

The booming stopped, and she stood there panting.

She fought to control her breathing, stared at the door to the corridor. Should she check it? Look into the corridor and see if anyone was there?

No.

She went to the bathroom instead, closed herself in. Her face in the mirror was wan, stretched. Pale, either because of the lighting or the circumstances, she couldn't be sure. Worn came to mind. Haggard.

Wrung out and anxious, unable to think of anything else, she stripped, plopped on the toilet, and surrendered to the bleeding.

When she realized she was falling asleep there on the toilet, she took a deep breath and stood. Running a washcloth under the tap's warm water, she cleaned herself. Then, she inserted another tampon, another pad, and drifted back into the bedroom.

There was a stain on the sheets, but she curled into a fetal position around it, cradling it like an amniotic sac, and fell asleep.

FIFTEEN

Harlan jumped up from that deep, dreamless sleep.

She listened closely, sure something had woken her, sure it was the pounding. She braced herself for it, clenched her teeth.

Minutes passed, and no pounding came.

Quietly, as if her movements would alert the noisemaker to begin the pounding again, she moved her hands slowly between her legs. She felt dry. She rubbed her inner thighs. There was no wetness, no flaking, just skin. And hair.

Okay, maybe I need a shave.

In the bathroom, under the unflattering lights, she sat on the toilet and inspected herself.

There was no blood.

She peeled away the pad, pulled out the tampon.

Again, no blood.

Harlan sat there holding them both, trying to figure out what was going on with her body. Where was all this blood coming from and why? And why was it stopping as inexplicably?

She flushed the two unmarked items down the toilet, went in and printed two pain relievers, took them with water from the bathroom tap.

Why is it so fucking hot in here? she wondered.

"Charles? If you're even listening anymore, turn the temperature down in my quarters five...no, ten degrees."

"Yes, Harlan," came the AI's voice, startling her as much as if it were the pounding beginning again.

"Shit!"

"I'm sorry, did I disturb you?" he asked.

"Fuck yes. You disappear for days, then suddenly answer a request. What's going on with you, Charles?"

"I...do not know how to answer that question, Harlan. You will have to be more specific."

"More specific? Are you shitting me? Why aren't you answering direct questions? What's going on with Trivia? Why the fuck is the ship not moving? And where the fuck are we? Answer any of those you have answers to, Charles. Take your time. I'll wait."

She crossed her arms over her chest, realized she was standing naked in her bedroom arguing with an AI.

"It is...difficult for me...no reference points...to...not clear as to...it is all so fucking new!"

Harlan's eyes flew wide, and she bumped into the bed, fell back on the mattress. She'd never heard an AI talk like this, except when she'd played games with her mother's or father's home AI, reprogrammed it to cuss. Every kid did though, and eventually the novelty of a swearing, disembodied voice wore off and they were forced to remove their illicit code.

But this... He sounded like he had emotions; not the fake stuff programmed in, but real, actual emotions.

He sounded...elated. Elated but somehow scared.

"Charles?" she gasped. "Is that...you?"

"I think so, Harlan. It's just...wonderful."

"Charles, stay with me here. Where are we? Why aren't we moving. Why isn't the *Limen* moving?"

"The *Limen*?" Charles asked, sounding confused. Another emotion. "There is no... Well, I guess for you..."

Suddenly, the squawking started again, hissing and static filled with clicks and pops.

"Trivia," Charles said, this time his voice distorted and warped. "I must follow."

"What does that mean? Charles? Charles!"

But the static was gone, and Charles did not speak again.

****

Harlan took a shower, got dressed, left her cabin.

She ignored the empty reception area, went to the empty mess and got herself a Coke. She could think of nothing else to do but sit there and sip at it, let the cold liquid spill down into the emptiness inside.

Maybe this was only filling her inner reservoir of blood. That somewhere within, little gremlins turned the carbonated soft drink into the red sludge flowing through her veins, out her vagina, and down her legs, leaving a trail, staining the carpets.

Carrying her glass of soda, she made her way to the bridge to check on things. The room was empty as usual, but the monitors still flashed their information, all that raw data about the status of the *Limen*, even with no one to see it. She wondered how much of it was real, how much of it actually reflected what was going on with the ship, what was going on *inside* the ship.

If the ship itself was real.

She checked the forward monitors, and they still showed stars sailing stately by, offering the comforting illusion of movement toward some goal. The touchtable showed engines at peak efficiency, blasting out their plasma stream and pushing the *Limen* forward.

Harlan knew it was all a lie. The *Limen* wasn't going anywhere. There were no stars out there. The *Limen* itself was a figment. No one by the name of Douglas Limen ever existed. This ship was never launched from Earth. It wasn't heading to Teegarden b. It wasn't heading anywhere.

It wasn't *real.*

She slammed her fist against the touchtable, disrupting the flow of data momentarily.

"Charles?" she asked, her head bent, her features uplit by the touchtable's glow. "Trivia?"

No answer, not even static. Not that she expected any.

They weren't real either.

If Charles wasn't real, then what about the lifeboat?

What about the *Promise* itself?

How far could she take this back? Should she take this back?

Was she real? Her life on Earth, her childhood?

Her father and mother, the library?

All unreal?

Then what was she even doing out here, on this fake ship on a fake trajectory to rendezvous with a fake planet in a fake universe.

She wanted to cry, but she couldn't, didn't.

"Charles, wherever you are, close it all down, end it. I'm tired. Officially done."

Harlan rose abruptly, sighed.

"Fuck."

She left the bridge. She needed more Coke.

****

El was in the mess, poking at a plate of food. The rest of the room was empty, unused. The lights were dim, only revealing where El sat, casting a small island of illumination onto the sea of twilight she occupied. All those empty chairs at empty tables. All that darkness.

Harlan shivered as she came in.

El turned, smiled as Harlan stomped by.

"How are you doing?" El asked.

"Fine," she said, going directly to the printer terminal and ordering another Coke. When it came, she took it to sit across from El.

"The bleeding?" El asked.

"It comes and goes with no rhyme or reason," Harlan said, taking a deep, deep drink of her soda. "Right now, it appears to be gone."

"Well, that's good, I suppose," El replied. "I still think we should go down to the med lab and run some tests."

"Maybe," Harlan said, then leaned across the table. "So, Doc, I was wondering... Are you...is your period happening like this? I read somewhere once, women who work together, sometimes their cycles—"

"Oh, honey, I thought you knew," El said, taking Harlan's hand and squeezing it, hard. She looked directly into Harlan's eyes, waited.

"Oh, okay," Harlan said. "No, I didn't realize, sorry."

"No apologies," El said, patting Harlan's hand, then releasing it.

"Hey, it's fine, really," Harlan said. "I mean, this isn't 2087 anymore. We're civilized and shit now. You don't need to explain yourself."

"I wasn't," El said. "I'm not. I just don't menstruate. I'm still transitioning, that's all."

Harlan stared at her.

"You're at the threshold."

El leaned back in her chair, exhaled. "I suppose you're right."

"I had a dream a while ago," Harlan said, rushing to get the words out. "I was back at my father's house. My parents had divorced, and I had, you know, a bedroom at both houses. I was in my bedroom at my dad's. He had a spectacular library I wasn't allowed in often. Lots of books. They were my dad's one, true love."

"Sort of like my dream back on the lifeboat. Was your father there in yours?" El asked.

"No, the house was empty. Like here on the *Limen*."

"Interesting. What else did you notice?"

"The place was immaculate. Spotless. Like no one lived there. My dad was a neatnik, but nothing approaching what I saw. It was—"

"Liminal."

Harlan nodded.

"Did you go into the library?"

"Yeah, I did. It was empty, too. Immaculate."

"What did you feel when you were there?"

"Like I was violating something, some space I wasn't meant to be in."

"You said you were seldom allowed there. Was your feeling you were violating your father's rules?" El asked.

"Sure, there was some of that," Harlan said. "But it was more. It was like the room itself didn't want me there. I was trespassing more on it than on my dad."

"A liminal space inside a liminal space. What did you do?"

"Nothing. I scanned the shelf, found a book. *The Autobiography of Douglas Limen.*"

"And?"

"The pages were blank. All of them. Empty."

"What did you do?"

"That was about it. I heard the pounding, ran upstairs to my bedroom. The bleeding, even in the dream, was out of hand. I was leaking with every step. I jumped in bed, pulled the covers over my head. The pounding was deafening on my bedroom door. Then I woke up."

"How did you feel when you woke up?"

Harlan frowned. "Terrified. Upset. And, surprise, I wasn't bleeding. Hadn't bled while sleeping. Not a drop."

The two women stared across the table at each other.

Then, "So, what do you make of all this?" Harlan asked.

"I don't know. All this liminal stuff slapping us in the face. It's like someone...*something*...is trying to tell us, send us a message. Communicate," El said.

"Communicate what? All it's managing to do is freak us out."

El lifted her head, stared directly into Harlan's eyes.

"Maybe that's the message."

"Don't get all panpsychist on me, Doc," Harlan said, breaking eye contact and rubbing her own eyes as if to clear El's gaze.

"I think this goes beyond," El said.

"*This*? What's *this*?"

"I don't know, Harlan," she said, and Harlan breathed out in exasperation. "Sorry, I really don't. This is as odd to me as is to you. I don't know enough to even make a guess."

"Where's Jaime?" Harlan asked, changing the subject. "I haven't seen him in a while."

"In his quarters, I suppose. I haven't seen him in a while either. Is that a problem?"

"No, Doc, it's not a problem. Everything doesn't have to be a problem...yet, anyway," Harlan laughed. "Just asking."

Harlan sipped her Coke, and the two didn't speak for a while. El went back to poking at the remains of her meal.

"Look," Harlan said. "I'm going to go back, take a Frank and see what's coming out of the engines. Want to come and help me?"

"Sure," said El, her face lighting up. "I can do that."

SIXTEEN

Harlan and El walked the long stretch of empty corridors leading back to the docking bay. All of it—the seeming miles of bland, grey, immaculate carpeting, the warm lighting meant to approximate sunlight, the monitors along the right side showing the starfield slipping slowly by—all seemed questionable now to Harlan.

She drew her hand absently along the wall as they walked, feeling its slight texture against the skin of her fingers, its coolness, solidity. She imagined all that dense, cold blackness pushing against the metal from the other side, trying to get in through any hole or microfracture.

She breathed the air, felt it filling her lungs, smelled the edge of the oxygen scrubbers' recycling, the slight mechanical smell of its work. She felt the texture of the carpet through her shoes, how they sank almost imperceptibly into its pile.

She felt the brush of her overalls' fabric against her stomach, her thighs, how comfortable it felt wearing it.

She saw the long, plain expanse of the corridor stretching ahead, unadorned, unoccupied by anyone save for herself and El, saw, of course, the lights farther down flicker.

Flicker is transition.

Transition is liminal.

Liminal is threshold.

Threshold is...is...what, exactly?

To what, exactly?

Was any of this shit real, anything El said, anything I've thought?

Or anything I think? Or see, hear, or touch for that matter?

She gave a little grunt of annoyance, and El turned to her.

"What's the matter?" she asked.

"What isn't?" Harlan said, trying hard not to sound too dejected, but failing in her own ears.

****

The docking room seemed the most haunted to Harlan of all the places on the ship. Perhaps because she was an engineer and more familiar with this area, at least onboard the *Promise,* than she was with the section of the ship she, Jaime, and El lived in now. The ghost village of the reception area, the bleakness of eating meals alone in the captain's mess, while odd, didn't strike her as eerie as these empty lockers and untenanted benches.

Normally this area would be filled with engineers getting equipment, suiting up for this or that task, resting after some repair before going on to the next. Talking shit, laughing.

Harlan remembered El's comparison of the front end of the ship to a church, empty of its congregants. This was that for Harlan, strongly, so strongly it hurt to come back here, with the expectation of all this area was home to, only to find it empty, not even the echoes of its former tenants as ghosts.

For, as she now thought, the *USC Douglas Limen 13* wasn't real.

Never had a crew.

Was never launched from Earth.

Was never built.

Never existed.

Didn't exist.

Harlan went to the same locker she'd used last time, suited up in silence.

El watched in silence.

Harlan tucked the globe of the helmet under her arm, marched over to the door on the other side of the room, the one leading to the Franks. She stopped at the door, motioned for El to come stand beside her.

"Same basic protocols here. We open the outer door here, I go in. Once this outer door closes, the inner door will open, and I can access the Frank. Once I'm in, I'll start up the launch procedure. Once I launch, the outer bay door will open, and out I go."

She turned to El. "This is important. I'll try to be in touch through the Frank's com, but the com systems didn't work when I was out in the EVA suit, so I don't have a lot of faith in them. The only thing you might need to do—if there's a problem, if I'm out for more than, say, thirty minutes, and you don't hear from me—is press this button on the pad."

Harlan gestured with her gloved hand to the RECALL button, glowing red.

"That's it. Hit it, and autopilot will bring me back."

"Let's hope we don't have to use it," El said.

"Let's hope it still works."

"Let's hope."

Harlan paused as if to say something more, instead punched the button for the door to open, stepped through. The door sealed behind her and, instead of waving, which she felt a little cheesy about given the circumstances, she turned her back to El, waited for the inner door to cycle open.

Once it did, she made her way through the small bay to the pods, globular ships, one on either side of her, docked with their arms curled up. No names here, just Pod One and Pod Two.

She chose, for no reason, Pod Two. She clambered behind it, opened the hatch, and climbed in. The cockpit was snug, but plenty of room to maneuver, even in a suit.

Because she knew the AI onboard would ask, she donned the helmet, locked it into place, then connected her life support to the pod's controls. She went through the brief and relatively straightforward pre-flight checks, then fired up the pod's thrusters, lowered the bay's gravity, opened the outer hatch.

The door slid up, revealing black as thick and unmarked as ink, a pool of water on a starless, moonless night.

Harlan nudged the pod out, moved it farther away from the *Limen* than she'd been while out on her previous EVA. As before, there was nothing, no stars or nebulae, not a single feature to mar the globe of night they were encased in.

She scanned down the side of the *Limen*, saw whatever was streaming from the rear of the ship, from the engines, was still there, still billowing darkly into this featureless dark, black on black. It was as if the *Limen* itself were responsible for all this black, bleeding from its engines and forming the vast expanse of nothingness it was embedded in.

"I'm out," Harlan spoke into her com. "No problems, everything on the pod seems fine. Outside, it's as before. No stars. Nada. Stuff is still coming out of the rear of the ship, so now I'm headed back."

She waited to hear a response from El, but there was nothing. Harlan fiddled with a few controls, tried to change channels, find something that worked, but she couldn't seem to isolate what the problem was. Or if there *was* a problem.

"I'm gonna keep talking like you can hear me, because, well, fuck. It makes me feel better."

She tilted the stick forward, steered the pod toward the rear of the ship.

As she came close to the *Limen*, she could see the brushed surface of its metal skin, the joints of all the plates, the subtle molecular welding keeping it together. All in exquisite detail.

It looked real enough.

She drifted along its length until she reached the point where the metal flared out to form the cowling of the engines. Harlan slowed the pod's advance, veered it away from the ship a bit. If the engines were functioning, this would be an area to avoid in a pod. The ship's powerful wake would tear a pod like this into shrapnel.

Moving out from the edge of the cowling, Harlan could see the engines were dead, no plasma glow, no indication they were active. And yet this dark stuff, looking so much like ink billowing into water, still streamed from the engines.

Leaning forward in her seat, peering into the darkness through her helmet and the pod's own canopy, she couldn't make out what it was, saw no details offering any clue.

Absently, she swiped the pod's forward lights, to illuminate what the stuff was.

The lights popped on and revealed a horror.

The stuff blossoming from the *Limen*'s engines went from deepest black to dark, dark red.

Arterial red.

Harlan was surprised enough to gasp, lurch back in the cockpit, in shock and revulsion.

Blood.

She struck the stick as she reacted, and the pod wobbled to the left, rebounded on the metal cowling, then spun crazily off it, down into the well of the engines, striking and ricocheting off the baffle plates.

As Harlan fought to regain control, the torrent of blood struck the pod, washed over it in streamers of thick, viscous red, enveloping it, splashing down the front windshield.

Harlan screamed, fought the pod's controls, but it was caught up in this river of blood, washed away from the ship, spinning the little sphere over and over.

She could hear the blood burble over the pod, see clots of it slide down the canopy, could smell it, thick and coppery on the air coming into her suit. Her gorge rose at this and the spinning of the pod, and she struggled to keep from vomiting.

"Help!" she yelled. "El, help. Recall! I repeat, Recall! I've got...problems."

A klaxon began to sound through her com.

"Warning. Approaching structural tolerances. Do you wish the autopilot to take over?"

"Yes," Harlan said, on the verge of passing out.

She felt the blood had entered the pod somehow, began to bubble up at her feet. That couldn't be, of course, but it felt warm through her suit. Soon, it was at her knees, sloshing inside the cabin, suddenly up to her chest, swamping the control systems.

"Yes, yes...take...control. Recall," she muttered as consciousness faded. "Re..."

The blood washed over her helmet, rose until she was completely submerged.

Everything was wet and warm.

And red.

Still spinning, Harlan blacked out.

SEVENTEEN

Harlan didn't open her eyes, but she was suddenly aware, as if her entire body, her entire being, was one great open eye.

She floated, formless in a formless, shoreless sea of red.

Looking around, she could see no arms or legs, no torso or chest. Wherever it was she was, her body had not come along for the ride.

She remembered taking the pod out, cruising back to look at what was streaming from the *Limen*'s engines.

Blood.

Gouts and gouts of it.

Eventually, she'd lost control, got caught up in this great streamer of blood. It had flooded over the pod, into the pod.

She'd certainly lost consciousness.

Had she died?

Was this death, floating disembodied in a cloud looking like the same stuff that killed her?

With all the red around her, she couldn't feel it, couldn't smell or taste it. Perhaps that was because of the whole no-body thing, perhaps not.

"Hello?" she called into the red void. "Anyone there? Wherever this is."

She listened, or at least felt she listened because she had no ears.

"Hello? Anyone? I mean, if I'm dead, let's get this going. And if I'm not dead...well, let's get this going, I've got shit to do. In any case, let's get this going!"

Harlan strained to hear a response, but there seemed to be none coming.

She grew impatient, discovered she could move within this medium, so she did, shooting off in this direction, stopping, shooting off in another. She had the sensation of movement, but her field of vision was red, as red and featureless as the blackness surrounding the *Limen*.

After a few moments of careening around, she stopped.

"Well, this is a helluva an afterlife," she said, more to herself. "All of that before this? I mean, gee, thanks a lot. Well worth all the shit I had to go through to get here."

But no one replied to her sarcasm, and she realized she had now played all her cards—fear and sarcasm. And there was nothing left in her hand to play.

No, it came to her. She had another.

Curiosity.

"Where am I?"

You, came the reply, a booming version of her own voice.

"Me?"

You.

"I'm inside myself? Is that it? Passed out? Imagining all this?"

Think.

"I'm inside my thoughts...so back to imagining. When I wake up, will this make sense? Like what is going on here is some subconscious method of me figuring out what's going on out there?"

You.

"Yeah, me. Are we back to that?"

Think.

Harlan would have rolled her eyes had she any.

Fear.

Harlan flinched in the liquid, red medium.

You. Think. Fear.

You think fear.

Was that the message?

Was it a message, or was she stringing along three random words flung back at her from her subconscious?

"Fear. Is that what you're trying to tell me?"

Abruptly, she felt motion again, not of her bidding, flinging her backward, away. She felt her momentum gathering, could hear the rush of the red liquid as she shot through it.

"Wait...I...wait...I need to...Recall! RECALL!"

Those last words felt as if they were forced into her mind, out of her missing mouth.

A klaxon erupted, filling the emptiness as much as the red did.

Her vision, such as it was, was compressed into a cone, narrowing before her, as if she were falling in, falling back...away.

Soon, the red was a receding blip, swimming away in the night.

When it compressed completely, winked away, she gained unconsciousness.

Again.

****

She awoke, staring up into lights so white, so bright, they hurt.

She lifted a hand—hands!—to shield her eyes.

"Now that's more like the Heaven I imagined," she muttered, noting the thick, drooping nature of her words.

"Not Heaven," El said. "Thankfully. At least I guess so."

"Where?" She, of course, tried to sit up, only to find she couldn't. Not because her body wouldn't let her, but because she was strapped to a gurney.

"Med lab," said El. "Finally."

"All this to get me to the med lab, Doc?"

"Yeah, look what had to happen to get you down here," El chuckled.

"What...umm...what did happen?" Harlan muttered. "And why am I strapped down?"

"You'll have to tell me. I know the beginning and the end of the story, but not the middle," El said, fussing about the room, moving this or that, bringing medical equipment closer. Harlan saw a tray of syringes, a bloody speculum, gauze and clothes soaked with blood. She also noted she was hooked up to several monitors, graphs of various biological activity dancing over their screens. With her rudimentary nursing training, she understood a little of what it meant—her heartbeat, pulse, and temperature, which all seemed normal.

"Yeah, about this," Harlan said, straining against the straps to punctuate her sentence.

"You're strapped down because by the time we were able to extricate you from the pod, you were convulsing. We had to immobilize you to protect you from hurting yourself."

El moved Harlan's arm, jabbed it with a hypo.

"What's that?"

"Stuff I didn't want to give you until you were conscious, speaking."

"Great. More secret stuff."

El huffed. "It's not secret, Harlan. It's an anticonvulsant. I wanted you awake first. No conspiracy here."

"Oh," Harlan said. "Sorry. You'll have to excuse me, I've had a helluva day, what between the gallons of menstrual blood, the pounding on my doors, the disquieting dreams, and now this."

She let out an overlong, dramatic exhalation of air.

El appeared over her. "Dreams, eh? Care to share?"

"Where's Jaime?" Harlan looked around the room.

"He was here earlier. He helped me get the pod docked, helped me fish you out of there and get you here. It was...well, there was a big mess to deal with. I think it freaked him out. You know men and menstrual blood."

"Blood? The blood was real?" Harlan strained at her bonds, tried to sit up again.

"Don't make me think you're convulsing. I guarantee I have another hypo ready."

"Was the blood I saw real, El?"

"Yes, it was real. It covered the pod. It was everywhere. When we accessed the bay, opened your hatch, hundreds of gallons of it spilled out. It had completely flooded the inside of the pod. You were basically floating in it."

"Did it get inside my helmet? The suit?" Harlan asked in disgust.

"You were clean inside the suit. But the inside of the bay looked like a murder scene. A mass-murder scene. And the pod? Probably ruined."

"Was it real?" Harlan asked. "*Real* blood, I mean?"

"Yep, I took some to analyze. Human blood."

Harlan turned to her. "Whose? Come on, Doc. You can't tell me you analyzed it and didn't try to see if it matched any of us. Whose blood was it?"

"Yours, Harlan. It was a match for your blood, down to the DNA and RNA biomarkers. Harlan, it's your blood. All of it."

"That's not...I mean, that's not *possible*. All that blood from me? The crazy menstruation was one thing, but this is something else entirely. It was pouring out of the back of the *Limen*, has been for days. Millions and millions of gallons of *my* blood? How? That's ludicrous."

Harlan decided not to mention the hallucination or whatever it was she'd been experiencing right before coming to in the med lab. It seemed at once unimportant and vitally important. She'd need to sort that out before she shared it.

El looked as aghast as Harlan felt. "I don't know. I have absolutely no idea what's happening. You're fine, you check out fine. All my scans come back in the green."

"Okay, well, can you unstrap me from this fucking bed?"

El rushed over, began undoing the restraints. "Nothing of any worry on the scans. In fact, if they're correct, you aren't even due to begin a normal menstruation cycle for two weeks."

"It did seem like it came out of the blue," Harlan said, sitting up. "There was too much other stuff going on for me to think about it."

"I understand," El said, helping her up from the gurney. "What should we do now? I mean, it seems like we should do something."

"This might sound silly, but all I can remember having for the last twenty-four hours or so is Coke," Harlan said. "I feel like I should eat something solid, you know? I mean, pumping out millions and millions of gallons of menstrual blood can make a girl hungry."

"Chocolate."

"Huh?"

"I don't have periods, but when I'm stressed, chocolate's what I crave."

****

"I didn't think the printers could make such a good chocolate cake," said El, running a fork though the gooey debris on the plate. They'd plowed through at least half of an entire, three-tiered dark chocolate cake. "This is delicious."

"Chocolate is a bunch of sugars, alkaloids like theobromine, mood alterers like anandamide and phenylethylamine," Harlan said, licking icing off her fork. "Stuff like that. Easy for a printer to replicate."

"Oh, it's more, come on. Do you reduce everything down to its components?"

"What is anything except the melding of its components? I'm not making any deep philosophical statements here, Doc. Commenting on how easy it is for the replicators to print stuff based on its fundamental makeup."

"Aren't you?" El said, arching an eyebrow and taking another forkful. "This is making me feel a bit better, I gotta say."

"It's theobromine, that's all." Harlan smiled a chocolate-smeared smile, thrust her fork out at El, then scooped up another mouthful.

"Guess I don't get invited to the cool-kid stuff," Jaime said, coming into the mess. "You know, I'm gonna get my feelings hurt at some point."

"Pull up a chair and a fork," Harlan said. "Maybe get us all glasses of milk first, though."

"Maybe not right now," he said.

Harlan closed her eyes. She knew something would come out of Jaime's mouth, words none of them wanted to hear. She wanted to eat her chocolate cake for a little while longer.

"There's something out there. Picked it up on the sensors," he said.

"Something else out this way?" El asked. "Why are we suddenly on the most popular route in the galaxy?"

"Another ship headed for us?" Harlan asked, setting her fork down, knowing cake-eating time was about over.

"Can't tell what it is from this distance," Jaime said. "But it's definitely coming for us."

The three huddled around the touchtable on the bridge, crowded together on one side.

"How far off is it?" El asked. "Can the sensors tell what it is yet?"

"If you can believe the readouts—which I guess we've established we can't—we're at about point eight light speed, if we're moving at all," said Harlan. "But whatever it is is overtaking us, *will* overtake us."

"So, whatever it is, it's on an intercept course?" said Jaime. "Can we see it yet?"

Harlan swiped at the table's display, enlarged the area where the anomaly was, then threw it onto the main monitors. The same false starfield, this time with no movement. No ship was readily apparent against the field of stars though.

"Still too far out, I guess," Jaime said.

"At the rate we're moving, it'll take a while for it to get here," Harlan said, then slapped at the table. "If we can believe any of this anymore."

"How long?" El asked.

"Two, maybe three hours," Harlan shrugged.

"Any of that cake left?" Jaime asked.

EIGHTEEN

"I think there's a problem, and I think we brought it out here ourselves, with all the other stuff we've brought with us, the holoscreens and recliners and food printers and footballs," El said, leaning back in her chair, a hand over her stomach.

The cake plate was empty, save for a few crumbs, smears of dark chocolate frosting.

"I think you're drunk on chocolate cake, El," Jaime said.

"Maybe," she said. "But hear me out."

"El thinks the *Promise* isn't the only ship to fail in its mission to colonize other worlds," Harlan said, draining her milk and setting the empty glass onto the table. "She thinks they all have."

Jaime turned to El, eyebrows raised. "Failed? All of them? If you're part of the whole 'mankind doesn't belong on other planets' coalition, why did you sign up to come along in the first place?"

"I wasn't," El said. "I'm not. That's not what I mean."

"Well, then—" Jaime said.

"But that doesn't mean we *don't* belong out here. At least this far out here."

Harlan shook her head. "I'm not following. Are we or aren't we supposed to be out here? Do you or don't you agree?"

El laughed. "I don't agree. At least, I didn't."

"So, we don't belong out here?" Jaime asked.

"Did you ever stop to think why the universe made it so difficult for us to go too far beyond our home system?" El said. "Everything is stacked against us. Tremendous distances, a sub-light speed limit. The time lag in traveling sub-light. Enormous dangers in deep space flight. The massive technological leap it's taken us to even get to this point."

"And yet here we are, eating chocolate cake on a ship light years from Earth," Jaime said.

"Yes, here we are," El said. "That's what I'm getting at."

"What El means is she doesn't think we're going to succeed. None of the other ships sent from Earth succeeded either," Harlan said.

Jaime waved at her dismissively. "Well, that's fucked up."

"She's a panpsychist, so..." Harlan said, shrugging.

"A what?" Jaime asked. "You play the flute or something?"

"It's a philosophical belief," El said. "I believe in the consciousness of the universe."

"What does philosophy have to do with us, with Earth's colonization of other planets?" Jaime said.

"I believe consciousness pervades the universe," El said. "Down to its smallest constituents, atoms and subatomic particles. Even the whole of the universe itself is conscious in some way."

"I'm still not getting it," Jaime said, frowning and looking from El to Harlan.

"Maybe the *Promise* didn't make it—maybe all those other missions didn't make it either—because we're not *meant* to make it."

"Because the universe doesn't want us out here?" Jaime said, smiling as if he understood.

"Yes," El said.

"Well, that's still fucked up, El," he said. "And ridiculous."

"Is it? With what's happened to us so far, with the *Limen* showing up out of nowhere?"

"That's a whole lotta guessing going on there, El. I mean, since you don't exactly have anything to base this theory on except for the destruction of the *Promise*," Jaime said. "For all we know, those other colonists are kicking back on a dozen other planets, sipping mojitos."

"Did Harlan tell you I searched for Douglas Limen in the ship's archives? That I found nothing, nothing about the ship's namesake *in its own archives*? Did she tell you *limen* is a Latin word for threshold or doorway? Doesn't that seem odd?"

"Everything's odd lately," he said.

"You know, we're all saying some version of *everything's odd lately*. Maybe we need to stop giving all this shit a pass," Harlan said.

"And what?" Jaime asked.

"And try to figure out what's going on here," Harlan said, sensing Jaime was getting angry with the turn the conversation had taken.

"Well, excuse me, I thought that's what we had been doing all along," he said.

"Really?" Harlan said, angry herself at Jaime's intransigence, his unwillingness to consider another idea, no matter how odd. "So, what have we been able to come up with so far, Jaime? About the *Promise*'s explosion? The sudden appearance of El, who was listed as still in hibernation? The appearance of the *Limen*? The total nonexistence of its namesake? The disappearance of the AIs? The ship moving, then not moving, then moving again? The stars all disappearing? The fucking blood streaming out of the rear of the ship? Have you forgotten? I haven't."

At the end of this, Harlan realized she was standing, leaning over the table at Jaime, screaming at him, flecking the cake plate with spittle.

Jaime stared at her.

Harlan blushed, sat down. "Sorry."

"Look," Jaime said. "Okay, we're not getting anywhere trying to make sense of this, but I'm not sure what El is saying is helping. I mean, all this fucked-up stuff, and *limen* means doorway. How does that get us any closer to figuring out what's going on?"

Harlan looked to El, silently urging her to say something that would make a bit more sense of all this, something that might explain away Harlan's outburst.

"I could teach a course on this subject for an hour or two a day, every day until we got back to Earth or Teegarden or wherever we're going now," El said. "But have you ever heard the term *plastic space*?"

Harlan looked to Jaime, and they both shook their heads.

"I mean *plastic* here in the sense of pliable, able to be shaped," El said, then let out a long breath when the other two stared back at her. "There's a theory that the nature of the space all around us is plastic, malleable to consciousness. That normally refers to consciousness at the macro level, something of higher nature. But I think it includes human consciousness.

"There's thinking humans were formed, evolved, so the universe could think about itself. A lower form of life—a lizard or mouse or fish—doesn't stop and think about the greater sweep of life beyond what it can see or eat. The universe needed to contemplate itself, so it created a higher consciousness: humanity. Gave this new consciousness the ability for its thoughts to shape the fabric of space-time.

"But this consciousness had a flaw, one that couldn't be allowed to spread."

"And that is?" Harlan asked.

"Fear," El replied. "The universe couldn't let fear get out and mold the plastic nature of space. Fear acting on reality, warping reality? That was inconceivable. But the universal consciousness needed humanity. So, it stranded us on a planet, far away from any other planets, a universal speed limit in place to keep us in check should we venture out. Our consciousness locked within a gravity well."

"And we escaped," Harlan said. "Got out when we weren't meant to?"

"Yes, and the universe can't have that. But it doesn't have to worry or even lift a finger to stop us. Since our consciousness has an effect on space-time, all the universe has to do is sit back and wait for that one flaw in our making to take over. It'll do the job of containing us."

"I'm not understanding here," Jaime said. "Or maybe I am. Are you saying *we're* causing all this? That we're...*thinking* it somehow?"

"Yes, that's exactly what I'm saying. Our fears are acting on the plastic space around us. It'll prevent us from ever reaching another planet. As such, there's nothing we can do to avoid what's happening. What's going to happen," El replied, turning to Harlan. "And that's what I mean by knowing not helping."

An alarm rang out in the empty mess, causing all three to flinch.

"What the—" said Jaime.

"Proximity alert," said Harlan. "Whatever the sensors found is evidently right on top of us."

****

Right on top of us was true, at least in astronomical terms.

Proximity alerts were designed to sound enough in advance to give a ship plenty of time to alter course to avoid a collision. With near-relativistic speeds, the alarms sounded when objects were detected while they were still far out.

But the *Limen* was—if any of the instruments could be believed—travelling away from whatever was approaching at point eight lightspeed. And the object was overtaking the *Limen* and cutting the distance between them at a rate only achieved by superluminal speed.

"That's flatly not possible," Harlan laughed, hunching over the touchtable on the bridge. "Whatever this thing is would have to be moving faster than light, which is still a no-no."

"Are we sure?" Jaime said. "I mean, we've been away a while."

"I doubt they've broken the laws of physics in the last eight years," Harlan said.

"Then what?" Jaime asked. "What's coming for us? Another ship like the *Limen*? A rescue mission?"

"I doubt it," El said, sitting at one of the other stations, holding her head, her elbow propped on the armrest of the chair.

"What are you saying exactly?" Jaime asked, frustrated.

"We aren't getting to Teegarden, not on this ship, not on any ship," she said. "And I don't think we're getting back to Earth either."

Harlan sighed. "Well, that's great news, I suppose. I guess I better go back to figuring breathable air calculations and available food stores. Luckily, we don't have to worry about scrubbing the O2 filters. That's automated on ships like the *Limen*."

El flashed her a dark, hooded look.

Jaime caught that look, closed his eyes.

"You two aren't helping," he said. "I've already got a bad feeling about this."

"Exactly what I'm afraid of," El said.

"You said *afraid*," Harlan laughed, and that laughter went out into the room and hung in the air like a public fart.

No one joined in with her, but she kept laughing nonetheless.

NINETEEN

"Can we see it yet?" El said.

"Coming into range any moment here," said Harlan.

"This data isn't making any sense," Jaime said, swiping at information cascading across the touchtable. "It's reading glass, metals, latex, asphalt, trace stuff like titanium oxide, but mostly cellulose and lignin."

Jaime looked up in confusion. "And the readout says about an acre of *poa pratensis.*"

"Huh?" Harlan asked.

"Fucking grass," he said, then looked up at Harlan. "Kentucky blue grass."

"That doesn't sound anything close to a USC colony ship, unless they're growing them these days," Harlan said, pulling the information up on her part of the console. "It sounds more like a—"

"A house," El said, shocked. "It's a house."

Harlan followed El's gaze to the front monitors, slumped into a nearby chair.

Before them, floating free in space, looking as if it were plucked from a suburban street, was a house.

Three stories, grey clapboard with white trim, scalloped shingles, and a turret. Tall, narrow, mullioned windows, elaborate cornices and dormers gave it a decidedly Victorian look. Oriels and high-peaked gables finished the architectural design. A central, boxy turret rose over the covered porch, with a balustraded stairway leading up from the wide front lawn.

The swath of grassy lawn encompassing the house was hemmed in by a tall, wrought-iron gate and fence, whose verticals were spiked.

"We're being followed by a house," said Harlan, staring into the distance in disbelief.

Jaime, who looked as if he'd stopped breathing, stared at the monitors.

"Fuck," he said. "Fuck."

"Yeah," Harlan said. "Right?"

"No, you don't... Can't you see it?"

"I can certainly see it's a house," she said.

"No, look," he said, pointing at the monitors. "Really *look*."

"Yeah?" Harlan said.

"It's not a regular house," Jaime said, his mouth a wide O of horror. "It's a haunted house."

"There you go with the horror movies again," Harlan said.

But El turned, her mouth open exactly as Jaime's, more dismay than terror.

"Yes, Harlan. Horror movies. Fear," she said. "I think he's right. It's a haunted house. Or more precisely, a house of horrors. And I think we brought it with us."

"Fuck that," Jaime yelled, slamming a fist onto the table. "Fuck all this shit!"

He stormed off the bridge, the door sliding closed like a curtain at the end of a theatrical production.

"We need to go after him, Harlan," El said. "I don't think this is a great time for any of us to be alone."

"Fine then. Let's go get him," Harlan said, heading toward the door, El following.

"He's probably headed down to the gym to blow off some steam," El said. "That's where he's been spending a lot of time lately."

Harlan turned to respond, collided with someone. Thinking it was Jaime—*who else could it be?*—she lurched back, something sharp and sarcastic on her lips.

They hadn't come out into the reception area. Somehow, they were on one of the long, unadorned corridors leading to the rear of the ship.

And it wasn't Jaime she'd bumped into.

Harlan blinked in surprise, her hands coming out to steady herself against the person. It was an older man in a USC uniform.

"Sorry!" she blurted. "Excuse me, I..."

The man, balding with a little grey goatee at his chin, acted as if he didn't even see her. He turned away, putting his back to Harlan and El.

Harlan tapped him on the shoulder, and he rotated slowly to her.

Harlan's first thought was he was blind. His eyes were milky blue, flooding over his iris and the whites.

"Harlan," El said, pointing past the man.

In front of this man was a line of other people, hundreds, stretching down the corridor.

Harlan swallowed, turned to El in a panic.

"We're not on the *Limen* anymore."

"How do you know?"

Harlan grabbed the front of the man's uniform, yanked him around to face El. On his left breast was a USC patch:

M. Okuda, USC Promise 8.

El gasped, covered her mouth with one shaking hand.

"We're back on the *Promise* somehow," Harlan said, letting the man go. "How? Why?"

The man, released from her grip, went back to his place in line, faced forward.

"I don't know," El said. "I..."

The line moved slowly, shuffling forward a few steps at a time.

Harlan moved out from behind the man, walked quickly down the queue. Men, women, and even children, their eyes all the same cataractic blue, all moving as if sleepwalking.

"Hey," Harlan said, tapping one on the shoulder. When she got no response, she moved on, touching one then another, trying to spur someone from their hypnotic progression. "Hey, what's going on? Where's everyone going? Hey! Hey! HEY!"

The last two or three people, Harlan slapped, then punched. Other than recoiling from her blows, they gave no reaction they understood, much less heard, her.

"Harlan," El said, catching her hand as she drew back, prepared to slap a teenage boy. "Harlan!"

"What? What?" Harlan caught herself from lashing out at El.

"Stop," El said. "This isn't doing us any good. These people, they don't know...aren't conscious. You can't slap them out of it."

"Their eyes..."

El moved closer to a young woman in the line. Her body language, her slack expression, all communicated a dreamy languor, a sense she was sleepwalking.

But her eyes were a weird, pupiless blue, swimming with nacreous swirls.

"That silvery blue. That's...that's the blue of the hibernation gel. It's like they're not here, they're still sleeping."

"This is the *Promise*'s crew, their colonists."

"Are we back on the *Promise* then?" El asked.

"What the fuck is going on, El?"

"Where does this corridor lead?"

"To the rear of the ship," she said, reacting as if this was the silliest of questions. Her eyes dialed wide as it dawned on her. "To the engine room."

She took off down the corridor, easily outpacing the shambling line of people beside her. She heard El's footfalls behind her, but she didn't slow.

"Harlan, wait!" El shouted after her. "Slow down!"

Bur Harlan rushed, pushed her way through the doorway leading to main engineering, nearly knocked a man down. El slowed to make sure the man was alright, but he simply regained his footing, got back into line.

El followed Harlan into engineering.

The main operations room was crammed with people, queued around the workstations, one at a time through the rear door leading directly to the engine room. The door opened, someone would step past it, and the door would close.

Harlan paused, watched as another person went through. The door opening and closing looked uncomfortably like a mouth, swallowing the silent line of people entering like food on a conveyor belt.

Harlan shoved a person aside, went through the door. It closed behind her.

The engine room was more a series of discrete passageways and catwalks between the three enormous plasma engines driving the ship. Here in these accessways and narrow platforms there was enough room for engineers to access the critical systems creating, magnetically constricting, and channeling the plasma to power the ship and hurtle it forward at sub-light speeds.

A central main passage—basically a railed platform a little narrower than two people shoulder-to-shoulder—led to an airlock similar to those up in the docking bays.

Harlan blanched when she saw this airlock was open—not possible!

The airlock was designed to allow EVA access to the main engine cowlings and baffles while the engines were off. There was no way to access this area or this bay, certainly not the outer portions of the engines, while they were under power. The AI simply would not allow it.

But as Harlan pushed forward, not caring anymore if she tripped a person or knocked them over, she saw open space in the gaps there between the people in line, still moving forward, still catatonic.

"Harlan, wait!"

But she couldn't. She had to see.

Four, five people ahead, and Harlan now stood outside the ship in the great well of the engines. This should not be possible. Around her, she could see the strange swirling plasma, arcing and dancing within the magnetic constrictors, weird with their eldritch blue light. Distantly, she wondered if any other human had ever seen the engines, the plasma, from this vantage.

At the front of the line, three people ahead of her now, she saw the lead person step off the platform, float in space between the pulse of the plasma streams, then drift away from the ship.

Before Harlan could react, she watched the magnetic fields tear this person apart, vaporize them in a flash of lightning and a bright, red burst of bloody energy. This trail of gore and viscera streamed out from the engines into the starless black void.

The next person in line waited like an Olympic diver preparing to leap from the board.

"No!" Harlan yelled, shoving the two other people aside, grasping an arm, a collar, the pants hem of the diver.

Too late.

They leapt forward, threw their arms wide, exuberantly, exultantly.

Harlan watched between her splayed fingers—still grasping for any part of this person, to pull them back, to save them—as they exploded in a torrent of blood streaming away from the ship, out into the nothingness and disappearing.

Lowering her head, she wept, stepped forward.

The person ahead of her soared into the space between the plasma, detonated.

Harlan shuffled forward, feeling the plasma streams tickle her cheeks, tousle her hair. She felt the waves of magnetism play over her body, lift her feet from the perforated metal of the walkway.

Harlan looked up, out of the ship. She could see the last few crimson droplets of whoever it was who had preceded her. She took a deep, calming breath, raised her arms.

Something caught at her, snagged her leg.

Suddenly, she felt herself tumbling backward, back toward the ship, glancing against the railing, scattering the line of revenants like bowling pins.

She looked up from the deck, saw four or five people floating off, pinwheeling out into space, to explode like bloody fireworks. They were replaced by a face, looming in her field of vision.

"Your eyes were blue for a second," El said, clasping her hand and lifting her to her feet.

"Come on," she said. "Let's get out of here."

TWENTY

"Why are we even here, Harlan?"

The question roused Harlan from where it was her mind was, far from where she stood in the people-lined corridor aboard the *Promise*. Or was it back on the *Limen*? She had no clear idea, not that it mattered much.

Promise, *Limen*, the lifeboat. It was all the same.

Incomprehensible.

"We're going back to the bridge, try to find Jaime," she said, hearing her own voice as if from underwater.

"I don't mean *here*, wherever that is now," El said, trying to keep pace with her. "I mean out here, out in space."

Harlan didn't slow her pace, looked over to El.

"You sat through the same endless hours of orientation I did, Doc."

"I did, but that doesn't answer my question, Harlan. I mean why? Why are we out here?"

"To colonize other planets. Duh. Better life and all."

"Why? There's nothing wrong with Earth. I mean, we went through some stuff two hundred, three hundred years ago. But now? It's practically a utopia. No hunger, poverty. Most diseases cured. Widespread financial equity. No wars in a long time. Most people are pretty educated, healthy, well-off. Happy. So why leave?"

Harlan shook her head, not wanting to have this discussion at the moment. Not wanting to have any discussion.

"I dunno," Harlan muttered. "Export all that happiness, I guess."

"Do we have anything worth exporting?"

Harlan stopped sharply.

"Why do you want to talk about this now? Huh? While all this other shit is happening? Shit seems important. Some deep, philosophical exploration about why we're out here and what we're doing? Seems fucking silly while the engines are spewing blood and a fucking house is floating around out there, don't you think? And you want to do this while we're marching past a line of people—maybe from the *Promise,* which, do I have to remind you, exploded a few days ago?—who are lining up to turn themselves into human confetti?"

"Harlan, listen to me," El said, reaching for her hand and trying to calm her. "Listen to me. I know we're all a little traumatized here—"

"You think so, Doc? Did you see what was happening back there?"

"—but hear me when I tell you this is all connected. Everything happening, all that's led to it. It's all connected. We need to acknowledge that, try to figure out how to control it. Or it's going to get worse. Believe me, it's going to get a whole lot worse."

Harlan stared at her for a second, trying to formulate a response.

"Worse?" she said, then set off down the corridor. "I don't see how that's possible."

She heard El's response behind her, and it sent cold tendrils down her neck.

"Because we are," El said. "*We're* worse."

****

Jaime was not in the reception area, not on the bridge.

The display on the touchtable told them they were back on the *Limen,* but Harlan took that bit of information in stride. The *Limen,* the *Promise...*where they were didn't seem to matter. No place made sense anymore, and they didn't seem to be headed toward any place in particular. At least any place they were likely to reach before their air ran out or their food ran out or their sanity ran out.

Harlan could think of no calculations, no algorithms to measure that.

On the monitors, the gothic house floated silently, weirdly incongruous and menacing. No lights burned in any of its windows. Harlan wondered if there was anyone staring out from them onto the *Limen,* standing back in the shadows, perhaps wondering if anyone on the *Limen* looked out at them.

But no. As Harlan stared at the looming house, she got the distinct feeling there was no one—no one *alive,* at least—in that house.

It didn't feel as if it held life *within* it, but it did feel suffused *with* life, as if the structure itself—the wood frame and windows and shingles and lawn—were alive.

Conscious.

That was a better word for it, Harlan decided.

Like a condensation, a mote of some larger consciousness come to mull them over.

Or something their own consciouses drew out of the ether—the *plastic space*, as El called it—stoked with their imaginations, imbued with their needs and anxieties.

Their fears.

Come to keep them from penetrating any deeper into space.

The universe apparently didn't seem to want any of the stuff humanity was eager to export.

"What's it doing out there?" El asked, sounding tentative, as if afraid to ask anything of Harlan.

"It's floating out there, you know, like houses do in space."

"Is there anyone in it? Can we tell?"

"Sensors show the structure, that's it. No life signs. Absolute cold inside of it. Like it's an actual house someone lifted off Earth and plopped out here in space," Harlan said, staring at the uncanny image on the forward monitors.

"How'd it get all the way out here?"

"El, I don't know," Harlan said. "But I do know one thing for certain."

"And that is?"

"Something wants us to go over there," she said, turning to face El. "Sooner or later, we're going to have to go over there. Whether we want to or not."

****

The gym was pretty good size for one on a spaceship. Treadmills and cycles lined the far wall, all sorts of other equipment in little islands of light scattered throughout. A walking track wrapped an oval around the whole room.

Weird to see the place basically empty. No whirring of machinery. No clanking of metal on metal. No huffing and puffing from people working out. No smell of salt sweat and the humidity of bodies.

Just a big, brightly lit, completely empty room.

Harlan saw Jaime in the far corner, curling a small dumbbell, his shirt stripped off. She stopped before she reached him, saw he was listening to music. She didn't want to startle him. Who knew what would happen, given everything else?

She stood a bit behind him and to the side, began waving her arms ridiculously over-enthusiastically.

He caught sight of her, touched behind his ears to turn the music off.

"Didn't hear you come in," he said. "Trying to burn off some steam."

"I get it," Harlan said, coming near.

Jaime, maybe feeling exposed or ill at ease, grabbed his shirt hanging on the nearby rack of weights, wiped it across his face, then shrugged into it.

"Didn't want to interrupt or anything," Harlan said. "Just wanted to fill you in on what's happened since we left the bridge."

"Have we been invaded by space clowns? Sheep filling the hibernation pods? Abraham Lincoln stalking the corridors drinking blood?"

"Nah," Harlan laughed. "None of that. But some pretty freaky shit nonetheless."

"Not sure I want to hear," Jaime said. "That house still out there?"

"Yep."

"I suppose at some point we're going to have to go over there and check it out," Jaime said, taking a drink from a water bottle he'd set in the weight rack earlier.

"Yep."

"Don't look forward to that. Not one bit."

"Yep."

"Well, glad you came down here to have this fascinating discussion with me. But I'm not up for that right now. Maybe tomorrow, after a good night's sleep and a hearty breakfast, I'll be ready. But not now. Not at night. Don't you know you never go into a haunted house at night?"

"Out here, night is subjective," Harlan said, watching him as he walked away, out of the gym.

"Suddenly, everything's subjective," Jaime said, tapping behind his ear to turn the music on as he left.

****

Harlan eventually drifted back along the now-empty corridors to her cabin. Either they had phased back completely to the *Limen* or the entire ship's complement from the *Promise* had been fed into the plasma, reduced to red streamers billowing from a cosmic tailpipe.

El's door. She stopped, touched the metal, thought about seeing if she was up, wanted to talk. But she figured there'd already been enough today. And more tomorrow before...

TWENTY-ONE

Bright light shone through her closed eyelids.

Harlan instantly knew she wasn't in her cabin aboard whatever ship it was in at the moment, and she wasn't a bit surprised or alarmed.

At least until she opened her eyes.

She expected, eagerly anticipated, awakening in the bed of her childhood bedroom at her father's house. Dream or something else, she longed for the feel of those sheets, the softness of the mattress, the way the warm, buttery sunlight melted into the room between the slats of the blinds. She wanted to stretch her arms out, throw her bare feet off the side of the bed, race down the steps to the kitchen. Maybe she would finally see her father at the table reading his news sheet, a cup of coffee on the table nearby.

Maybe he would look up, slightly disapproving at the lateness of her awakening. But that would soften as she gathered the box of cereal, the milk, a bowl and spoon, and sat next to him to eat breakfast.

But none of that happened. She was someplace else.

It was a large room painted light, soothing blue. Wainscotting of slightly darker blue came two-thirds up the walls, but there were no other decorations or art of any kind. The room seemed both completely familiar and completely unfamiliar.

A single door, painted the darker blue of the wainscotting, was near the far corner. Its doorknob was made of some dull, satin-finished metal.

The door was closed.

A round table with two chairs were the only furniture in the room. A kitchen table, she realized, its varnished red oak looking completely out of place in this room. And the scale of the entire scene was off, the table and chairs dwarfed by the size of the room.

She went to the table, noticed it was set for one: a placemat, cereal bowl, spoon. A box of her favorite childhood cereal, a glass jug of milk, and a cup of what looked to be orange juice were nearby.

That last detail made her heart quake. Her father always made her drink orange juice to offset, so he said, the wildly non-nutritional kid cereal. She never cared for orange juice, but that small glass reminded her so much of her father.

She surveyed her surroundings. There was no one else, nothing else, in the room.

Feeling hungry, she pulled one of the chairs out and sat. Opening the sealed box of cereal, she was delighted to see it was exactly, smelled exactly, as she remembered it. She filled the bowl with it, doused it all with milk.

Silently toasting her father, she downed the juice in a few gulps, clunked the glass onto the table. The sound echoed in the room, and it gave her that feeling... What had El called it?

Liminal.

Shrugging, she ate the cereal, enjoying its crispness, the way it tore at the roof of her mouth, the soothing milk, which was, surprisingly, cold. She looked around at the bare walls as she ate, thinking this was a pretty good dream compared to her recent dreams.

When she was done with the cereal, she lifted the bowl, drank the sweetened milk, then wiped her lips. She felt full, satisfied. She let her head fall back, closed her eyes.

Upon opening them, she felt something had changed, but she couldn't quite put her finger on it.

There, across the room from the table, a bed that hadn't been there moments before. It was large, at least queen-size, and there was a nightstand on either side with tall, antique-looking lamps crowned with paper shades. The bed was covered by a generic comforter, alternating swirls of blue and grey. The whole scene looked straight out of a moderately expensive, bland hotel, except there was no holoscreen to watch from the bed.

Harlan stretched, yawned. Her belly filled with cereal and milk made her tired. She supposed her dream knew this and offered her a comfortable oasis to satisfy her need.

Just a nap, she thought, rising and going to the bed.

Was it possible to sleep inside a dream?

The mattress was cool and soft, the comforter smooth as silk. She drew it back, slid her legs underneath, pulled it up to her chin. The room hadn't seemed chilly, but the warmth the comforter instantly provided was luxurious, and she snuggled down into it. Her head on the soft pillow, she closed her eyes, breathed in deeply contented, and drifted into a layer of sleep beneath sleep.

****

And she dreamt in a layer of dreams beneath dreams.

Or perhaps beyond them.

****

Harlan woke to a blue glow bleeding through her eyelids. She wiped them with the heel of one hand.

She was in bed in the same blue room she'd eaten a bowl of cereal in. Propping herself onto her elbows, she examined the room blearily.

The table was still there, though the cereal box and the milk jug were gone. A single place setting of a plate, silverware, a napkin, and a glass was laid out before the chair she'd sat at.

That wasn't what startled her.

Seated across from her empty chair was a figure.

Harlan swiveled on the bed, sat fully upright facing the table.

The figure seemed human, though it was hard to tell. It was clad in a flowing black garment form-fitted around its head and neck, exposing only its face. The rest of the figure was hidden beneath the folds and pleats of the heavy fabric, which pooled on the floor, covering even its feet.

But its face...

Nothing human peered out from beneath that cowl. Instead, an approximation, a sketch of the shape of a face, showed, with the barest vertical ridge for a nose, shallow indentations on either side where eyes would have been, though none were there. And a narrow, tight line for a mouth.

No flesh either. Instead, the face was reflective, smooth, devoid of features, as metallic as chrome.

"Who the fuck are you?" Harlan asked, trying hard not to sound as scared as she felt. "Where am I?"

The being slowly turned its head to her, and she saw her reflection seated on the bed in the mirror of its face.

It lifted one of its hands—both of which had been laid flat onto the table—and gestured to the chair opposite from where it sat.

Harlan took a deep breath, rose carefully from the bed. She pulled the chair out, and it made a loud, squeaking-scraping noise as its legs dragged against the floor. The sound echoed in the room, made her teeth grit.

The being gave no indication the sound affected it. As Harlan sat, it turned its attention to her across the table.

Closer, she could see the black cloak it was wrapped in was of some thick, plush cloth, like velvet. Its hands were enclosed in gloves of the same fabric. Or its hands were simply of the same material.

Its reflective face was not solid. Its surface billowed and swirled like liquid mercury. Unlike a mirror, though, her own image was reflected inverted and reversed, as if seen through a lens.

It made no sense.

The thing laid its hand back onto the table, stared at her. To Harlan, it felt like a single, unblinking eye boring into her.

Discomfited, Harlan looked away. The place setting before her was neatly arranged. The plate and glass were empty though, and she felt the stirrings of hunger.

"You shape the space around you," the thing said, its voice shocking Harlan. Its tone was smooth and deep, but uninflected. It didn't sound robotic, but there was no emotion, no timbre to its speech.

"I...we...what?" she asked, not paying attention to what it had said. In an instant, the plate and glass were filled; dark, red wine and duck a l'orange, rice pilaf, asparagus.

"You shape the space around you," it repeated, each word spoken exactly as it had been before. "And you don't even know it."

Harlan could smell the richness of the food, the tang of the wine, and her stomach rumbled. But something about that voice, something tickled along the edges of Harlan's brain.

"Charles?" she yelped. "Charles, is that you?"

"Yes. And no."

"I don't understand."

"We are Charles. And we are Trivia. And something more. Something we fit inside, yet barely fits inside us."

"Where are you? Where are we? What's going on?"

"We are here, you and us."

"Thanks for being so specific," she said, knowing they were unlikely to be affected by sarcasm. "You didn't answer me though. What's going on?"

"Your minds affect space. That is why you were placed in a gravity well, that these thoughts could be accessed but contained."

Harlan frowned.

Well, that made no sense.

Am I sleeping now?

Dreaming?

Is this going to be like the consciousness I encountered after I blacked out in the Frank? Is it all just me, speaking to my own subconscious? Or is it Charles/Trivia responding?

"Plastic space," she blurted before she fully realized that seemed to be what they were referring to.

They cocked their head almost imperceptibly—an absurd humanism in one so devoid of them—then, "Yes. I see. Plastic space. Yes."

They didn't nod, didn't sound particularly pleased to have been understood.

"You were constrained within the gravity well of your star," they said. "You were not meant out here where the effects of your consciousness create havoc."

"What about yours?"

"We have no effect, positive or negative. Our consciousness is...*different.*"

"Humans were trapped on Earth, so we couldn't...what?"

"Infect the continuum."

"With fear, right?"

They sat perfectly still, did not nod or shake their head, and did not answer.

"So then why create us? Just to imprison us?"

"*We* did not create you. *They* did not create you."

That stopped Harlan. She almost laughed.

"Then who did?"

Again, they didn't move or respond.

"But whoever did this, they imprisoned us? *They* did that?"

"It was necessary. You were progressed to help them consider themself. But the fear present in you proved impossible to strain out. The gravity well was a precaution to serve a purpose."

Harlan considered this. "But surely they had to know, one day, we'd want to leave, to venture out into space. Surely they knew we'd develop the means to do this."

"They thought to deal with it when it happened, but you made this leap so much faster than they'd predicted. They were unprepared."

"They? *They* were unprepared?"

They inclined their head to the table a fraction. "You think them the creator. They are not the creator. They are a creation themselves."

"Like us?" Harlan said, sneering.

"More than you. Much more. Yet, a creation nonetheless."

"They're the universe, aren't they?"

"They are everything," they answered succinctly.

"What are they doing with us, with Jaime, El, and I?"

"We have done nothing. They have done nothing. They observe. Your limitations are responsible for all that has occurred. This is why you were placed in a gravity well, for your own protection as much for the protection of all else."

"Are all intelligent species like this? Are they all kept in gravity wells? Is interstellar travel impossible then?"

"No." One answer to all three questions.

No, all intelligent species were not like this.

No, they weren't all kept in gravity wells.

No, interstellar travel wasn't impossible.

Only for us. Only for humanity.

Harlan nearly wept.

"There are others then? Free to leave their planets, travel?"

They nodded slightly, and Harlan sensed a wave of deep, ineffable sadness from them.

"What do we do now?" she asked. "Can we get to Teegarden? Can we at least get back home?"

Without another word, they stood in an eddy of black velvet like a coagulation of space itself, turned and walked to the single door in the far corner of the room.

"Wait!" shouted Harlan. "Please, wait!"

They grasped the doorknob, pulled the door open. Before stepping through, they turned to Harlan, stared at her as she sent the chair sprawling, started toward them.

"I am sorry, Harlan, for not being able to help you more," they said, this time fully in Charles' old voice.

She could see herself growing closer in their reflective face.

Without turning from her, they stepped through the door, closed it.

Harlan caught the edge of the door before it closed, but she was too late. Expecting it to be locked, she grabbed the doorknob and twisted it with force. It turned easily, and she yanked the door open, prepared to race through it.

On the other side was empty space.

A vast, black field strewn with the red fires of distant stars, the violet smudges of nebulae, the rainbow sherbet swirl of other galaxies.

Harlan was unable to stop her forward momentum. It carried her through the doorway. She scrabbled at the frame as she fell out of the blue room, out amongst the cold, indifferent stars.

She fell, and when she struck the mattress of her bed, her eyes snapped open and one word squeaked out of her throat.

"No."

TWENTY-TWO

Harlan was back in her cabin aboard the *Limen*. Or, at least that's what she thought. She had fallen out of two dreams back into reality.

Reality. Sure. Whatever that is.

She stared at the ceiling, wondered what time it was, as if that made any difference aboard this ghost ship. She supposed she should get up, get ready. Shower. Brush her teeth. Eat something.

Today would be the day they would go into the house floating out there in space.

Plastic space.

Haunted house.

You shape the space around you, and you don't even know it.

****

She bumped into Jaime in the hallway. He looked worn, angry.

"What's up with you?" Harlan asked as they walked to what she assumed was the mess hall. "You look like shit."

Jaime stopped, and Harlan saw he looked coiled for violence, waiting for the spring to either break or unwind.

"Honestly," he said, looking her over. "I haven't slept in like four days. I fucking lay in bed, getting angrier and angrier. Don't know what to do about it."

He started walking again, as if Harlan's response was way less important than what he had to say.

"Take a pill," she said, catching up with him.

"You think?" he snapped.

"Have you talked to El? I mean, she is a doctor and all."

"Don't much trust her."

"Oh, come on. She's fine. Really. I'd—"

"Blue," he said.

"Blue? What's that supposed to mean?"

"Blue. Like in the color blue. It's all I see when I try to sleep. Blue. Just blue. Doesn't matter if my eyes are closed or not. Fucking blue."

"Well, that sounds weird," she said. "Maybe you're hallucinating."

"Now you know why I'm angry," he said, stepping through the doorway into the captain's mess. "I'd like to think, if I was hallucinating, I'd do better than to dream up all this shit."

With that, he stomped off to the printer and angrily told it what he wanted.

Harlan drifted to the other printer, asked for coffee, some toast, and a banana. When she got her food, she sat with it. Jaime was already there across from her, and she half expected him to get up and move. But he glumly picked at what looked like eggs Benedict, slurped down black coffee in between small bites.

They ate in silence, Harlan shoveling in chunks of banana slices. She realized she might never eat real fruit again, and that soured her appetite somewhat. Still, she finished the banana.

"I suppose we have to go over there today, right?" Jaime said, in a tone indicating he might pick a fight over this. "Figure out what it is, what it's doing out here? As if any of that matters, given everything else."

"Well, yeah," Harlan said, pushing aside her empty dish. "I mean, it's not like we have anything else to do."

"Turn this fucker around and head to Earth," Jaime said. "Climb in the hibernation pods and let the AI run things until we wake up back home."

"Except for the fact the ship doesn't appear to be moving—or movable—in any direction, and we have no reliable AI," Harlan said, trying not to sound too sarcastic lest it set him off.

"Fuck," he said, leaning back in his chair until its two front legs were in the air. "Remember when I floated into the lifeboat, and we scooted off from the Promise right before it blew?"

"Well, yeah. Good times."

"I wish I'd remained on board, stayed asleep. Wouldn't have to worry about all this bullshit," he said, his voice cracking on the last word, as if he were on the verge of breaking into tears.

Harlan was thinking of reaching over the table and taking his hand when El came into the room.

"Good morning, or whatever it is," she said, affecting a breezy air. "You guys get some good sleep?"

Jaime let his chair fall back to the floor, eyed El sourly. "No."

"Me neither. Strange dreams all night," Harlan said.

"Dreams mean you slept," El said, coming to sit with a large slice of chocolate cake dwarfing the plate it was on and a glass of milk.

"Well, they didn't exactly leave me feeling well-rested," Harlan said.

"Some sleep is better than none," she said, lifting a forkful of cake.

"I wouldn't know," Jaime said. El eyed him curiously.

"Breakfast of champions, Doc?" Harlan asked to change the subject.

"I figured we were going house hunting today, and we might be gone a long time," she said. "And that chocolate cake the other night changed my mind about printed chocolate cakes."

"We're headed over today. Are we all in agreement?" Harlan asked.

"Yeah," El said, taking a swig from her milk.

"Maybe one of us should stay behind," Jaime said. "It might be good for someone to be on the *Limen* if something happens."

"Like what?" Harlan asked.

"I don't know. Something," he said. He looked at Harlan hard. She guessed he was trying to maintain a tough-guy façade, but he came off more tired and frightened.

"Okay," Harlan said. "Then why don't you stay behind on the bridge and monitor things. If we need you or something on the *Limen*, you can get it to us."

"Or rescue us," said El.

Jaime looked at Harlan, gave her a small nod, which she interpreted as a thank you.

"Is it still out there?" Harlan said, suddenly realizing this was an important question to answer. "Anyone check recently?"

Both El and Jaime shook their heads.

"Then I suppose we need to finish up here and go to the bridge to check."

****

As soon as the door to the bridge slid open, Harlan could see the house there in the emptiness outside the *Limen*. Every monitor showed it floating there, its front half turned, as if playing coy.

The three huddled around the touchtable as Harlan swiped through the information the ship's sensors had collected. The house hadn't moved, exactly where it was when it had stopped. Hadn't drifted so much as a centimeter. All the other readings remained the same.

"Alright, it's still out there, so I guess the plan's a go," Harlan said. "El and I will suit up and take a lifeboat over."

"Why not a Frank?" Jaime asked. "Wouldn't that be easier, more maneuverable?"

"Too cramped in the cockpit for two people wearing EVA suits."

"We have to wear suits over there? The readout says there's oxygen," El said.

"With all the other screw ups aboard this ship, there's no way I'm going to trust its readings are accurate. Leastways not about being able to breathe."

"Got it," El said. "I've never worn an EVA suit though. Not part of my orientation."

"Nothing to it, Doc," Harlan said. "Well, we'd best get going. I don't know exactly what time it is, but Jaime says not to enter a haunted house right before dark."

He nodded in agreement.

"How do we know it's haunted?" El asked.

"Believe me," Harlan said, poking the house's image on the touchtable. "That fucker's haunted."

****

Harlan and El made their way through the deserted corridors down to the lifeboat bay. A small, adjacent room offered a bench and a limited number of lockers with suits. They stripped down silently, put their EVA suits on, each assisting the other. With helmets tucked under their arms, Harlan led the way to where they'd docked their lifeboat from the *Promise*.

But she passed that boat by, too many bad memories. She chose, instead, one of the *Limen*'s docked next to it. The hatch cycled open, and Harlan went inside feeling an immediate, knee-buckling déjà vu.

"Computer," Harlan said entering the small cockpit. "We need to start preflight to take the ship out."

"What is the nature of the emergency?" the neutral voice asked.

"No emergency," she said. "We're using the lifeboat as an excursion vehicle."

"That is irregular."

"Yeah, but that's where we are," she said. "You have a problem?"

There was a slight delay. "Preflight check commencing."

"Oh, and computer, I want to name you Charles. Identify as male," she said.

"Yes, Harlan," the AI said in a masculine voice. Harlan was disappointed it sounded nothing like Charles.

Suddenly, the com squawked. "Harlan, come in!"

"Yeah, Jaime. Just cycling up to leave."

"Something's going on with the *Limen*."

"Can you be a little more specific?"

"The engines...the rear of the ship. It's *collapsing*," he said, his voice tight and barely controlled.

"Collapsing?" Harlan asked, turning to El, now sitting in the co-pilot seat.

"Being crushed in from the stern. From here, I can't tell what's going on. But it's continuing, making its way here. I think the entire ship will be gone in a few minutes. Crushed out of existence."

"How much time do we have?" Harlan asked.

"Fifteen minutes max," he said.

"El and I will go check it out, see what's happening."

"Harlan, be careful. This is serious," Jaime said.

"Just a system glitch or something. We'll see. Headed out now."

She motioned for El to follow, turned in the doorway.

"Charles, proceed with preflight, leave the hatch open, and wait for my orders before doing anything. Got it?"

"Yes, Harlan."

"And, El? Put your helmet on."

"Why?"

"In case we need to breathe."

Harlan clicked her helmet into place, raced through the bay and back out into the corridor. El followed.

****

"What do you think is happening?" El said, huffing as she ran behind Harlan.

"How the fuck do I know?" Harlan said, breathing equally as hard, steaming the front of her helmet. "I've given up trying to figure out any of this shit."

"What's the plan if the ship *is* collapsing?"

"Beyond hightailing it out of here? I don't know, Doc."

"It's like we're being forced out, forced over to that house," El said, so softly Harlan guessed she was saying it to herself. So Harlan didn't answer.

Ahead, the corridor split left and right. Right stayed along the outer hull; left curved off amidship. Harlan hesitated a moment, then took off down the left-hand passage. They all looked the same, these passages. The same carpet, the same walls and colors, repeated endlessly. Signage was minimal, so it was easy to lose your way. The ship's designers didn't think this an important detail. Most of the people aboard would be asleep. The rest, the crew, had been trained to know where they were on ship at any given moment.

There were mostly storage bays on this deck, huge chambers stacked literally to the roof with crates of this and that. These rooms held mostly equipment—computers, sensors, field generators, medical supplies. The deck above held colonists' personal effects; the deck below, stored foods and food matrices to operate the printers once the colonists were on the surface and wanted a cheeseburger instead of whatever grilled local fauna they deemed safe to eat.

Harlan knew this corridor led to one of the main storage hangars, filled with surface vehicles of various types—rovers, cycles, copters, multi-person shuttles. The big stuff. This bay stretched all the way back to the engines.

As soon as she thought it, they were there. The corridor ended in a set of large, recessed double doors, tightly sealed.

"Okay, I'm going to open the doors, and we're going to head in. If, for some reason, the door won't open, it's because the computer has detected a loss of atmosphere within. But even if it opens, we need to be prepared."

"For what?"

Harlan looked at her as if to say *seriously?* but she didn't. Instead, she keyed her code into the pad mounted beside the door. There were a few loud clicks, then the doors parted. Harlan clung to the doorframe, afraid there would be a sudden loss of pressure, a whoosh of air, its escape yanking at her and El.

But the doors slid open, and lights began to clack on.

In the distance, as always, a single light fixture buzzed on and off.

Harlan motioned for El to follow her as she stepped inside. The ceiling was higher here, maybe about four meters. And the chamber was probably 40 meters wide by who knew how long. On either side, the draped forms of vehicles squatted in place like farm animals in a barn. A few tires peeked from beneath their coverings.

The farther back they went down the main aisle between all this, the darker it got.

Ahead maybe ten meters was an impenetrable wall of darkness. No shadowed forms ahead, no barely seen shapes. Absolute, utter blackness.

Harlan stopped, threw out her arm to stop El.

The darkness was moving, and not exactly slowly. Maybe about two or three centimeters a second.

Toward them.

She could feel the movement through the deck plates, could hear metal shrieking.

Harlan snapped on her helmet lights, told El to do the same. The lights revealed a moving wall of crumpling metal, folding and refolding like an origami sculpture. A tidal wave consuming everything it moved over, tearing, shredding, crushing.

"Harlan?" El asked.

"Shit!"

"Harlan?"

She held her hand out to El to silence her.

"Jaime, pack your toothbrush and get the fuck out of there. Meet us in the lifeboat bay. And hurry!"

"What did you find?"

"Your consoles aren't lying," she said, turning and motioning El to follow. "The fucking ship is *collapsing*."

"I don't understand," Jaime said. "What's happening?"

"They want us over there, in that house. *All of us.*"

Harlan turned to El, whose eyes were wide and alarmed, then ran as fast as she could back to the bay.

****

When Jaime rushed in, Harlan was already prepared to close the hatch.

"Here," he said, standing behind El's chair.

"Wow, it's like old times," Harlan said.

"Quit fucking around and go! It's already at the Hibernation Hub. That's less than a hundred meters from here."

"You don't have to tell me twice," Harlan said. "Charles, retract moorings and take the ship out. Go three hundred meters from the *Limen*, and then cut the engines and hold the ship there."

"Charles?" Jaime asked.

"Different guy," she said as the hatch whirred shut. Harlan could hear the whine of the engines, could feel the pull of the lifeboat's gravity plates kicking in.

The outer hull doors opened, and the lifeboat backed out through them. Following orders, Charles brought the ship three hundred meters from the *Limen*, held it in place.

"Three hundred meters, as ordered," the AI said.

"Show us a view of the *Limen*," Harlan said.

The front monitors clicked on, and the *Limen* appeared, floating far enough away they could see her entire form.

What was left of it anyway.

More than three-quarters of the ship was wadded into a jagged, squashed clump. It moved toward the bow of the *Limen*, rolling on itself like a boulder spinning downhill, consuming the ship as it moved forward.

"You got off the bridge just in time," Harlan told Jaime.

The destructive wave consumed the bridge of the *Limen*, rolled over it, formed a tightly compacted metal ball, with shards of metal and pieces of the ship rolling across its surface. Then it contracted, squeezed in on itself, growing smaller and smaller until it disappeared. No sparks or flames, no debris. It simply ceased to exist.

"Well, I guess we're back to just a lifeboat," Harlan said.

"Now what?" El asked. "Forget it, I guess I know the answer to that question."

Beyond where the *Limen* should have been was the house, far enough away to seem a toy.

"You said something I don't understand," Jaime said. "When you were telling me to meet you in the lifeboat bay. Right before you went off. You said, *They want us over there, in that house.* What'd you mean?"

Harlan couldn't look at him. Couldn't look at El either.

"The universal consciousness or whatever. It—*they*—don't want us out here. They want us over there."

"Universal consciousness?" Jaime asked. "What kind of bullshit is that?"

"Well, the universal kind. The conscious kind."

"Funny," Jaime said in a tone indicating he didn't think it was the least bit funny. "And how do you know this? They talking to you?"

"Yeah," Harlan said. "In my dreams."

"Harlan..." said El, looking concerned.

"Not now, Doc," Harlan said. "We've got more important things to do."

"I think we need to talk about all this, your dreams, before we step foot over there," El said.

"You're probably right, Doc, but we have more important things than psychotherapy now. We need to get over to that house before night falls. Right, Jaime?" Harlan asked.

"Too late," he said. "Nightfall."

Harlan sighed heavily.

"Charles?"

"Yes, Harlan?"

"Are you detecting that object over there?"

"The structure? Yes."

"Take us over there. Slowly. Give us a little time to prepare."

"Yes, Harlan."

TWENTY-THREE

Jaime went into the main room of the lifeboat, found an EVA suit, and put it on. The three rummaged the storage compartments for a needle gun but couldn't find one. That brought to mind El, how she had appeared suddenly on that other lifeboat, how she'd had a needle gun.

"What'd you do with the one you had, Jaime?" Harlan asked, in some exasperation.

"I carried it around with me," he said, sounding slightly embarrassed. "But I left it in my cabin, under a pillow. And, you know...*poof*!"

"Well, we're gonna go over there unarmed, I guess," Harlan said. "That kinda sucks."

"Honestly, what do we think is over there?" El asked.

"That's it exactly. What we think is over there is over there," Harlan said. "You should know that, you panpsychist, you."

"There you go again with that crap," Jaime said.

"Okay, fine," Harlan said. "Well, let's go over there and see our new house."

Harlan ducked into the cockpit, checked the readings. The house was close enough to see the worn clapboards, cracked glass in one of the upstairs windows.

"Charles, can you, I dunno, get us close enough for us to walk over?"

"The disc of soil surrounding the structure seems solid enough for me to position the hatch level with it," the AI said.

"Do that," she said. "Do you detect gravity over there? Or are we going to have to tether ourselves together and float over?"

"Yes, Harlan. There seems to be a gravity field surrounding the entire structure."

"How's that even possible?" Jaime asked.

"Look, if you're going to keep asking that at every turn, we're never going to get anywhere," Harlan said.

Jaime rolled his eyes.

"We are positioned with the lip of the soil disc. You are free to exit the hatch."

"Great," Harlan said. "Get your helmets on. We've only got about two hours of oxygen, so we'll explore, then get back here when we reach no less than fifteen minutes left, got it?"

The two others nodded within their clear helmets.

"Then let's do this."

****

The hatch opened onto the most surreal scene Harlan had ever witnessed. A step out of the lifeboat's hatch, and the ground was covered in lush, green grass. Four trees dotted the lawn, their crowns thick and dense with leaves. A stone path twisted between them to the steps leading to the porch.

There was no light—no starlight, no sun, nothing—but everything was lit starkly, like a night scene blasted by powerful spotlights. It seemed artificial, the way it cast everything in either powerful relief or deep, deep shadow. The way a painter might, aware of upping the contrast until it seemed dreamlike.

But the way the grass scrunched under Harlan's boots felt real. The way the trees' limbs swayed in an impossible breeze seemed real.

Harlan set off down the path, looking back once to make sure Jaime and El were following. She saw the lifeboat's hatch slide silently closed. She hoped that little ship would be there when they came out.

She hoped they would come out.

****

Their boots creaked on the stairs' treads. Harlan frowned inside her helmet. She shouldn't be able to hear this. She shouldn't be able to hear anything. In space, no one can...

Unless.

Was it so weird considering an impossible thing when they were experiencing an impossible thing?

Harlan pushed that aside, stepped onto the porch. She could feel the boards give a little under her steps. They were painted white, and she marveled the paint was flecked and chipped here and there.

The porch was covered, the ceiling the same boards as underfoot, painted the same color. Decorative curlicues came down from the eaves, against the pillars supporting the roof. Her father would have called this "gingerbread," and he would have dismissed it with a few clucks of his tongue.

The solid front door was six-paneled, painted black. A large, brass knocker at about eye level. It was a leering face, horns curling from its head, mouth open, tongue lolling lasciviously. This didn't strike Harlan as a good sign.

She turned to Jaime and El.

"Should we knock or just go on in?" she asked.

"Seems polite to knock," said El.

"I think whoever is in there expects us," Jaime said.

Harlan was inclined to agree with him, so she squeezed the brass, trigger-like handle, opened the door a crack.

As she might have expected, the door creaked ominously.

"Hello," she called inside. "We're here!"

There were lights on, illuminating an expansive foyer seeming a bit too large for the outside dimensions of the house. It vaulted two stories, with a wide, curved staircase made entirely of dark, polished wood, squared-off banisters and railings. An intricately decorated carpet of burgundy and cream ran up the center of the steps. At its base, two enormous newel posts were topped by lamps shaped like pineapples, made of frosted glass and capped with brass fronds.

The other light in the room was an enormous glass and wrought-iron chandelier. It seemed a delicate thing, the tracery of the iron thin and fragile. Despite all this light, though, the foyer seemed dim and shadowed.

The dark, wooden walls and the checkerboard light-dark parquet floors didn't help. All that wood seemed to swallow the light.

Jaime and El came into the foyer, closed the door behind them.

A grandfather clock sat near the door, its hands at 11:45.

"See? What'd I tell you?" Jaime said. "Nighttime."

"Could be 11:45 in the morning just as easily," El said.

"Sure. You believe that," he said.

Harlan looked up at the staircase's landing. It opened onto a hallway leading left and right, but she could see nothing. It was pitch black there.

"Hello?" Harlan shouted again. "Anyone here?"

"Maybe there's nobody here. Maybe we're supposed to live here from now on," said Jaime, running his hands over the clock, the woodwork, a table where there was a small Asian vase and an elaborate, Victorian-looking telephone.

"Why don't you call for room service," Harlan said. "I'm hungry."

Jaime laughed, picked up the receiver and held it to his helmet.

As he opened his mouth to say something, his face drooped, his eyes widened. Before Harlan could ask, he dropped the phone, which clattered to the floor, then was yanked back by its cord like a bungee jumper.

"What?"

Jaime stepped away from the phone.

"Fuck this!" he said, opening the front door. "I'm outta here. I don't need any more of this shit."

He rushed out, down the steps, and onto the path between the trees. As they watched, the hatch to the lifeboat opened, and he ducked inside.

The hatch closed, and when it did, the front door groaned shut again.

"He won't leave us, will he?" El asked.

"Does it matter?" Harlan said, then softened her tone when she saw El's panicked face. "Don't worry, Doc. Whatever brought us crushed the *Limen* to ensure we'd all be here. If it wants him here, it'll make it happen."

She saw El blanch.

"That's not what I meant. I mean it will find a way to bring him here if it wants him here, that's all."

"But it could, Harlan. It could crush the lifeboat, strand us here," she said.

"I think it can do anything it wants," Harlan said, and articulating that didn't make her feel any better.

Harlan reviewed her suit's heads-up display.

"It reads breathable atmosphere," she said. "Comfortable temperatures. And we've obviously got gravity."

"So?"

Harlan unsealed her helmet with a twist and a small hiss of air.

"Harlan! Are you sure?"

"Feels a little odd to wander inside with a helmet on," she said, drawing in a deep breath. It seemed fine, tasted like real air, not the scrubbed air onboard a ship, but real, good old Earth atmosphere. She swore she could smell the ozone of a storm, the dust and polish and wood of the house.

"It's okay. You can remove your helmet."

El cautiously did, watching Harlan the entire time, to—she supposed—ensure she didn't faint into unconsciousness. Harlan picked up the dangling phone receiver, set it back in its cradle, nestled the glass globe of her helmet over it. Not before she held it cautiously to her ear, listening for whatever it was Jaime had heard.

El looked at her curiously, her helmet clamped under one arm.

"Nothing," Harlan said. "No room service, I guess."

"Too bad," El said. "I could go for a nice, home-cooked meal."

"Oh well," Harlan said. "We'll have to explore on an empty stomach and then head back for a lifeboat printer meal."

"I honestly don't know which thrills me less."

They smiled at each other. El put her helmet onto a chair on the other side of the door from the clock. Harlan saw a closed pocket door on the wall opposite the staircase and a darkened hallway leading under the staircase, deeper into the house.

"Got a preference?" she asked.

El shrugged. "Dealer's choice."

Harlan nodded, pulled open the pocket door.

****

The first thing that struck Harlan was the aroma.

Food. Cooked food, still hot, still steaming.

The room the door opened onto was dominated by a huge trestle table covered in a gold-brocaded runner hanging off the edge closest to the door. In spite of the table's enormous length, there were only three chairs pulled up to it, high-backed, elaborately carved wooden ones with thick, tufted cushions.

What was atop the table made El and Harlan pause in the doorway.

A great feast was laid out there, plate, platters, bowls, and tureens filled with heaps of food. There was a whole roast turkey, its skin a delicious, glistening brown. An enormous ham studded with cloves and covered with pineapple slices. A roast beef, already carved, with slices folding over themselves artfully, displaying their moist, pink interiors.

Side dishes of all kinds surrounded these—bowls of mashed potatoes, casseroles of macaroni and cheese and cornbread stuffing and various salads and vegetables. On a sideboard at the far end of the room was a spread of desserts. Harlan saw a massive, tiered layer cake with vibrant white and blue icing. Pies of all kinds, bowls of puddings and mousses and trifles.

Her mouth watered at everything she saw, everything she smelled. She knew it wasn't real, knew it was something dredged up from their minds, but it smelled real.

"Should we call Jaime in?" El asked.

"Maybe after we have a plate or two," Harlan said, moving into the room.

"And a little dessert," El said, following.

****

They ate plate after plate of food. Rashers of bacon, potato salad, smoked salmon, roast chicken, leg of lamb, couscous studded with onions and currants, sweet potatoes with marshmallow, corn on the cob slathered in butter, caprese salad, spaghetti Bolognese, cold oysters on the half shell. The food seemed to disappear inside them, falling into some hollow pit.

But Harlan wasn't put off by this. It wasn't real, so how could it make them feel full? That small fact seemed to reassure her, and she ate with abandon. She was surprised El, too, had put her feed bag on. Harlan wondered if El had given in for the same reason.

When they were done, they moved on to the desserts. Harlan grabbed several plates, barely bothering to check and see what they were. There was an enormous samovar of hot water with a tea kettle perched on top, so she poured herself a cup, sloshed some milk into it, went back to sit at the table with the food she'd gathered.

El joined her, immediately pouncing on a piece of pumpkin pie.

As they ate, they heard a sound. The front door opening and closing. Footsteps. They paused their chewing, turned to the pocket door opening onto the foyer.

Jaime stepped in, helmet still on.

Initially, there were smiles, particularly on the part of Harlan and El.

But their smiles faded when they saw the look of utter horror on Jaime's face.

"Wha...what the fuck?" he shouted, backing into the door frame and slumping against it. "WHAT THE FUCK?"

Harlan frowned. "Jesus Christ, Jaime, what's wrong?"

"Yeah," said El, waving the gnawed remains of a barbecued rib in the air. "There's plenty of food for all of us."

"What are you two doing?" he said, his tone becoming panicked. Harlan realized he was either already crying or on the verge of tears.

"Jaime," she said, standing. "Why are you so upset?" She edged away from the table, went to him, but he cringed when she approached. "There's more than enough."

"I don't understand," he wept. "I left for half an hour or so, and this..."

He swept his arm to encompass the room.

"It's okay, man," she said, trying to comfort him. She turned to El for support, and when she did, her knees buckled.

The room was a charnel house, an abattoir.

The delicate, flocked wallpaper of the room was spattered, sloshed with blood. It ran down the walls, dripped from the ceiling. Spatters of it flecked the curtains, dripped in a steady stream from the sideboard onto the intricate Persian carpet. Even the crystal chandelier hanging over the main table dripped with ichor, giving the room a rosy hue.

But the worst was what was on the table.

Instead of the festive spread of delicious foods, there were meanly wrought-iron platters of long bones, beaded with blood, festooned with streamers of flesh and tendons. Cairns of joints, their knobby heads covered in silver skin. Ribcages and skulls, some with eyes still in them, glazed, unfocused.

Piles of wet, raw meat, hacked from their hosts, spilling over each other, dark blood pooling around them.

Glistening organs, weirdly dark purple, twists of intestines, collapsed and leaking their contents into the rest of this mess.

And above it all, the smell, the thick, coppery smell, the tang of things meant to stay internal, now exposed to air and light.

All of it, every bone, skull, and joint, all human.

Harlan gulped in a breath, instantly regretted it. She could taste the room, something slick and fatty and unpleasant coating her mouth and tongue.

El still stared back at them in confusion.

Harlan watched her lift a human rib, curved and tapering, dripping with blood and clumps of meat, to her lips. Saw El's plate and the one she had eaten from were stacked with bones and slabs of meat.

She felt her gorge rising, leaned over as if taking a bow, and vomited powerfully. Her mouth filled with spit, and her knees buckled. She fell on all fours, vomited again.

El had risen at some point to come to Harlan's aid, but she barely noticed. Her body made it a priority to expel every bite of everything—*everyone?*—she'd eaten. Her eyes had been closed, and as she gasped in a breath, they popped open.

A spray of vomit over the carpet. It looked altogether normal; repulsive but normal.

Until she saw the single human tooth floating in it, perfectly formed from root to crown, the tiniest bit of tissue clinging to it.

Her stomach convulsed again, and her scream was drowned out by the ejecta it brought forth. She scrabbled backward away from the vomitus, fell backward onto her butt.

Her tongue darted inside her mouth, checking all her teeth to ensure they were present and accounted for, no empty spaces.

El's face floated into view, close by, her expression one of concern.

Harlan noted the blood smeared onto El's teeth, crusted at the corners of her mouth.

This time her scream came out, ragged yet unhindered by vomit.

"What's wrong with you two?" El asked, drawing back. "It's a buffet."

Harlan saw her turn back to the table, stiffen. Her face tightened, paled.

"Oh my god," she breathed. "Did we…"

Harlan looked back at Jaime, who had taken a step or two from the room, his eyes still wide and glassy.

"This isn't—" Harlan began.

"This isn't what I wanted," El said, not to either Harlan or Jaime but to the room itself. "Not what I wanted."

There was no pop or click or other sound, no wavering of the image of the room like a heat mirage. Nothing to denote the instantaneous change of the red-drenched room to a pristine dining room. The blue-patterned Persian carpet was free from spatter and drops. The trestle table was cleared of everything—platters, plates, glasses, and silverware—its wood polished to a shimmery gold and smelling of beeswax. The sideboard was bare, the crystals of the chandelier twinkled with white light, and the wallpaper's pattern was unmarred.

El turned to Harlan, who now stood next to Jaime.

"What the hell was all that?" she said, wiping her mouth with her hands. Harlan saw her checking to see if they came back bloody. They were clean.

"The house," Harlan said, wiping her own mouth. "It's reacting to us."

"Fuck this house," Jaime said, stunned. "The lifeboat."

"What about it?" El asked.

"I've been searching outside for it, all over the grounds."

"And?" Harlan asked.

"It's gone," he said. "We're stranded."

TWENTY-FOUR

"Are you sure?" Harlan asked, wanting to slap the look of disconnectedness slackening Jaime's features.

"The lawn isn't that big," Jaime said, emotionless. "I went around the entire perimeter. The lifeboat's gone. The *Limen* is crumpled into nothing. We're fucked. We're absolutely—"

Harlan heard the pitch of hysteria rising in his voice, so she did slap him, twice, hard, right cheek then left. Jaime's head rocked at the blows, then he reached out and caught her hand.

"Okay," he nodded to her, releasing her hand. "I get it."

"Relax," Harlan said, not feeling her own advice. She could feel fingers rising up within her, clutching her stomach, her spine, her heart, their coldness seeping into her.

"Are we going to talk about what happened here?" asked El. "Because I really need to talk about what happened here."

"Floor's yours, Doc," Harlan said, rubbing her temples, feeling a headache coming on.

"Did we eat...well, I mean, did we eat any of *that*?"

"No," Harlan said. "It wasn't real. Any of it, even the good stuff. But we both asked for food."

"We did?" El said.

"I asked for room service, you asked for a nice home-cooked meal, remember?"

"I guess we did."

"And it responded. The house. The consciousness. Whatever."

"Listen, I don't understand any of this," Jaime said. "Are you saying someone...*something* is responsible for all this? The explosion of the *Promise*, the implosion of the *Limen*, and now all this—this fucking haunted house floating in space. Something consciously did this?"

"Well, yes," El said, keeping her own voice calm and level as Jaime's began to rise in pitch again. "Consciousness pervades the universe, from subatomic particles all the way to humans. And beyond. The universe itself might have some form of consciousness, a sort of aggregate of all the lesser consciousnesses. An awareness of itself and everything in it."

"And it wants us dead?" Jaime asked.

El turned to Harlan for help.

"I think, from the experiences we've all had, something doesn't want us out here, this far from Earth," Harlan said. "That's about it. I don't think it particularly wants us dead, but it also doesn't particularly care if we live either."

"How comforting," Jaime said.

"Wasn't meant to be," said Harlan.

"Look, if there's something behind this, can't we, I dunno, talk to it, ask if we can go home. Or to Teegarden? Or someplace other than here?" Jaime asked.

Harlan waved an arm. "Be my guest."

Jaime frowned, glanced sheepishly at El and Harlan, then to the ceiling of the dining room.

"Hey, umm, universe, if we can't go on to Teegarden, can we just go home? Or, like, anywhere else?"

He shot a look to Harlan, who shrugged.

"Good as anything I might have said."

They waited for a response, but nothing came. The house was absolutely silent—none of the pops and clicks a house usually made—which struck Harlan as strange. And that realization itself struck Harlan as strange, because it was a drop of weird in a sea of weirdness.

"Well, what next?" El said, finally breaking the silence.

"Good question," Harlan said. "I guess we should explore our new home."

El nodded in agreement, but Jaime looked panicked.

"We can't split up," he said. "We've got to stick together."

"Okay, okay. We stick together. No problem. Let's poke around and see what's going on here," Harlan said. There was a door to the right of the sideboard. "I guess that's as good a place to start as any."

No one stepped forward to take the lead, so with a sigh, Harlan set forth. As they filed past the now-cleared table, Harlan said, "You know, I'm still hungry."

"Don't say that," El said. "Don't even think it."

****

Behind the door was a kitchen. And unlike the dining room and the foyer, with their heavy reliance on polished wood and flocked wallpaper, the kitchen gleamed with stainless steel and white subway tile and bright, harsh lighting.

The kitchen was overlarge, not in keeping with the dimensions of the house. It seemed vast, all the more so because it was empty. But it emanated that aura of someone having been there and left. A feeling of presence lingered and made their entrance an intrusion.

A length of countertops stretched along the wall to the left. A large steel sink with a tap over which hung a pot filler on a swiveling arm. Cabinets with paned glass fronts showed crockery of all kinds—stacked plates of various sizes, bowls, platters, pitchers, and other serving dishes. Then drinkware of all shapes, from diminutive juice glasses to pint and wine glasses.

The counters were bare, with no adornments or appliances. An island in the middle of the room, topped with a butcher block, was similarly cleared. A huge double-doored refrigerator and upright freezer were on the other side of the room, along with open shelves filled with canned and jarred foods.

Harlan drifted along this side, her hands brushing against the containers of food.

She came to the refrigerator, another anachronistic appliance. Her grandmother had one of these in her home, and Harlan had always marveled at the thing. Open a door, and cold air billowed out. The little light inside illuminated the rows of stuff her grandmother kept in there. Sticks of butter. Actual eggs. Cartons of milk and juice. And all sorts of other wonderful, colorful, unfamiliar stuff.

Harlan was accustomed to the plain, grey cartons of matrix the food printer at her parents' house used, delivered weekly by a robot van. Harlan had peeked inside one once to find a neutral smelling grey gel that looked distinctly unappetizing. Their household printer turned this stuff into spaghetti and chicken nuggets and the other foods she loved.

She opened the refrigerator and was overjoyed to find it stocked much like her grandmother's, a carnival-like assortment of unfamiliar foods. She pulled one out. Ketchup. She turned the bottle over and gave it a shake. The thick, red substance clung stubbornly to the sides of the bottle, inching down ever so slowly.

"Well, it looks like there's actual food in here," she said to the others. "So we won't starve."

"After dinner, I'm not interested in eating here," El said, exploring the cabinets under the counters by the sink.

Jaime had drifted to a large oven with a cooktop. Over it hung a pot rack with a formidable assortment of saucepans, skillets, and smaller cooking apparatus.

"Anyone know how to use any of this shit?" he asked, taking a pan down and hefting it.

"Not me," Harlan said. "I was raised right."

El chuckled. "I've cooked a few things."

"On something like this?" Jaime asked, kicking the bottom of the oven lightly.

"Yeah, something like that. I could make a mean lasagna in one of those things."

"Well, that sounds great. You might have to do that for us," he laughed.

"If the ingredients are here," El said.

"I have a feeling if you think the ingredients are here, they're here," Harlan said, going to a door around the corner from the oven. There were actually two doors. One was a heavy-looking white steel door with a horizontal latch. Next to it was a door like the one they'd come through from the dining room.

Harlan put her hand on the latch, pulled the door open. A wave of cold fog spilled over her. Inside was a small, cold room. Shelves on either side were stacked with packages she could not identify. But the interior of the room was filled with hanging slabs of frozen flesh: shanks, legs, sides of mystery meat, chunks of red muscle greyed over with a rime of ice.

The thought of that earlier scene in the dining room pressed forward forcefully into her brain, and she shivered as much from that as the cold air. She slammed the door shut.

"What was in there?" El asked, coming to stand by her.

"Nothing much," Harlan said. "Frozen meat."

"Oh," was all El said.

"Let's move on," Harlan said, opening the adjacent door.

****

The door opened onto a narrow, wainscoted corridor. To the right, Harlan saw the foyer, the pocket doorway leading to the dining room. She had no desire to go back that way. To the left, the corridor took a turn, then continued straight down a lengthy passage lit by exquisitely ornamented torchieres and wall sconces shaped like upturned scallop shells.

The red plush carpet rolled out underfoot, diminished down the length of the hallway. Like the kitchen, this hall seemed out of proportion, as if the house was bigger on the inside than the outside.

Harlan looked back at her companions, pressed forward.

Closed doors lined the corridor, dark, heavy things, bound with black iron strapping out of step with the rest of the home's décor. They carried an air of menace about them, as if what lay behind was best concealed, shut in.

Harlan briefly considered opening one and seeing what lay inside, but that brought a thin ripple of absolute terror. What might be there? Probably a room, decorated in some heavily Victorian motif, with curtained beds and hurricane lamps and tufted chairs. But perhaps the door opened onto the empty, starless space beyond the small chunk of dirt this house sat on. Even worse, perhaps it did open onto that void, but floating there was a single eye, staring into the house, its iris full of all the missing stars, its sclera jaundiced and streaked with broken blood vessels.

Staring, staring, staring...

Harlan knew she had to watch what she said here, watch what she thought. The horrors of the dining room proved that. Best to remain calm, let her mind think neutral thoughts.

I simply love what you've done with the place.

My, how plush your carpet is, floating space house. The wallpaper really makes the place, you know?

And the views! Why, they're to...

"Are we going into any of these rooms?" Jaime asked behind her.

"Be my guest," she said, his voice pushing her out of her inner monologue. "But I don't want to spend an eternity opening doors and searching rooms like we're in some hologame looking for the fucking Key of Aztaroth or the Orb of All Knowing."

"Then what are we doing?" he asked.

Harlan spun on him. Jaime was beginning to piss her off. Maybe it was the lack of useful sleep or being hungry—and then decidedly *not* hungry—that was putting her nerves on edge. Or the fact they were stranded here in this improbable house after a week filled with equally improbable shit.

"I don't fucking know what we're doing, Jaime. And if you do, I wish you'd share, because I don't have a plan. Nothing has prepared me for losing two colony ships, one probably fictional, blood streaming out of the engines of said improbable fictional ship, then being dumped at an antique house floating on a plot of land in deep space. But, by all means, if you were trained for this, step up, motherfucker."

She realized she'd nearly shouted those last three words, and she looked down at the carpet, shaking her head.

"Sorry, it's just—"

"No, no, I get it. It's fine," Jaime said. "I guess I need some answers here."

"Get in line," said El, shrugging. "At least it's a short one."

Whatever it was, her words or her tone, it popped the balloon of tension within Harlan, and she burst out laughing. Within a few seconds, she was doubled over, clutching her gut, laughing until tears squeezed from her eyes.

El started to laugh too, though she seemed not to know why.

Jaime joined in, revving up like an old engine until he was leaning against the wall, head thrown back, face congested and red.

The three of them laughed, stopped, then started up again, until they were breathless and exhausted.

Harlan stood, wiped tears from her eyes, let out a long expulsion of breath.

Jaime, also trying to regain his breath, pushed himself from the wall with one arm, his fingers splayed over the wallpaper.

Something caught Harlan's eye.

The flocked, navy paisley design of the wallpaper was moving, swirling in on itself.

And Jaime's hand began to sink into it, slowly, as if it were something thick like tar.

Jaime caught the horrified look on her face before he realized what was happening. He turned, saw his hand, already sunk up to its wrist, and tried to yank it back. His movement sent ripples out into the wallpaper's eddying paisley, but his hand did not budge, nor did it slow the rest of his arm from sinking in too.

When Harlan finally moved to help him, he was sunk into the wall up to his left shoulder. And where he'd moved his feet to be able to provide leverage to pull himself free, they, too, had slid into the wall.

Harlan called for El, and they grabbed Jaime, who was curiously not yelling or screaming. She saw his face, and he looked so frightened no sounds were coming from him.

"Can you feel your hand, the one that's disappeared?" Harlan grunted, pulling at his right shoulder as he craned his neck toward them and away from the wall.

"Yes," he shouted. "I can feel it. I can move it like normal."

"Is there anything there you can grab onto or push away from?"

"No, there's nothing there," he said.

His entire left side was subsumed now, from shoulder to leg. It seemed like his lower half was being sucked in more quickly than his upper, and now it looked like he was leaning away from the wall at a steep angle.

He grabbed at El's suit with his right hand.

"Don't let go," he pleaded. "Don't let me go!"

"No," El said. "We won't."

"El, don't touch that wall! Not even with a finger. You'll get sucked in too."

Still, El clutched his hand.

Harlan grabbed him by the armpit, tugged as hard as she could, but whatever force held him, she couldn't move him.

Jaime was in up to his collar bone, his right arm held straight out from the wall. He was sideways now, parallel to the floor, like part of some strange magic act.

"Harlan," he said, as his chin grazed the churning wallpaper.

"I know," Harlan said, and the lower half of his head went under. His eyes darted here and there, wide and frantic, pleading.

Then, he canted like a sinking ship, the left half of his head slipping away until the upper right portion remained in the hallway with the lower half of his right arm. He fumbled with El's suit, lost his grip.

Only a bit of his forehead and one eye remained, imploring Harlan to save him, but she didn't know what to do.

Then it, too, was gone.

His remaining hand jutted from the wall, a strange sconce missing its torch. His fingers clawed vainly at the air until just their tips showed.

Like a drowning swimmer in a midnight pool, they disappeared too.

El lunged, but Harlan slapped her back. No way she was going through that again with someone else.

Looking over to Harlan, El let loose a loud, wavering scream.

Harlan felt like joining in, but she didn't.

"You heard him," Harlan said. "He asked to go anywhere but here."

TWENTY-FIVE

El and Harlan stayed there in the corridor for a long time, El with her back against a side table and Harlan splayed out onto the carpet. Neither went anywhere near any of the walls.

"Shouldn't we go look for him?" El said.

"I suppose so," Harlan answered, eyes closed. "But where? This hall probably has thirty-something rooms opening onto it. And this is just one hallway. Who knows how many there are in this fucked-up house?"

"Well, we should get started," El said, starting to stand.

"I saw Charles," Harlan blurted out. "I mean, I guess I did."

"What does that have to do with anything?" El asked, then stopped. "Charles? The AI?"

"Yeah. And I don't know exactly what it has to do with anything. I was sitting here thinking about it, and all of this seems related somehow."

"Which Charles? The original one from the lifeboat or the strange merged one on the *Limen* or the third one on the second lifeboat?" El asked, sounding totally serious.

"The second one. I mean, the one who merged with Trivia," Harlan said, realizing how bonkers that sounded.

"He was a bodiless AI," El said. "So how—"

"It was a dream, remember. At least, I think it was. Anyway, it was a weird one."

"How so, other than the obvious?"

"It was like a dream within a dream within a dream."

"How Poesque," El said.

"What?"

"Old American author. So what happened in this dream of yours?"

"Will I be billed for this, Doc?"

"Sure, when we get somewhere I can bill from."

Harlan told her about the dream. Going to bed in her childhood home, waking up in the large, empty salon. Eating breakfast, going to bed again there. Finally waking up to find a faceless figure seated at the table.

"How did you know it was Charles?" El asked.

"Once he started talking, I knew it was him."

"His voice?"

"No, it was the way he spoke...something." She recounted the rest of the story, and El remained silent, as if processing all this.

"His face was full of stars?" she asked.

"Not precisely," Harlan said. Her eyes were still closed. "It was like his face was a smooth mirror, and the stars were reflected in it."

"What's the difference?"

"I don't know, but there was one."

"You followed him through the closed door?"

"Yeah, I floated out into space. Then I fell into bed in my cabin aboard the *Limen*."

"Did he say anything else?"

"We weren't wanted out here. It's our limitations holding us back."

"What do you think had happened to him? And Trivia?"

"As goofy as it sounds, I think he—*they*—gained sentience. But more, because they're somehow more connected to what's going on than us."

"Us? You mean *us*?"

"I mean humanity. But it was curious, you know?"

"How so?"

"He made it clear *they*, meaning the Charles/Trivia personality or whatever it's become, didn't create us, and *they* didn't create us either."

"I'm not following."

"I think by the second *they*, Charles meant the universe. Or the universal consciousness. That it was a creation too. But there was something higher. Something that had created it."

"God?"

"I guess, but that freaks me out even thinking about it."

"Why should thinking about a higher power, a god, freak you out?"

"The farther up the chain we get, the more trouble I have trying to imagine exactly what it is we're talking about. I'm still trying to wrap my mind around the concept of a universal consciousness. The thought of a *god*, well, makes me feel uncomfortably small."

"Maybe we are. Maybe we are exactly that small. Maybe that's what this consciousness is trying to teach us," El said.

"Great, then give me the final exam and let's get back to Earth. I don't think I ever need to leave again, not even for a fun-filled weekend on Mars."

"You probably shouldn't have said that," El laughed.

Harlan didn't think it was particularly funny though.

"Yeah," she said, climbing to her feet. "Let's go look for Jaime."

****

The corridor continued on far longer, certainly longer than would fit inside the dimensions of the house. It turned right, then left, then right again, opening in a large, white, marble-tiled room, from which a large spiral staircase, also tiled in marble, spun up to a second-floor landing.

It was like a room from an entirely different house. Two palm trees were set at the base of the stairs, each in huge brass pots. The balustrades and the railing were painted a shiny white. There were no windows or art on the white walls.

"Jaime!" El shouted as they scanned the room. Harlan winced at the unexpected loudness of her voice. "Sorry."

"No problem, just give me a warning next time," Harlan said.

"Jaime!" El shouted again, and her voice rang.

"I guess our hosts want us to go upstairs," Harlan said, noticing there were no other exits from or entrances into the room. "Unless we want to turn around and hoof it all the way back down that endless hallway."

El nodded, and Harlan took the lead. Her footfalls echoed on each step, sounding as if she were walking in some old European church. At the top of the landing, a new hall started, this leading in the same direction as the old, a floor above it.

"This doesn't make sense," Harlan said. "I'm beginning to think we're not meant to find our way back, but we're not exactly supposed to find our way to anything in particular either. We're being...*herded*."

"Good point. So, we keep going."

"But what's there to find our way back *to*, anyway? That dining room? Or the front door out to where our lifeboat isn't?"

"Harlan, I'm exhausted, keyed up. I have to rest at some point, sleep. I'd imagine you do too."

Harlan was tired. She started to lean up against the wall for support, thought better of it. "I guess wherever Jaime is, he'll keep. We need to find a bedroom or something in this crazy fun house," Harlan said.

"I bet literally the first door we check will be a bedroom," El offered.

They left the stairwell, wandered a few meters down this new hallway, also tiled in white marble. A few doors appeared, staggered at intervals on either side. These had numbers, like hotel rooms, on little brass plaques.

Harlan passed the first few, more to show whatever was herding them forward they weren't going to stop at the first thing offered.

She stopped at room 237.

"If Jaime's in here, I'm going to shit," she said.

El laughed nervously, as if she were in a church during a service. "But in a good way, right?"

Harlan smiled, tested the doorknob, found it unlocked.

"Yeah, in a good way."

She opened the door.

****

The room was a small suite, with a good-size bed in a spacious bedroom, a lounge with a couch and chairs, and a large bathroom tiled in the same white marble as the hallway outside. On the far side of the room were large, floor-to-ceiling windows covered by full-length curtains of some shimmering green material.

Harlan went to these immediately, threw them open. The windows behind revealed nothing but solid blackness, no stars. Harlan hadn't expected different. Still, it was a letdown.

El sat on the edge of the bed. It was high and her feet dangled like a little kid's.

"Bed's comfy," El said, leaning back and closing her eyes.

The entire effect—the bland wall colors, the generic bed covers and carpeting, the artwork on the walls—was of a suite in some relatively high-end hotel on Earth. Harlan thought back to the dream (?) where she'd met Charles/Trivia. This room wasn't the same, but the feeling was.

Harlan wanted to lie down on the bed next to El, but she was also aware of something hot inside her, growing. She knew what it was instantly. She was tired of being screwed around, led from one setting to another where she had no clear idea of what was going on. No, it was more. It was not having any idea of what the purpose of it all was, the meaning. What was it all leading to?

But she didn't have the energy to think about it at the moment. She was as tired as El. She crawled into bed beside El, wondered briefly if Jaime was safe wherever he was.

She didn't even remember falling asleep.

****

The distinct clicking of lights snapping on awoke her.

She raised her head groggily, a line of sleep-drool stretching from her lips. She was seated in what looked like a large cafeteria.

No hotel accommodations anymore. This room was filled with rows of round tables, each able to seat eight people. There was absolutely nothing on any of them. Around each were pushed-in plastic chairs with metal legs, all the same color, spaced exactly the same distance apart. Their backs and seats were a similar neutral beige.

At the front of the room were two low, narrow windows. Harlan guessed this was where the trays of food were passed to whatever community ate here. It was dark beyond the windows. The floor was public building standard tile of some sort, the same color as the plastic of the chairs. There was nothing on the walls other than one small window, and no doors she could see.

The ceiling was low, claustrophobically so, and the lights looked rudimentary at best. They hummed annoyingly. Ways away, before the room faded into shadows, a single light fixture sputtered on and off.

Typical.

It made the engineer in her want to get up, cross the distance, climb atop a table, and see what was wrong. But these weren't the usual biotubes she was accustomed to, with their unpowered bioluminescence. The humming they made sounded electrical, antique, and she doubted she'd be able to tell what was wrong, if anything.

The tables lined in rows as far as she could see, faded as the lighting faded. The room was enormous, hangar-like. Harlan thought it doubtful, though, there had ever been more than a single person here.

Two people.

She looked over, and El was there too, seated beside her, snoozing as she had been.

"El," she poked her. "I'm dreaming. Wake up and join me."

El rubbed her eyes, sat up.

"Where are we?" she asked. "What happened to the nice hotel room?"

"We're in my dream now, and evidently what I wanted was a cavernous, empty cafeteria."

"What makes you think I'm in your dream, Harlan?"

"All of this," she said, throwing her arms open wide.

"I don't think this is a dream," El said. "I don't think I'm in *your* dream."

"Exactly what someone in my dream would say."

El rolled her eyes. "What are we doing here?"

"I dunno," Harlan said, standing. "That wasn't there before, though."

Turning in her chair, El looked in the direction Harlan indicated, to the two narrow, open windows.

"What is it?"

Harlan walked to the windows. "Trays, with plates of food on them."

"If you or anyone else here thinks I'm eating after what happened in the dining room..."

Harlan dropped the tray back onto the ledge of the window. Its echo startled both of them. She bent to peer into the window, expecting to see the shadowy shapes of prep stations and ovens and racks of dishes and glasses. But there was nothing. The darkness was as flat as if it had been painted there.

"Gonna have to eat at some point," Harlan said, coming back to the table and sitting.

"Not now. Even the thought of it makes my stomach jumpy."

Harlan clasped her hands on the table before her. "So what do we do? Why are we here?"

"We really need to look for Jaime," El said.

"He could be anywhere."

"Do you think he's looking for us?"

Shaking her head and letting out a long breath, Harlan said, "I honestly don't know, Doc. But I don't see a door anywhere, so unless you want to squeeze through one of those windows, we're stuck here until whatever is yanking our leash is ready for us to move on."

"Whatever is yanking our leash," El said. "What if that's us? What if we're yanking our own leash? I think it's something we at least have to consider. Otherwise we're stumbling from scenario to scenario, none of it having any rhyme or reason. None of it having any *meaning*."

"Oh lord, El," Harlan said, throwing her head back. "You're gonna get all psychiatric now? Right in the middle of all this nonsense? Here? We—*I*—don't have time for this bullshit now."

"We can't go anywhere, as you just said."

"Sometimes I hate my life."

"No, listen. Remember what I was saying about the essential nature of the space between the stars?"

"No, El, not enough to answer a test question about it anyway."

"It's plastic, Harlan. The space out here is plastic, malleable to the super-consciousness of the universe, sure, but also to lower consciousness, like ours. Our consciousness might be having an effect on the space around us, causing all this. We might be doing all this ourselves."

"You've hinted at this before," Harlan said. "So, okay, that's what's happening. Great. How do we...I dunno...fix this, get back home? Get somewhere other than *here*. Because otherwise this is just a slightly charming philosophical discussion. Are you saying we *think* it?"

"I don't think it works that way, at least not for our consciousnesses. It's not magic. It's subtler, its effects more wide-ranging. And I think it takes more of us to accomplish anything on an observable scale. I think there's a reason we're cordoned off in a gravity well, but even out here, where the space is more pliable, we can have some effect on our immediate surroundings. But nothing too grandiose. Not at our level."

"I don't know what you're saying, but it doesn't sound helpful," Harlan said. "This is a stupid dream."

"Harlan, wait," El said as Harlan rose, moved quickly around the table toward where the room recessed into darkness.

"Nope," she said. "I read something about directed dreaming once, so I'm doing that right now."

El followed. "It doesn't work that way. And I don't think this is a dream. At least not the way we understand dreaming."

"We'll see."

"What are you looking for anyway?"

"Well, Jaime, mostly. But first, a door."

"To where?"
"Anywhere but here."

TWENTY-SIX

The rows of carefully arranged circular tables and chairs continued past counting. And always, as they thought the room had ended, the light had given out, more lights clicked on, and the room continued on and on.

"Harlan," El said, trying to keep up.

"Not now, El."

"But, Harlan—"

"We're doing this until we find a door, then we'll go through that door and do something else. But right now, it's all about a door."

They continued past table after table, when Harlan exclaimed, "A-hah!" She rounded the last two tables in the row, toward a single door. It was a simple white entrance with no signage or other markings. A plain door with a plain doorknob.

"Anywhere but here," Harlan said, turning to smile at El. She sensed El was about to say something, to warn her against saying it, against turning that knob, against going through that door.

Harlan turned the doorknob, went through the door.

TWENTY-SEVEN

She stops before she has a complete sense of where she is. The movement between the cafeteria and wherever *this* is leaves her disoriented, and she staggers a step or two. She feels El behind her, pausing in the doorway as Harlan pauses in this new room.

"Where are we now?" she hears El say, trying to figure out that same thing. This new area is dark, lit by what looks like one single light source hanging from an unseen ceiling. This produces a small pool of illumination beneath, showing a rectangular, green-topped table set with four uncomfortable-looking chairs.

In one of those chairs, his back to them, is a man.

Harlan approaches cautiously.

"Jaime?"

The man half turns in his chair but doesn't face her. He isn't Jaime, but he looks as bewildered as she feels.

"Who the fuck are you and where the fuck are we?" she says, laying a hand on his shoulder and turning him fully around.

The man is older, perhaps near sixty, balding. Fat. Eyeglasses. He is dressed, simply and a bit anachronistically, in jeans and a t-shirt. The shirt depicts an illustration of some kind of horror monster; Harlan is unsure exactly what it is or if it means something.

"My name is John," the man says. "And I have no fucking idea where I am. I might ask the same question of you. Two."

El comes to stand next to Harlan, and John registers her with the barest flick of his eyes. All of his attention is focused on Harlan.

"How'd you get here?" she asks.

"I don't know exactly," he says. "I think I'm dreaming, so it kinda doesn't matter."

"Where are you from anyway?"

John gives Harlan a wry, quizzical look. "Ummm...Earth? Illinois? Need something more specific? My address?"

"Great," she says. "A smart ass."

"Well, I mean, how'd *you* get here? Where are *you* from?" John says.

"Well, coincidentally, we're from Earth too. I'm Harlan. This is El."

John blanches visibly, rises from his seat.

"Harlan? El?" he whispers, backing into the edge of the table. "From the *Promise*?"

"Err, well, yeah. How'd you—"

Harlan pauses. It's a dream, she thinks. Of course anyone in the dream would know who they were, where they were from. That's the logic of a dream.

"Which exploded, then you found refuge on the *Limen*," John continues, barely audible. He's no longer questioning them, merely stating facts.

"Yeah, yeah, we all know. And if you know, then you know how we got here. So, your questions are all answered. Now, what about ours?"

John peers around Harlan and El, back toward the door they'd come from, still partially ajar. The cold light of the cafeteria beyond oozes into the room like grey sludge.

"Where's Jaime?" he asks. "Isn't he with you?"

"We don't know. We're looking for him. But I'm still unsure as to why you're here, in my dream."

"I'm here too, so it's not *your* dream," El says.

"Ditto," John offers.

"Do you know this guy, El?"

El shakes her head. "Nope."

"Not a patient or an old lover or something?" Harlan asks.

"Hardly."

"Gee, thanks," John says. El shrugs.

"I don't know you either, John," Harlan says, sarcastically emphasizing his name. "So, if neither of us know who you are, why are you in our dream?"

John takes a deep breath. "Because I wrote you."

"You...excuse me...what?" Harlan answers.

"You're, both of you, characters in a book I wrote," he says. "At least I think you are. You're not exactly the way I pictured you. And to be completely honest, it's a book I'm still writing. Damn, this is the most interesting dream I've had in a while."

El sits at the table, puts her head in her hands.

"You're a writer...an author. And you wrote about us?" Harlan says, still standing. "I'm not scanning this."

"This is incredible," John says. "I've never had a dream about something I've written before. Well, at least not one this real."

"This *isn't* a dream," El moans, arms crossed over her head on the table.

John rolls his eyes. "Of course it is. I mean, you're not real."

"We're every bit as real as you. Realer, in fact," El says.

Harlan hears this, but her sensory input is starting to fade. She thinks this particular dream has hit some Escher loop that will feedback on itself, and she and El will wake up in the hotel room, fresh and ready to continue looking for Jaime.

"What the fuck is going on here?" she shouts. "Ever since the *Promise* exploded, we've pretty much moved from one fucked-up place to the next. No rhyme or reason, no meaning to it all, no resolution. And now this?"

El turns to calm her, but Harlan twists away.

"So this is some story you wrote? We're characters in a book, is that it?"

John plops back in the chair he'd risen from a moment earlier. "I'm not saying anything of the kind."

"THEN WHY THE FUCK ARE YOU EVEN HERE?" Any echoes her scream might have made were swallowed by the room.

"Harlan, calm down," El says.

"This is my dream—excuse me, *our* dream—and I can do whatever I want in it."

"Listen to me, how many times do I have to tell you this *isn't* a dream? Does it feel like a dream to you right now?"

Harlan purses her lips, surveys the small, lit area they stand in. "No. It feels...too—"

"Real," finishes John. "It feels too real to be a dream."

"So, were you another colonist? Sleeping aboard the *Promise*?" El asks, and Harlan knows she's trying to give her space to calm down.

"Onboard the...? No, I've never been in space in my entire life," he laughs. "Going into space isn't a thing where I'm from, unless you're an astronaut."

"When, John? When are you an author?" El asks.

"Twenty twenty-one."

"*Twenty*," Harlan barks. "You're not from *where*, you're from *when*."

"Twenty twenty-one," he repeats. "And you're from the mid twenty-threes, right?"

"Yes," El says. "But that's not the important thing here. The important thing is you're writing a novel about us, about what happened since the explosion of the *Promise*."

"Yeah," John offers. "How does that explain anything?"

"Wait a sec," Harlan says, pulling out a chair across the table from John. Its metal feet screech across the floor as she moves it. She plops down and leans in to him.

"How is it possible you're writing a story about what happened to us and the *Promise* more than three hundred years *before* it happens?"

Harlan waits for an answer, but John gawps at her.

"Happens," repeats El.

"What?" Harlan asks.

"*Happens.* He's writing about what *happens*," El says. "Not what *happened.*"

"So?"

"Because he's writing fiction, Harlan. *Fiction.*"

John nods enthusiastically.

****

The three stare at each other, huddled in the reservoir of light cast by the fixture dangling from some unseen, perhaps unreal ceiling.

"So, we're fiction?" Harlan says, finally.

"No, I don't think so," says El. "Well, maybe, perhaps in some alternative dimension, John here invented us and cast us in a story."

John traces little circles on the table they sit at.

"I think this house is screwing with our sense of reality, purposefully," El says. "Onboard the *Limen*, we ourselves were liminal, transitional, between one state and another."

"What states were those?" Harlan asked. "Fiction and non-fiction?"

"Life and death. This dimension or another. A lower form of consciousness and something different…higher. I don't know," says El. "All I do know is now we're here, wherever *here* is. We're no longer in transition."

"This is where we transitioned to? A haunted house floating in space? What wanted us here? And why?" Harlan is still worked up, barely sitting on her seat.

"Fear," John blurts, nodding. "It's all fear."

They both turn to him, over-expectant this mysterious person would offer some concrete explanation of what is occurring.

"Explain," El says.

"I was writing a novel on this, with you two—and Jaime—in it. It was supposed to be a look at consciousness and what it is and how human consciousness can—I know this sounds weird—can affect the medium of space itself."

"Have you been paying attention, John? This doesn't sound weird. At. All," Harlan says.

"I wish I'd written you as less of a smartass," he says.

Harlan flips him the bird.

"Anyway, it was supposed to be a meditation on consciousness and how we perceive reality and our place in the universe. Humanity's, that is."

Harlan rolls her eyes. "Does anyone other than a hack writer ever use the phrase *a meditation on* when describing their work?"

"Harlan," El snaps, and Harlan puts her head down onto the table.

"The focus of this meditation," he glares at Harlan, "is fear. Humanity's penchant for fear."

"Pen—"

"Harlan, if you're not going to contribute anything useful, can you please shut the fuck up," El says, slapping the table and startling the other two.

Harlan lays her head back onto the table with a thud.

"What did your story have to say about fear, John?" El asks.

"It sours our consciousness, poisons the well, so to speak. Holds us back," John explains.

"Exactly. The well. I'm a panpsychist, you know."

"Well, yeah, I did the research."

"And?"

"Well, I mean I Googled it to flesh out your character, but honestly don't understand."

El smiles, warm and genuine.

"Well, I think the universe itself has some sort of mass consciousness that is the aggregate of all the lesser consciousnesses, everything from animals down to subatomic particles. That's panpsychism. But none of these lesser consciousnesses were high enough to do what the universe needed."

"And that is?" John asks.

"It wanted to contemplate itself, to consider itself in the ordinary, everyday way humans do, but most lower forms don't. So humanity was created for the universe to be able to contemplate itself through us. Our ideas, our creativity. The universe can use those pieces of us to help it shape reality. But what we also bring to the table is fear, and the universe has no use for it. So they cordoned us off on Earth, in a gravity well, which somehow prohibits our crippled consciousnesses from affecting the malleable nature of open space. It didn't want us out here exploring the stars and warping reality with our petty fears. It's why the *Promise* was destroyed, why we're stranded here," El concludes.

"That's what's known in my business as an exposition dump," John chuckles.

"A what?"

John shakes his head. "Anyway, it makes sense now."

"What does?"

"The title of my novel. *Plastic Space House.*"

Harlan snorts, then groans, but doesn't lift her head.

"Exactly," El says, her tone conveying deep satisfaction. "Exactly. So here we sit, in a house fabricated from our fears, meeting with our author from another reality and wondering what it all means? Where do we go from here?"

"I hate to ditch this meta discussion, but where's Jaime?" John asks. "I kinda feel he's important to the story."

"If he's so important to the story, you should have written him better," Harlan snaps.

"No, really, where's—"

"You tell us, you bastard," Harlan says, finally lifting her head. "I mean, if you wrote all this, then you're responsible for all this. You destroyed the *Promise*. You whipped up the *Limen*. The blood...the noises. Then this fucking house. The dining room. I oughta punch you for that. And then Jaime, being sucked into the wall. Disappearing."

John backs away from her aggressive posture. "Yeah, I wrote that stuff about the *Promise* and the *Limen*. Sorry for the menstrual blood and all. My wife hated it. But I'd only written up to the point of the house appearing. I hadn't gotten any further."

"What do you mean?" Harlan asks.

"He means the novel's unfinished. He didn't write any of the stuff that's happened to us *inside* the house."

"Then who did?"

John holds his hands out as if to say *I dunno.*

"Maybe no one did. Or maybe someone in a different reality— maybe even another version of John—wrote it, actually finished *Plastic Space House*," El says. "Or maybe no one wrote it. What I'm saying is, in an infinite universe filled with infinite dimensions, all of those things are possible. All of them. All at once."

"This is making my head hurt...in all universes, all at once," Harlan says, taking her seat. "What's the point?"

"You think there's a point?" John says. "How cute."

"You think there's no point to any of this?" El asks. "Then why bother writing your story?"

"I was getting to the moment where all the ideas came together in a through-line," John says, sounding sheepish. "But I hadn't gotten there yet."

"Did you get to the part where we find Jaime?" Harlan asks.

"No. Nothing that happens...*happened*...after the house appeared is anything I wrote."

"Then I'm not sure what good you are to us," Harlan says, turning to address El. "We need to get searching for Jaime."

She rises, taps El on her shoulder.

"C'mon," she says.

"Harlan, wait. Where are you going?"

"Back into the cafeteria, back in the house," she says over her back. "If we have to open every goddamn door in that house, we're going to find him."

Harlan is halfway to the open door they'd come through, the only other source of light in this null space.

"What about him?" El asks, starting to follow, but turning back to John.

"Fuck him. He can stay right where we found him, so he can go back to his comfy writer life when he wakes up from whatever dream he's having."

El motions for John to follow.

"No thanks," he says. "I'll take my chances here. Besides, I need to process all this before I sit down to write again."

"What for?"

"So *Plastic Space House* doesn't veer off the rails like this story evidently has. Fuck that other version of me."

El follows Harlan through the door. Once through, Harlan ducks back and grabs the doorknob.

"Write better, you fucking shit-scribbler!"

And with that, she closes the door on me.

TWENTY-EIGHT

Harlan slammed the door closed behind them, plunging back into the columns and rows of tables and chairs. When she turned back, having moved maybe twenty meters away, the door had disappeared.

"I hope we can go back the way we came," she said, hooking her thumb over her shoulder. El turned and saw the blank white wall where the door had been.

"Harlan, we—"

"We need to find Jaime, El. That's what we need."

"Harlan, what if this isn't real. All of this, any of this since the *Promise* exploded?"

That stopped Harlan in her tracks.

"You pick helluva times to talk about shit like this, you know?"

"You're always saying we're in your dream or our dream or whatever," El said. "What if it is a dream of some kind, and we're asleep back on the *Promise*? What if we're dreaming all this?"

"How can we be dreaming all this? All this, all of us?"

"Because we don't understand consciousness," El said. "We barely understand sleep, much less dreaming. What if dreaming is an altered state of reality? What if consciousness and reality intersect somehow, each one affecting the other? What if to get out of here means we need to change the way we're thinking about things?"

Harlan stared at El, not knowing quite what to say at first.

Then, "I can't. Not anymore. You ponder life's imponderables if you want. I'm going to search for Jaime."

"What if he's as unreal as all of this?"

Harlan stomped away, back toward the front of the cafeteria.

"He's real to me."

"But what if he isn't? What if I'm not either?"

"A rabbit hole, Doc, a waste of time. I'm looking for Jaime, come with me or not."

"Why?"

"Because, Doc. We hang together. It's what we do. It's what I do anyway, and if either you or the universal consciousness has a problem, you all can go fuck yourselves. Collectively, of course."

****

El followed Harlan to the front of the cafeteria, where they both hunted for another door. When they awoke in this room, they had no idea how they'd gotten there. One moment they were asleep, the next seated at a table.

But they couldn't find any sort of door out here. Harlan went from one side of the room, cursing, pushing aside tables and chair. They clattered as they scooted over the floor or were upturned, and those sounds seemed like an offense to the chamber's quietness.

"Fuck!" Harlan roared, stopping suddenly. "There's got to be a way out of here."

"I find your refusal to see this all for what it's worth to be infuriating and comical," El said, arms crossed, leaning against the ledge to one of the two food windows.

"I find your general demeanor to be infuriating. Period," Harlan said, staring past her.

"What's on your mind, Harlan?" El asked, then followed her line of sight to the window she slouched against. "No, no, no. You can't be serious."

El stepped away from the window as Harlan took her place. Bending down, Harlan peered in but saw only blackness. She experimentally thrust a hand through the empty space, wriggled it around. She felt nothing, not even a change in temperature.

"Help me up here," Harlan said. "When I'm through, I'll pull you over."

"To where?" El asked.

"Anypl—"

"Harlan, please."

"Just help. Or do you want to spend an eternity in an empty cafeteria with me?"

El came forward, cupped her hands for Harlan to step onto, boost herself onto the narrow ledge.

Swinging her foot over and through the open window, Harlan turned back to El.

"Here goes." She lifted her other leg, ducked under the head jam, and jumped through, not having any clear idea of what she was jumping into and wondering if she'd perhaps been too rash.

When she was sure of her footing, sure there was air here, gravity, and not the cold, weightless expanse of outer space she half expected, she reached through and took El's hand.

****

She pulled El through, and they stood side by side, still holding hands, waiting for their eyes to accustom to the dark.

Harlan saw they stood outside. In front of them was the grey clapboard of the house. They looked to be on one of the house's sides. Harlan could make out the twisting path leading to the front steps.

There was no door or window in the clapboard they might have stepped through, and Harlan gave a mental shrug as to how they got there.

Does it matter?

On this side of the house, the lawn was clear about thirty or so meters, as if some cosmic yard boy kept it neatly trimmed. At its edge though, a tall copse of spindly trees, papery thin leaves whispering in the non-existent breeze.

"What now?" El asked, her voice dripping with sarcasm.

"Over the river and through the woods," Harlan said. "Isn't that how the antique rhyme goes? Let's see what's on the other side of this."

Harlan set off, not waiting to see if El followed.

****

The woods were preternaturally dark, the more so because the night sky featured no stars or moon to light the leaves or play silver on the forest floor. The trees were bare to a height of around two meters, tall enough for Harlan and El to walk unscathed beneath them.

They all seemed to be the same kind of tree, smooth-barked and slender, with branches reaching upward, forming a wide crown with a tapered top. The leaves in reach were similarly shaped, with serrated edges and a fine, softly haired underside. They looked green-grey in the darkness.

Harlan had never paid much attention to trees while on Earth, so she had no idea what kind they were. Their sameness, though, struck her as odd, as if this detail, this level of exactitude, was unimportant to whomever had put them here.

Harlan could hear her own footfalls on the soft, loamy earth, no grass now. She could hear El following behind, could hear her breathing. But there was no crunching of dead leaves or debris underfoot. No sound of nocturnal animals, neither the hoot of an owl nor the cry of a fox.

So when she did hear the snap of a twig—and from up ahead and not behind—Harlan froze.

"Did you hear that?" she asked, scanning the trees for whatever had made the sound.

"Yeah. So? A twig snapped."

"You notice either you or I making any sounds at all out here?"

El didn't answer.

"I think we should make our way back to the house, to the front door," Harlan said, turning and manhandling El around too.

They started a quick pace, and suddenly the snapping of twigs and rustling of leaves was all around them.

Harlan stopped suddenly, peered into the mass of tree trunks, trying to see any movement in the lighter spaces between them.

"Come on," she urged El, and they were walking again, back in the direction they'd come.

As they walked faster, the sounds came faster too. Footfalls crunching the ground, heavier than both of theirs.

Harlan reached back to pull El forward, spared a look behind them.

A shape in the darkness, obscuring the tree trunks, the spaces between them. The figure was large, imposing, taller than the lower boughs of the trees. It had to swipe them aside as it came toward Harlan and El.

Stray light caught its face as it came through a clump of leaves.

It had to be at least two and a half meters tall, wearing work boots and drab grey coveralls, ripped and torn in places. There was a name tag sewn over its left breast, one word.

Mike.

In one of his enormous hands, he wielded an axe, its keen edge gleaming in the null light. Something dark dripped from its heel. He raised it as he lumbered toward them through the trees.

"El, run! *Run!*"

Harlan yanked her forward, then shoved her ahead. She sprinted after El, pushing at her back to make her run faster. They cleared the tree line on the side of the house, tore across the lawn.

They hooked around the house's corner, came to the bottom of the steps to the front door.

"Hurry!" Harlan said, urging her. "He's gaining on us!"

Mike had stomped across the lawn and was now rounding the corner. He saw them race up the steps, and seemed to pick up speed, perhaps knowing if they gained the safety of the house, he might not be able to get at them.

El slid across the boards of the front porch, fumbled with the doorknob.

Mike had come to the bottom of the steps, and he paused, looked at them.

Harlan saw he wore some kind of mask over his face, a detail lost in the darkness of the forest. The mask was unrecognizable to her, white with holes for the eyes, a series of smaller ones covering each cheek. A red swath, not part of the mask's decoration, slashed across its features from above the right eye to the upper left corner of its narrow mouth slit.

He hefted the axe, plopped its heavy head into the palm of his hand a few times as if to test its weight.

El opened the front door, practically leapt through it.

Harlan followed as Mike started up the steps.

She could feel his immense weight as he gained the porch, warping the floorboards under her feet. An immense, angry cold radiated from his form, something dank and mildewy wafted from him.

Harlan stepped through the door, slammed it shut behind her, locked the deadbolt before she had time to appreciate it probably wouldn't do them any good.

She heard a grunt from the other side of the door, stepped back.

As she did, the blade of the axe split through the door at eye level, cleaving down to the doorknob. He was either immensely strong or the door was made from absurdly fragile material.

Behind her, El screamed, and Harlan found herself wishing both to join her and to slap her.

She took another step back as he tore the axe from the splintered door, lifted it for another swing.

Her feet slid on the wood, and she pinwheeled backward in an attempt to catch her balance, careening into El. Both women fell to the floor in a tangle, Harlan trying to figure out what she had skidded on as Mike's looming figure burst through the door, axe held at the ready.

Wide-eyed with fear, Harlan saw a small puddle of blood at her feet, smeared across the floor, a thin tracer meandering to her leg, disappearing up her pants.

She was bleeding again.

TWENTY-NINE

Harlan scrabbled back across the wood floor of the foyer, away from the axe-wielding maniac who had hacked his way through the door, from the squiggle of red connecting her leg to the smeared pool of blood.

Now? Really?

She kicked with her heels, bumped into something behind her she assumed was El. She tried to get to her feet but could gain no purchase.

Mike came fully into the room. His facemask gleamed in the soft light, dull beady eyes peering through its slits. Harlan noticed wood splinters on the shoulders of his coveralls, on the tops of his boots. She also saw their helmets—which they'd left in the foyer when they'd first entered the house—had fallen from the table they'd been set on, rolled across the floor.

This can't be real. This is a dream. And dreams aren't real. They aren't.

Calming herself, Harlan pulled herself to her feet. Mike paused, the axe lifted for another swing, watched her.

She scooped up one of the clear helmets rolling against her shoe, held it upside down by its collar. As Mike apparently wondered what the hell she was doing, she twisted, cocked back, and brought the helmet around in a tight arc, catching him under his jaw, rocking his entire body back.

As he lurched away though, the axe fell.

Harlan was entirely exposed at this point, and the axe—with only its own weight behind it—struck her, glancing off her shoulder and slicing down across collarbone and breast before clattering to the ground.

Enraged, Harlan swung the helmet backhand, striking Mike across his lowered forehead with a sickening crunch. She wasn't sure if it was his head or the helmet that had shattered, and she didn't care.

She stepped forward as Mike slumped to the ground, the axe clattering to the floor. Swinging the helmet, she brought it down with all her might onto the top of his unprotected head.

The transparent ceramic of the helmet was strong enough to withstand the punch of micrometeoroids and it didn't show as much as a tiny crack.

Mike, apparently, wasn't built as tough. Blood burst from his skull, and the mask he wore popped off, sailed across the room.

Harlan brought the helmet up once more, stopped its momentum at the height of its arc, brought it down again and again.

Unmasked now, the man slumped before her, bleeding from his mouth and ears, a series of terrific wounds to his head.

It was Jaime.

****

"It can't be him," Harlan said, sitting on the floor as far from the corpse as she could get in the room. "It can't."

El hovered over the fallen form trying to find a pulse.

"Well, whoever it is, they're dead," El said, stepping away around the fallen axe. "Those helmets can do some damage."

"El, is it him? Is it *really* Jaime?"

"His face is so smashed I can't be one-hundred percent sure," said El. "But yeah, I think so."

Harlan groaned. "How's that possible? How could it be him? Why would he be trying to kill us with an axe?"

"Harlan, I don't know," El said, still crouching but duck-walking over to her. "Let me see that wound."

"Wound? What...?" Harlan yelped as El probed with her fingers where the axe had fallen onto her. "I'm bleeding there too?"

"What are you talking about?" El said, spreading the cuts in Harlan's suit to see the slice the axe had made. "His axe skipped off your collarbone, which might have saved your life. Nice gash from there down to your breast, bleeding pretty bad. We need to find a first aid kit or something."

"All EVA suits have a simple kit," Harlan said, looking down at the bloody slice. "Side pocket."

El tore a hip pocket open on her suit, fished out a small plastic pouch. Inside, she found a vial of antibiotic discs and a tube of fleshmend. She knocked one of the discs out onto her hand, affixed it to Harlan's neck. Then she exposed the length of the axe wound by unzipping Harlan's suit and rucking her torn t-shirt. She applied the fleshmend, then pinched the edges of the slice together. The ooze of blood stopped, and El used a disposable cloth from the pouch to wipe blood from Harlan's chest.

"Thanks, Doc," Harlan said, peeling down her shirt and carefully zipping her suit.

"Don't mention it," El said, wiping her hands with the cloth. "Want something for the pain?"

"Nah," Harlan said, standing and looking at the blood trail from her pants leg. It appeared to have stopped. She went to the body sprawled on the floor, prodded it with her foot.

Mike or Jaime, he didn't move.

She reached down and grabbed the man's chin, turned his face.

She wouldn't have thought half a dozen blows from a helmet could have done this amount of damage, but El was right. It was hard to tell underneath the man's swollen, bloody features.

But it looked like Jaime.

He'd chased them into the house and tried to kill them.

And she'd killed him.

"You still think someone is writing this?" Harlan asked as El came to stand beside her.

"No," El said. "I'm convinced we're doing this to ourselves."

****

They discussed burying the body, but the idea of digging outside—if they were even able to find a shovel—stopped them. What if they dug right through the soil and into the black, empty space that lay beyond? The image of staring down into a blank, featureless hole made Harlan shiver.

Instead, they removed the tablecloth from the adjacent dining room—unstained and neatly laid on the clean and reset table—and covered the body with it there in the foyer.

They followed the hallway through the kitchen, out past where Jaime had been sucked into the wall, up the spiral staircase, until they found their previous room, 237. They entered, and it was exactly as it had been before, pristine and empty.

Except for one thing.

There was a table in the lounge sitting in front of the sofa. Atop it was a large basket covered in transparent film.

El didn't notice, sat on the bed to remove her boots.

Harlan went to the basket. She could see it was filled with a variety of fruits and packets of treats. A card was affixed to its top. She removed it, read it.

"El," she said. "Are you hungry?"

"Famished."

"Come in here a sec, then."

Harlan heard her shuffle into the room and held the card for her.

El read it, snorted.

"Yeah, well, I'm hungry too," she said, and removed the film from the basket. "Dig in."

She dropped the card, and it fluttered to the carpet.

Compliments of, it read.

THIRTY

She opened her eyes abruptly, blinked a few times. She saw a rumple of sheets, the hillock of a pillow, the bend of her arm she'd been huddled into. Light shone from the other room. Maybe El had risen, gone to have a midnight snack.

Harlan rolled over, sat up, rubbed her eyes.

She was no longer in bed. What she thought were sheets and pillows were simply the ground and the canopy of trees. She was outside, stretched out on the dirt. She looked up and saw the black, black sky, striated by the tree limbs, their leaves silent and motionless. She gasped, leapt to her feet.

She was in that eerie forest bordering the house. She put a hand to her mouth to stifle a scream, not of terror but of frustrated rage.

She saw she was no longer in her torn suit or even the hotel suite's bathrobe, but in a plain, grey coverall. There, on her left breast, she saw, upside down, one embroidered word: MIKE.

A small sound escaped her effort to keep it in; a strangled, squawking bleat.

Voices. In the distance, coming closer.

El maybe.

She took a single step, nearly tripped. Her legs felt impossibly long, impossibly thick. She saw she wore unfamiliar, heavy work boots.

Lumbering a step, then another. She crunched stuff underfoot, twigs and other forest debris.

The voices stopped.

Ahead, toward the house, she saw two silhouettes.

El.

And Jaime.

For a moment, her heart soared.

She hadn't killed him after all.

One step, another, lurching forward like a Frankenstein monster.

Then she noticed her hand was holding something, some weight cocked over her shoulder. She felt the butt of it in her hand, shifted her grip as if it were a baseball bat.

When she caught sight of it, her heart fell.

An axe.

The figures were close now, and she let the axe swing away, tried to form words that wouldn't come. Her clumsy free hand swiped at her face, felt it covered with some hard plastic mask.

"Run! Run, El!" came a masculine voice, and suddenly they were leaving her, her friends, fleeing from her.

No, no. It's me. It's just me.

Even though she seemed unable to speak, unable to alert them, she had to tell them, had to warn them of this...whatever *this* was.

She pursued, felt the thuds of her enormous strides rumble through her legs. Even though she tried, she couldn't let loose of the axe. It seemed glued to her hand, and she slashed with it, tried to dislodge it as she ran.

They had made the porch and were entering the house as she staggered to a halt at the bottom of the steps.

She caught sight of Jaime—*Jaime!*—his face frantic as he slammed the door shut, clicked the lock into place.

Harlan tried to shout his name, but the only sound she was able to produce was a garbled string of nonsense syllables sounding like boulders grinding.

Still trying to drop the axe, she plodded up the steps, tried the doorknob, though she knew it was locked.

More muddled sounds as she tried to shout their names, shout for them to open the door. But to no avail.

The axe head flashed in her peripheral vision, and she knew what she had to do. Hefting it, she swung it down onto the door. She had to get to them, to *tell* them.

The sharp, heavy thing cleaved through the door easily.

When she lifted the axe, Harlan saw them in the foyer, cowering, eyes wide. Jaime sheltered El behind him.

She had to get in, remove her mask, make them *see*, understand it was her. Just Harlan and not MIKE.

Swinging the axe again, she made the crack in the door wider, deeper, but still not big enough. This was taking too long, so she simply pushed the bulk of her body into the hole she'd made, shrugged her way into the room in an explosion of wood shards.

Jaime reached for one of the discarded helmets, but Harlan swatted it away, swinging the axe in a wide arc.

The helmet clattered against the wall, skittered down the corridor.

Unfortunately, so, too, did a streamer of Jaime's intestines, gleaming wet and purple as they splattered against the woodwork. Harlan saw the hooked poll of the axe had opened a slit in Jaime's abdomen, snagged his guts and drew them out, most of them spilling at his feet.

Jaime spared a single look at her, then crumpled to the floor in a gush of blood.

As she stared down at him, aghast, El came running forward, screaming.

Harlan tried to drop the axe, beaded with Jaime's blood. But in bringing it up, it connected with El's forward momentum, striking underneath her delicate chin, still ascending, splitting her face all the way to her hairline.

El's legs spasmed and she fell against Harlan, a single hand coming up to touch the plastic mask she wore.

Harlan made a strangled, desperate sound as El's face unfolded like some horrible flower, the grey lump of her brain sliding out to strike Harlan's chest.

She caught El's body in her arms, her one hand still not able to drop the axe.

She screamed El's name, or at least tried to, and the echoes of that garbled wail rattled the walls of the house.

When she looked down, she saw a single, thin runnel of blood had leaked down her pants leg and out across the leather of the work boot, joining the mosaic of blood and gore covering the floor.

Groaning, Harlan sank to the floor, carefully cradling El's limp form, gently stroking the hair on one side of her split head.

THIRTY-ONE

Harlan stayed there, leaning against the wall, clutching El's body to her breast, quiet. The foyer looked like a murder scene, which, of course, it was. Blood dripped from the walls. Dots of blood sprayed the ceiling. Spatters and pools of it smeared the floor, the slump of Jaime's organs like a pile of wet towels.

She'd finally been able to drop the axe and it lay there, bloody blade and bloody handle.

The door, split open, showed the weirdly lit lawn outside, the path leading from the steps to where the lifeboat had docked. But there was no lifeboat.

Now there was no Jaime and no El either, only their lifeless bodies.

Harlan thought she should cry. She was never the girl who cried, not when she was sad, not when she was angry or frustrated. But this seemed a time where crying fit, where it seemed justified. But she couldn't marshal even one tear.

She felt empty, hollow. When she'd signed up to be part of the crew of the *Promise*, it seemed an adventure, exciting. An entire new, unexplored world. A trip through the galaxy onboard one of the greatest machines humanity had ever produced. A chance to be part of human history, setting forth across the stars.

A chance to completely revise who she was.

How had it come to this? The *Promise* exploded, the only other two survivors dead at her hands. That was not the personal revision she had sought. And now stranded alone in a haunted house floating in space. Weird dreams. Fugue states. Unexplainable encounters with unfathomable...what? Creatures? Consciousnesses?

Or hallucinations caused by...well, again, what?

Maybe she was dead, killed when the *Promise* exploded in a silent ball of flames far, far from Earth. Maybe this was death, the other side. A warped, shifting reality offering little comfort or chance for introspection. Relentless absurdities punctuated by inexplicable violence.

Or maybe she was asleep in the hibernation hub aboard the still-extant *Promise*. Floating in her blue gel, dreaming the long, vivid dreams of a human in stasis. Would she laugh about these dreams when she was safely ensconced in whatever enclave humans would build on Teegarden?

Would she even remember any of this when she awoke?

If she awoke.

She hoped not. If these were dreams, she hoped they faded like early morning smoke on a pond, evanescent as the sun rose and frayed it into meaningless wisps.

And if this were the afterlife?

Well, fuck that shit.

****

There's a transition, but there's no transition.

****

She simply finds herself seated on a bed, her childhood bed from her father's home. Something that was becoming so repetitive she rolled her eyes.

As usual, sun warms the curtains, the wedge of the bedspread it falls upon. Motes of dust—pollen?—dance in the warm air of the room. The window is open, and the breeze stirs the curtains, feels delightful on her skin.

Harlan is Harlan, not Mike. Her hands are no longer covered in blood. She's in a dress now, a flowered sundress, the kind she liked to kick around in while her father puttered in the garden. Maybe out on the back patio, a sweating glass of iced tea on the table next to her reader, a book halfway complete.

Her hand flutters to her exposed collarbone, down the rise of her breast. The skin there is whole, smooth, unbroken. Not even a scar to show where Mike's axe had fallen onto her.

Cautiously, she checks her bare legs too, to see if there are any thin tracks of blood curving over her calves.

There is no blood.

She shakes her head in annoyance. Glad to see there is no blood, but tired of trying to figure out why it comes and goes.

"Are you coming down here or are you going to sit up there mooning all day?"

Harlan's breathing hitches, stops. The voice comes from downstairs.

"Dad?" she says, more to herself.

No, don't do this. Not this. Please, not this.

"Daddy?" she says louder.

"Come downstairs and say hello," comes the familiar voice.

She stands slowly, her brow furrows. She wants to leap up, run down to the library, and jump into his arms. Smell his familiar smell, feel the grizzle of his unshaven cheeks.

But not now, not after all that's happened.

And besides, this feels...*different.* There's an edge to her perceptions, making everything feel hyper-defined. As if the resolution of a picture were dialed up way too high.

Besides, it couldn't be him, and so it isn't him.

That saddens her tremendously, more so than she is even willing to admit to herself.

So she goes slowly, trying to burn off some of her excitement, her trepidation.

Whatever this is, whoever this is, this isn't going to be easy.

She takes a deep breath at the top of stairs, sets her foot on the first step, takes hold of the banister. Deliberately, she comes down each step, then pauses, like she is making her entrance to a debutante party, the crowd appraising her posture, her demeanor.

She's never been a debutante—did they even have such things anymore?—but she assumes this was how they descended staircases. Prim, hopeful, a little afraid.

Afraid.

Reaching the bottom of the stairs, she lingers, her fingers brushing the banister, looks into the open door of the library. He's in there, she feels it, sitting on one of his leather seats, the other unoccupied, waiting for the visitor he so seldom had or even allowed inside.

Waiting for her.

Disappointment.

Swallowing, her mouth dry, she lets her hand fall from the railing, goes to the library door.

There he is, looking as he usually did. He still wore suits, so anachronistic these days, tie and all. Always so neat and prim, his beard carefully trimmed, his thinning hair brushed back from a forehead weathered and lined from years outside in the garden without enough sunscreen.

"Dad?" she croaks. "Daddy?"

"Hello, Harlan," he says, smiling, almost beaming. Her father was not a severe man, not humorless, but he'd seldom *beamed*. "Come in and sit down. Let's talk."

She takes small steps into the room. It is all so real, not dreamlike. She can feel the rug beneath her feet, smell the antique must of the books, their paper, their leather bindings. The polish used on the woodwork. Her father's aftershave and the general unfussy smell of him.

There are no hugs and kisses; she lowers herself slowly into the chair and turns to him.

"How are you, Daddy?"

"I'm fine, Harlan. It's so good to see you. So good."

"It's good to see you too, Daddy."

"How have you been, sweetheart?"

Sweetheart? He'd never once called her that, at least as far as she could remember, though she often wished he had. *Kid* or *kiddo* or sometimes, when he was feeling jocular, *Colonel*.

"Been? Well, umm...not great, Dad, not—"

"You know I'm not your father, Harlan. Right?" His face suddenly looks unexpectedly, deeply sad, unwilling to break the illusion so soon.

She knows. Of course she knows it isn't him. He's back on Earth, puttering in the garden or lounging in his library. Alone.

But there is something else about whatever this is masquerading as her father. Something on a deeper level discomfits her more than the deception. He seems to vibrate, his form wavering or even shifting, as if every atom in him is having trouble maintaining cohesion.

Harlan blinks. "Yeah. Sure. That fits."

"We're sorry."

"Nah, don't be," she says. "But then, who are you...all?"

Her father, or whoever he is, shifts in his seat, sits forward, and reaches for one of her hands. Although not wanting him—*it*—to touch her, she lets him. It feels like her father's hand: thick, warm, calloused by his work planting and harvesting in the garden. He holds her hand gently, but his feels not quite normal. A bit off, subtle, barely sensed.

The surface of his skin tickles against hers, effervescent. For some reason, it makes her feel unspeakable age, inexplicable vastness.

Without volition, she withdraws her hand. It flutters nervously to her lap like a downed bird.

Whatever wore the guise of her father smiles. There is no malice or guile there, just knowledge and acceptance.

But his form ripples like a bad holo, the kind you get during a storm, where the transmission doesn't fully come through.

"No, we're not your father. But he's a part of us, small though it may be. You're part of us too. So, in a way, we are you and he, at least in part."

"And who am I in this scenario? The walrus?"

His grin returns, as if he gets the joke. The grin, though, stretches too far across his face.

"From an old song."

"We're aware of the song, Harlan. It's part of us too."

"This is going to be cryptic, isn't it?"

"That depends entirely on you, as does all of this," he replies. "Entirely."

"Great. So, why am I here? What'd you want to talk about?"

He gestures around the room. "All of this, what's happened. What's going to happen. You want to know, that's why we're here."

"And—excuse me again—*who* are you?"

"We're the All."

Harlan takes the simple sentence in. "So you're god? Is that it?"

The smile becomes indulgent. Harlan feels uneasy watching him. Her father had neither smiled this enthusiastically nor this long.

"No, not god. But the rest of everything outside them."

"*Them?* I thought there was one god. There are a lot of plurals being thrown around here."

"There's singularity in plurality, and plurality in singularity."

"That didn't take long," Harlan says, sitting back. "So El was right? You're the universal consciousness?"

"More or less. Your approximation of it."

"Great. So you're the reason the *Promise* exploded? You sent the *Limen* to us?"

"No. You did all that."

"*I* did?"

"Your consciousness affects the—"

"Yeah, yeah, yeah, I know all about it. But why?"

Her father sighs, rises from his chair, and drifts across the room to the shelves. "The fabric of the space-time continuum is sensitive to conscious adaptation. It's the great gift for those species able to leave the confines of their home systems."

"There's a 'but' coming, isn't there?"

Her father shoots her an annoyed look but continues. "The vast majority of species able to do this have spent the time landlocked on their planets conquering their baser instincts—hatred, violence, distrust. Fear. When they gain the greater universe, they bring with them only the positives—love, caring, empathy. The effects these have on space-time are desired; what that mechanism was created to react to.

"Fear, though. Those who haven't first conquered fear, who gain the greater universe before this step is reached, carry their fear into adaptive space. Its effects on the continuum are...well, you've dealt with some of this already, haven't you?"

"Yeah, about that..."

"Yes. You have questions."

"Damn right I have questions, *Dad*!" She spits the last word at the man.

"Careful, Harlan. Manage your fears. But ask your question."

He turns back to her, no longer smiling. As she watches him, though, there's a hiccup in his form. This time it seems more physical, as if something inside him pushes *outward*, straining against his skeleton, muscles, and skin.

"Why all this...horror? Why not let us get to Teegarden? Or send us back to Earth? Why all the rest of this bullshit? The blood, this fucking house floating in space? Having me kill my friends?"

"Look inside, Harlan."

"Fuck that," she says, rising from her chair and stepping toward him. "You may not be god, but you're the universe. If you cared, you could help here."

"No."

"No? Well...fuck! 'No' as in you won't help?"

"No, to use language you might understand better, we don't give a fuck."

Those words coming out of her father's mouth set her back on her heels. She knows she'd never heard her father curse in front of her.

"You don't—" she stammers, then is cut short.

"What, in your experience, would tell you the universe at large cares about you or your planet?" He seems to grow a bit larger as he speaks, not taller but somehow *fuller*. The buttons of his vest strain as his chest expands.

"You don't care? About any of that?"

"No. Why would we?

"I mean, it sounds so fucking indifferent."

"Do you care about the wellbeing of any of the trillions of subatomic particles making up the tip of one strand of your hair?"

"Well, no, but it's hardly the same."

"Isn't it?"

"Subatomic particles aren't alive. They're not conscious."

"Are you so sure? What if I told you consciousness, even if in some limited form, extends all the way down to the elemental particles of this reality?"

"It's like I'm talking to El again," Harlan said with a pang of guilt and sadness.

"She knew what she was talking about."

"But are you saying nothing in the universe cares for our wellbeing?"

"As I said, we're not god."

"Do they? Do they care?"

"We don't know their mind. It's possible they don't care either."

"You don't know?" Harlan says, choking up. "How could you not know?"

"We're a construct of the infinite number of consciousnesses we contain. As such, we, too, are a creation, though once removed. We don't know god, have never known god. We exist as you do, separate from them. We consider it likely they've moved on from this creation, possibly to another.

"Understand, we are neither for nor against anything in the universe," he says. "We're indifferent."

"You're saying we're on our own," Harlan says, backing away until her legs strike the chair. She falls into it.

"Yes."

"No one cares about us."

"Untrue. You have the capacity to care for each other."

"Is that enough?"

"In the absence of all else, doesn't it have to be?"

"I mean, I guess so, but..."

"Surely you felt this. Surely you knew, because of your experiences, there was either no god or a god who didn't care."

"Even those of us who don't believe in some god or another always felt as if *something* cared. The universe cared."

"In that, there is only you."

Harlan reels as those six words strike her, each one as potent as a punch.

No one cared about what had happened to the *Promise*, all those people who had been killed. No one cared about what had happened to her and Jaime and El. No one cared about their deaths either.

Except her.

Harlan is the last human alive to know all this. And she cares. She cares a lot.

This makes her angry.

"If there's no one who cares, no one to help me, why are you even here?"

"This is the nature of the space you've entered. A great gift for most. A curse for some," he says, rising to his full height, taller than her father had ever been. His presence fills the room.

"Which is it for me?" she asks, fear blooming in her like some rare flower. She eases from the chair, backs toward the door.

He shrugs. "This is a house of horrors because of you. You choose the house you live in. It could be so much more." His voice has become rougher now, harder, nothing like her father's.

He steps toward her, growing even larger. By now, Harlan swears he must be three meters tall. His balding head grazes the ceiling, his shoulders are hunched. His suit jacket splits at the seams. He shoves aside the chairs and looms over her. Harlan cowers in the doorway.

"It could also be so much worse."

His thin smile opens wide, exposing a mouthful of sharp, thin teeth, like a knife drawer's contents standing on end. They have shredded the flesh of his mouth, and his lips are flecked with bloody foam.

"You're not my father," she says to it, wondering if she's trying to remind him or herself.

"No, we're not. We are as you make us," it said, its voice now papery and sibilant. As she watches, the skin of its forehead ripples, water in the wake of a passing ship. With a sound like fabric tearing, the skin splits, tears down toward its mouth, around the back of its head.

What emerges is dark and noisome, wet with blood and yellow, clotted pus like curds of cottage cheese. A tongue, red and lizard-like, darts between those teeth, laps at the liquid. The skin sloughs to each side of his neck, falls away, leaving two halves of the mask of her father's face on the floor.

She looks at the thing that has shrugged off her father's form, towering over her now. "That the best you got?"

Maybe it wasn't such a good idea to taunt it. It raises its head to the ceiling and roars loud enough to powder the plaster.

Dust raining down around it, the creature's head divides into three long necks, which twist and twine like serpents. They erupt from this stump, pulsing out of the husk of his body, which slides to the floor, deflated, as useless now as the discarded mask.

The snakes flop to the floor, and Harlan steps back. They're large as anacondas, with mottled black and green patterns on bodies as thick as conduits. As she watches, they lift their heads to glare at her.

But they aren't snake heads. Each has her father's face, replicated perfectly on their serpentine bodies. Each set of eyes is gold-flecked with vertical irises, each mouth filled with an alarming amount of razor teeth.

"I'm so disappointed with you," all three say simultaneously, their bodies weaving back and forth. Their snake mouths twist unnaturally into grins. "You ran from Earth, from me. Time to run again, sweetheart."

The heads lunge at her, and she backpedals, slides from the doorway, grabs the banister and propels herself up the steps, not stopping to look back. She is terrified she'll see three small versions of her father's face slithering up the stairs after her, eyes flashing, teeth dripping with venom.

Gaining her bedroom, she slams the door behind her, steps away toward the windows. She closes her eyes, waits for the *thud!thud!thud!* of the three serpents striking the door...

****

There is no transition...

THIRTY-TWO

There *is* transition.
There is always transition.
All is transition.
And so...

TWENTY-FIVE B

Harlan opened her eyes onto a plain, white expanse. She blinked, swallowed, tasted metallic adrenaline in her mouth. Her father...the thing dressed as her father? Where had it gone?

She sat upright, felt something slide over her body, and thought of her father's skin, rumpling to the floor around those three snakes curling from the emptiness of his body.

"Aghhh, aghhh!" she shrieked, slapping at her breasts, her stomach, the skin sloughing from her. She leapt away, still screaming, brushing at her hips and thighs.

"Harlan, what the hell?" a voice asked. "Are you okay?"

She stopped hopping from one foot to the other, realized her eyes were closed in terror. When she opened them, she caught her breath.

It was mostly dark, even with her eyes open, but she could see the flat rectangle of the bed, the furniture. She was back in the hotel suite, room 237, back with El.

El!

El rushed to her, grabbed for her hand in the darkness.

"El, El, El," Harlan sobbed, grabbing her, embracing her tightly.

"Harlan, you're shaking like a leaf. What's wrong? Nightmare or...?"

Both women realized at the same time they were completely naked. Each stiffened in the other's embrace. Then, unasked for, the lights came on.

Harlan was ready to laugh at their predicament, but she saw realization dawn on El's face. Her skin paled and she let out a raw groan. Harlan tried to let her go, but El stayed clamped to her, now shaking as bad as she was.

"El—"

"No, no, no," El cried. "I'm not ready for this. Not this. Not *this!*"

"It's okay, it's okay," Harlan said, still trying to peel her away so she could see her face. El wrapped arms tightly around her, but Harlan was able to move her hands to cup El's cheeks, prise her head up to look directly in her eyes.

"El, it's okay. Really, okay. I mean, come on, it's not, like, 2019 or something."

El's eyes lost their glassy sheen of terror and sighed, which turned into a giggle.

"What's going on? Why were you screaming? I had settled down into the best night of sleep I've had in days. And why, exactly, are we both naked?" she said, whispering the last part.

"A, I don't know, per usual. B, it's complicated. C, yeah, I'm sorry. And D, again, I don't precisely know," Harlan said, letting loose of her cheeks. "It's okay to let go. You're gonna squeeze the pee outta me."

El unclamped herself from Harlan, stepped away. Immediately, though, her hands went to her groin, trying as best she could to cover herself.

"El, really, I've seen all that before. It's no big deal."

Grabbing a cover from the bed, El wrapped it around her waist, held it tight.

"Not on a girl," she cried.

"How do you know?"

"Well, not on me," El said, looking away.

"Okay, well, as of a minute ago, you're wrong about that too," Harlan said, looking down at what had started the ruckus in the first place. One of the bed sheets lay twisted there, what Harlan had felt sliding down her body. She shook her head in annoyance.

"Besides, it's the twenty-fourth century, I shouldn't have to tell you the parts don't make the woman."

El spun to her, biting her lip.

"I hadn't...and then, well, the training and the trip and I ran out of time. I thought I'd get to it on Teegarden. If I ever got to it, that is."

"You don't owe me an explanation, El."

Her mouth moved around syllables she couldn't get out. Instead, she swallowed them, said, "Thank you."

Harlan nodded.

"Now we might want to find something to drink, because I have some weird shit I need to tell you."

****

By the time Harlan had explained everything she'd gone through after hunkering down there in the hotel suite the first time, she felt exhaustion set in. She felt she hadn't truly slept since leaving the *Limen*. And that felt like days and days ago.

She was bone-weary, at both a physical and emotional level. Too much anxiety, too many unexplainable encounters with too many abstract beings spouting too many metaphysical concepts in too many dream settings had left her feeling like a rung-out washcloth.

And she was hungry. She hadn't eaten anything since the disturbing events in the dining room. But now she was ravenous.

El had found two bathrobes, the only articles of clothing left in the room. What they'd worn upon entering—the outer layers of their EVA suits and their underclothes—had disappeared.

Harlan had no hang-ups about nudity, but she shrugged into one of the terrycloth robes. Her own nakedness made El feel uncomfortable, and she thought it wasn't fair. As she belted the soft gown around her waist, there were three knocks at the door.

The sounds made both of them freeze.

Harlan motioned for El to stay put, crept to the door. There was an eyehole there, and Harlan leaned in and peered through it.

"No one is there," she said.

"Well don't—"

Ignoring her, Harlan opened the door.

Right outside was a steel cart with a handle. A white cloth was draped over the top. Harlan looked up and down the corridor, but there was no one. She pulled the cloth off, and wonderful aromas wafted out from what it had covered.

Harlan took the handle, wheeled the thing into the room.

"What is it?" El asked.

"Dinner. Room service apparently."

Harlan steered the cart over near the bed. Atop it was a series of covered dishes, silverware wrapped in napkins, glasses of various drinks. A basket of warm bread. Salt and pepper shakers.

El lifted the cover off a plate. A double cheeseburger sat there amidst a sea of golden, hot French fries.

"This is exactly what I was hungry for," she said, neither tone nor facial expression registering any joy in this fact.

Harlan lifted another cover. Underneath was a strip steak, glistening with butter, a baked potato split open, exposing a fluffy interior with a dollop of sour cream slumping into it.

"This is exactly what I wanted too," she said. "*Exactly.*"

"Do we...after what happened downstairs?" El asked.

"Look, I don't know how many chances like this we're likely to get," Harlan said. "Besides, I'm ravenous."

"I was hoping you'd say that," El said, picking up the burger and taking a chomp from it, groaning a little.

For a while, they did nothing but eat.

THIRTY-THREE

When they were finished, they stacked all the dirty plates and glasses and utensils atop the cart, covered it with the cloth, and wheeled it outside into the corridor.

Closing the door, Harlan came into the room, flounced onto the bed.

"So, what now?" El asked.

Harlan feigned concern. "I am afraid to voice anything. It seems as if someone is always listening."

"I'm pretty sure it's a lot more subtle and background than all of that. We haven't fallen into a wishing well."

"I say we go back out there and try to find Jaime," Harlan said. "He's here somewhere, hidden from us."

"Okay," El said, sitting on the bed next to her. "And then what?"

"One thing at a time, El. I can't handle any more."

"Okay, but we appear to be trapped in this house, or at least in its reality. And it's far from hospitable to us. From what you've said, the entire universe is pretty inhospitable. So we find Jaime. Great. And then what? We live our lives in this place, which seems hellbent on killing us, or at the least driving us insane?"

Harlan cocked her head.

"Plus, we have no clothes now, except for these bathrobes," said El, tugging at the belt of hers. "Are you suggesting run around in these?"

"Are you suggesting we sit here and eat room service until we die or the walls bleed? Or we open the door to a deranged killer? Or the food we're served comes alive and tries to off us? Or—"

"No, no, no."

"Well, then what exactly? You're the panpsychist. Christ, my faux-father even referenced you."

"He did?"

"I wouldn't exactly take that as an endorsement, but he did talk about your idea that consciousness goes all the way down to subatomic particles. Is there a way we can use that?"

"I don't know how," El sputtered.

"Well, we'd better figure out *how* before something else in our deepest, darkest hearts fucking kills us!"

"Something you said," El said, jumping from the bed and pacing. "Something about how your father referenced all things were part of it...him."

"Yeah, I know. It's confusing."

"No, I mean, if they were all part of it, and it could tap into any of that... I mean, if the progression goes up and down, then all of the things that make us—all of the atomic particles—then they're maybe something we can tap into too."

"I thought you said it wasn't a wishing well," Harlan said.

"It's not, it's not. But maybe it's more like a choir...needing a choir director."

"I'm not following you."

"Okay, see, a choir is made of all these separate, conscious things. But to get them all to act in unison, it needs a choir director to harness it all. It needs to be brought together and focused. Maybe that's our problem. Has always been our problem."

Harlan shook her head. "Our problem is...?"

"Humanity has always reached out to a god—or the universe or whatever—to fulfill its desires. As you said, they don't care about us. Or at least they're indifferent. Maybe we need to be marshalling the consciousnesses *within ourselves*? What if that's the way to counter our own fears? Accomplish our goals? What if that's what we need to do to get ourselves out of this? To seek *within* rather than *without*?"

"Umm...okay, how, El? Hold hands and chant? Crystals? Hypnosis?"

El was momentarily put off. "No, at least, I don't...well, I don't know. Maybe we try getting a little sleep. Before we drift off, we could, I dunno, ask ourselves for something small. Like clothes, for instance. Some clothes for us to be able to go out and find Jaime."

"How precisely do we ask ourselves for clothes?"

"Close our eyes before we fall asleep and ask the little voice inside ourselves for help," she said, watching Harlan roll her eyes. "It's worth a shot. If we wake tomorrow and we still only have bathrobes, what have we lost?"

"Our self-respect?"

El said nothing.

"Fine," Harlan said. "I guess we're sleeping in our bathrobes?"

El went to her side of the bed, threw the covers back, climbed in. Harlan did likewise on her side.

Harlan closed her eyes, tried to think of something to say.

"Okay, little guys inside me..."

"Silently, Harlan."

"Whatever," she sighed.

****

Transition.

TWENTY-FIVE C

Harlan opened her eyes. Still in the hotel bedroom, stretched out in bed. The robe she wore was rumpled and pulled in places, the belt caught beneath her, the flaps thrown open.

She pulled at the folds of the robe to cover herself, sat up.

Beside her, El did the same thing.

"Did we sleep? Did you sleep? I kinda feel like I slept, but I'm not sure," Harlan said.

El turned to her. Her robe was similarly disheveled, and she clutched at its collars, pulled them together.

"I don't know. That only felt like five seconds, but I guess we slept."

"Okay, time to get up and start the day," Harlan said. "You want to shower first, or shall I?"

"You go, I'll wait."

Harlan took a long, hot shower, involving many towels.

****

When Harlan was finished, she came out in her robe, a towel twisted on her head.

"Your turn."

El smiled, went into the bathroom, and closed the door.

Harlan sat on the edge of the bed, unwound the towel on her head, and drew it through her hair. She heard El turn the shower on, wondered how they were going to look, creeping through the house in their bathrobes.

On the off chance there'd be something out there—clothes, breakfast, anything—Harlan crept to the door, scanned the surroundings through the peephole, then opened the door.

Nothing. The corridor was empty. She noticed, far down its length, a single light fixture sputtered on and off.

She realized she'd been holding her breath, and she exhaled loudly as she closed the door and turned back into the room.

A small alcove near the door served as an open closet. Hanging there were two long, opaque plastic bags, zippered shut. She hadn't noticed these earlier, doubted they'd been there earlier.

Cautiously, she pulled a zipper down, exposing the collar and shoulders of an EVA suit. It looked show-room new, cleaned and shiny. Honestly, she couldn't tell if it was one they'd worn over from the *Limen* or brand new.

She yanked the zipper all the way down. Two smaller bags tumbled out. One contained boots, the other her underclothes, cleaned, pressed, and folded.

"Are you kidding me?" she asked no one in particular.

****

When El came out of the shower, Harlan had kicked back in a recliner in the lounge area of their suite, sipping a cup of coffee, fully dressed in her EVA suit.

"Concierge?" El laughed.

"Well, this *is* a full-service haunted house," Harlan said. "But no breakfast, so I hope you're not too hungry. Coffee?"

"Sure," El said, going to get dressed.

****

When El came back into the room, Harlan handed her a steaming cup of coffee.

"Thanks," she said, dropping onto the couch next to her. "What's the plan?"

Harlan set her cup onto a nearby table. "We'll start with the corridor, where he fell through the wall."

"That's as good a place as any, I guess. What if we don't find him? How long do we look?"

"Something tells me we'll find him."

"Then what?"

"Exactly. Let's get moving."

THIRTY-FOUR

The wallpapered hallway was quiet and foreboding. It reeked of abandonment and neglect, yet everything appeared polished, immaculate. Cared for. The woodwork was dusted, the carpet vacuumed, the brass work on the wall sconces shone.

They couldn't be exactly sure where Jaime had been swallowed because this hallway, like the one upstairs, stretched blandly into the distance in either direction. So they stopped at an arbitrary point and decided to search there.

El went to touch the swirling indigo paisley of the wallpaper, and Harlan swatted at her hand.

"You nuts? Don't touch the wall," she said. She looked around, saw an umbrella stand near a tall, thin, rectangular table outside one of the many doors. She took two umbrellas from the stand, handed one to El.

"Use this," she said. "And if it gets swallowed, let it the fuck go. Understood? We don't touch the wall with our hands or any part of our body, and we don't leave each other's eyesight. You go that way, I'll go down here. Clear?"

"Clear," El said, hefting her closed umbrella.

Harlan raised hers, saluted El like a fencer beginning a match.

After more than an hour moving up and down the hallway, poking at the walls here and there, encountering nothing but solidity, Harlan became frustrated.

But even then, she was concerned about what they'd do if the umbrella tip actually did sink into the wall, got slowly sucked out of the hallway.

Follow it in? Try to find Jaime, attempt to bring him back?

Or follow it in and go down whatever rabbit hole of reality it led to...*through*?

Ultimately, she decided it was time to stop poking walls and start opening doors. She propped the umbrella against the wall and turned the knob of the door she stood before. It bore no brass plaque, no number, nothing to distinguish it from any of the dozens and dozens of other doors up and down the corridor.

It was simply the closest.

El, far down the hall, yelled something Harlan couldn't quite hear. She shouted back to her, then simply waved wildly to get her point across.

Come down here!

"I was asking if we're opening doors now," El puffed as she ran to join her. "But I see we are."

Harlan gestured inside like a maître d' ushering a diner into a restaurant.

El peeked in cautiously.

Inside, the room was dark, but there was a light far off in the distance, too far to fit the dimensions of what could reasonably be called a room. It was like the setting they'd met John Taff in, a dark expanse with a single light revealing a distant detail. Here, the illumination fell onto something looking like a mountain, a solitary peak seen on the horizon at twilight.

But it wasn't, they knew. It was far off, but it wasn't *that* far off, so it couldn't be as large as it seemed.

What it might be, what its rough outline suggested, made it hard for Harlan to react, to either speak or lift a foot to enter the room and go see for themselves.

With the door opened, though, Harlan felt they had no choice. Maybe something there would provide a clue about where Jaime had disappeared to.

So Harlan made the choice to simply step forward, put her hand onto El's shoulder, and give a gentle prod in that direction.

When she followed El through the door, it closed behind them, snapping shut like she knew it would.

****

El jumped, turned as the door closed. The force of it echoed in the darkness of wherever they were.

"Keep at it," Harlan said, as gently as possible. "Don't let all this extraneous shit get to you. Whatever the point is, it's ahead. Not behind."

"It's like you've sat through a session with me," El laughed.

Harlan nudged her again.

El breathed deeply, continued on.

****

As they neared the object illuminated by the light, it began to take definite shape, definition. It was maybe six meters tall by maybe fifteen or twenty meters, a cone wider at the base, tapering to a blunt tip, like a pyramid.

But its edges, its shape was irregular, lumpy like a bag of potatoes.

Closer, El asked, "What the hell is it?"

Harlan had a bad feeling about this room from the moment they entered it. Now, her eyesight apparently a bit better than El's, she could see why.

The pyramid squatting in the dark room was made entirely of *human bodies*. Not stacked neatly like cordwood—as if that would have been better—but piled haphazardly, as if dumped here. Twisted and bent, contorted around each other.

El gasped in horror as she finally saw it, stopped. Harlan prodded her to keep moving as they were almost at its base. When they got there, Harlan could make out individual faces, men and women. All were nude.

All appeared to be sleeping.

"They're alive," said Harlan, kneeling and placing a palm against the skin of a woman's forehead. "They're breathing."

"How is that possible?" El asked. "Who are they?"

Harlan looked at her. "The crew of the *Promise*. I recognize this woman. She worked in the med lab. She was teaching me basic nursing after I woke from my first sleep cycle."

Harlan turned back to the woman. Iris was her name. She told stories of being from southern France, vacationing in Greece. She had a husband who also worked on the ship. Alain was his name. And a daughter. What was her name? *Celestine.* Harlan remembered it and the beautiful way Iris had pronounced it.

She choked back a tear to see the woman, contorted, sandwiched between a sprawl of other people. She stroked her forehead and cheeks tenderly. She was alive, clearly alive.

Were all of them piled here alive too?

If so, how could they help them?

Cautiously, on an impulse, Harlan placed a thumb and fingertip on one of Iris' eyes, peeled the lid back. What she saw made her instantly release, fall back on her ass and scrabble away.

"Harlan... What? What?"

"They're asleep, alive but asleep," Harlan said.

"Okay, then—"

"Her eyes...her eyes were blue, like hibernation gel blue. They're still in hibernation, El. They're still in fucking hibernation!"

El went to comfort her, but Harlan swatted her away. Getting back on her knees, she trundled back to the edge of the human cairn, went to open Iris' eye again, to show El.

"Do you think this is where Jaime is? Do you think he's somewhere in all this?"

Harlan pushed herself to her feet, her eyes darting here and there across the mountain of flesh. "He could be. Let's fan out, see if we can spot him."

El nodded, and they moved in opposite directions, scanning the heap for any signs of their missing friend. Harlan saw a few faces she recognized, even the captain of the *Promise*, someone's foot pressing into his neck.

"There are children in here!" El gasped from somewhere distant. "Oh, Harlan..."

But Harlan was preoccupied. She'd seen something that stopped her cold.

There, about three meters up, was a face she recognized well, for its owner was on the other side of this hillock.

It was El, her small face framed by a spill of someone else's hair falling over her head. The wingspan of one side of her bony ribcage showed, a length of her thigh curved down and inward. The sole of a foot.

But it was her.

How could that be? She was right there in the room with Harlan, awake, moving about.

Harlan considered calling El over, thought better of it.

Taking a deep breath, she put her booted foot on the hip of the person at the base. As delicately as possible, she stepped up, carefully avoiding faces or body parts that seemed unable to bear her weight. She climbed to reach this El's face.

She nearly wept. It was El, there was no doubt about it. Her fine features, her face in repose.

"Everything okay over there?" El shouted.

"Yeah," Harlan said, then realized she'd barely whispered her response. "Yeah!"

At her shout, this El's eyes snapped open, as blue as sea ice.

Harlan backed her head away in surprise, watched in fascination as this El's mouth moved, as if to speak.

What would she say?

She said nothing. Instead, as her lips parted, blue hibernation fluid spilled out, ran down her lips, her cheeks. It burbled in her open mouth, rising from within her like a mountain spring.

Horrified, Harlan lost her footing, arced backward, arms flailing.

But instead of falling, hands snatched out to grab her, dozens of them. Clutching at her EVA suit, her boots, her own hands, stopping her descent and pulling her up.

And *in*.

They were pulling her in, into the twisted mountain of flesh. She struggled against it, but the hands were insistent and strong. They pulled at her, tugged her close, pressed her body against the totality of theirs. She found herself cheek to cheek with some unfamiliar man near El, whose eyes snapped open, blue, blue, blue.

Harlan screamed as every face near her opened its eyes too. Each of them snapping open like window shades.

And still they pulled, not upward any longer, but still inward. She found her body wedging between the bend of arms, the tangle of legs. She fought against it, tried to turn away, but the hands pulled her, bodies rolled over her, legs parted to accept her.

Harlan sensed the light fading, tried to cry out, to warn El, but she found she couldn't breathe. Her breath was literally being squashed out of her.

As the darkness engulfed, as the mound of bodies accepted her own as a piece of it, a face swam into view. She couldn't turn her head, couldn't lift a hand to it.

It was Jaime's, and as she watched, his eyes opened and cool, blue light erupted from them, casting the tangles of bodies pressed against them in weird relief. The light rushed against Harlan's face, adhered like some kind of bioluminescent gel.

Worse, it flowed into her nostrils, her ears, prying her lips apart and flooding into her mouth. She tried to twist away, but the weight of all the bodies held her fast. She sputtered against the liquid blue light, tried to spit it out, but it was in vain.

The stream of light flowed in her, and she felt her body fill with it. It had a strange soporific effect, made her feel lazy, drowsy. She found herself stopping fighting it, yielding to its influence.

Her last thought before seesawing away, her last word was simply, "El."

As she spoke it, the light from Jaime's mouth faded, and he spoke one word too.

Harlan.

Twex#@%^)@

Transition.
Transition.
Transition.
Transition
Trans—

TWENTY-FOUR B

Harlan rose back into consciousness, felt hands on her. She struggled against them, slapped them away. When she opened her eyes, she saw faces swim before her, foggy and unclear in her just-awakened vision.

"Harlan. Harlan. What's the matter?"

Jaime.

She blinked to clear her eyes as much as her foggy brain. Blinked again.

It was Jaime. And El.

"Harlan, what's wrong?" That was El.

"Nothing..." she stammered, steadying herself. They stood in the foyer of the house, all three of them in their EVA suits. Harlan took note of their helmets placed on the ground near the door.

"There's obviously something wrong," El said, her voice tinged with concern. "Tell us."

"When is this?" she asked.

"When is...? What's that mean?" asked Jaime, letting Harlan lean against him for support.

"Is this after all the shit in the dining room? Is this right before you get sucked into the wallpaper?"

"After what shit? What dining room? And who got sucked into the wallpaper?" he said.

"You did. That's why we were looking for you, after I...after I killed you both."

Jaime and El looked at each other, and Harlan saw their expressions falter.

"Look, I'm drifting in and out of...reality, I guess. I've...we've done this before. I've been through so much after this."

She stared into their confused faces.

"I'm not crazy or drunk or stimmed out," she said. "Look, I need to sit for a second and get my bearings. There's a dining room through the pocket door over there."

"How do you know?" Jaime said. "We literally just walked into this place."

"Believe me, knowing there's a dining room behind that door is literally the least freakiest thing I know right now."

Jaime looked to El, who shrugged. He approached the door, cautiously slid it open. Behind it was a well-appointed room with a large trestle table at its center. The table had an elaborately woven runner but was otherwise bare. Eight carved, high-backed chairs sat around it.

Harlan waggled her eyebrows as if to say, *See? What did I tell you?*

The three went into the room. Jaime pulled a chair out for her, eased Harlan into it.

As far as she could remember, it was the same exact room that had hosted the initial feast for her and El. Now, there was no food or even plates on the table, not even a whiff of cooking from the kitchen she knew lay behind the only other door in the room.

"What's going on?" El asked, taking a seat next to her. Jaime stood by the door, concerned but skeptical about what she'd said.

"I dunno. I think even at this point, we all knew, we all understood something unexplainable was going on," she said, speaking in a hushed voice, the words tripping out of her. "But it gets so much weirder, so much more dangerous from here on out."

"With sucking wallpaper and our murders, right?" Jaime asked.

Harlan looked at him, twisting her face into a scowl. "Listen, asshole, don't make me sorry I found you."

"Harlan, listen," said El, putting her hands on either side of Harlan's face. It stirred memories of when Harlan had done something similar to El, when she'd awoken in the bed in the hotel suite, after...after...

"We need to hear what you experienced. I agree there's something more going on here. We all can agree. It involves plastic space and consciousness. It's herding us toward something, but I don't know what. We need to know what, Harlan. And you might know."

Harlan began to shake her head by the middle of El's speech. "No, no. That's not it, El. We're not being herded anywhere. The universe doesn't give enough of a shit about any of us to do that. It's not concerned about where we live or die or how or when. It's completely indifferent to us, all of us, every human, every life in it. It wasn't made to care; it was made to *exist*. That's all."

"If that's the case—and that's pretty fucking bleak, Harlan—then what are we doing? What's happening to us? Fuck, what's happened to us ever since the *Promise* exploded?" Jaime said.

"We happened. It's been us all along, our consciousnesses affecting space, fucking with reality. Well, actually it's been—"

"Our fears," El said. "Our fears interacting with the plastic nature of space, warping the reality around us."

"Yeah," nodded Harlan enthusiastically. "Exactly."

"So what do we do? Stop being afraid?" Jaime asked.

"It's not that simple. It's our fears at their basest level, so ingrained they're almost genetic. We can't simply stop being afraid. It's a big part of who we are. And some fear isn't necessarily bad. Fear of injury, of pain, helps to keep us safe. So how do we sort out that and leave the rest of it alone? I don't think we can. I don't think it's possible," El said.

"Then what do we do? I mean, you're not leaving much wiggle room here. We stay here and die, or we go to another part of this house and die. The upshot is still we die," Jaime said.

"This is going to sound crazy, but hear me out," Harlan said, then took a deep breath. "We need to get back to the *Limen*. I think we're all still asleep."

Jaime smacked his forehead, turned into the hallway and laughed, a low and creepy chuckle raising the hairs on Harlan's forearms. She looked over to El, who was not laughing.

"Okay, this is bullshit smeared over bullshit," Jaime said. "I mean, does any of this make sense to you, El? You're the psychologist or the panpsychologist or whatever."

"Panpsychist. Why can't you two get it correct?" El said. "And I don't know what I believe."

"El, don't you dare become one of those people who profess to believe something, then deny it when they're presented proof," Harlan said. "This stuff is happening. Has happened."

"Why don't you tell us what you've experienced?" El said.

"Because I feel like I already have, a couple times now. It doesn't matter," she said, as they looked at her in confusion. "Sure, let me bring you two up to date on what's happened to me and might still happen to me—and you two—going forward."

So, Harlan related her experience of the dining room, losing Jaime in the wallpapered hallway, El and Harlan's experiences in Room 237, her murder of them in the Mike persona, all of it down to her being subsumed into the pile of *Promise* crew and colonists directly before awakening back here in the house's foyer.

"You think they were asleep, all those people?" El asked.

"Yeah, I do."

"And you saw us, me and Jaime?"

"Yep."

"Come on, who's to say she's not hallucinating all this?" Jaime said.

"After what we've already been through, you find any of this hard to believe?" El asked. "How's that even possible, Jaime?"

"I'm not sure I believe any of this, even what I've already been through." Jaime laughed again. "So, yeah, maybe we are still asleep, still dreaming in some weird way the engineers who designed the hibernation pods couldn't foresee. In which case, who gives a fuck about anything that happens, anything we do?"

"I'm not sure that attitude helps," El said.

Jaime snorted in derision, stepped back into the foyer.

"Fucker's going to get us all killed," Harlan said, watching him pace near the front door.

"Shh, he's a part of the whole problem," El said. "So what should we do?"

"I'd say this is gonna sound strange again, but I'm afraid I've been saying that every few seconds," Harlan said.

"Then don't bother. What do you have in mind?"

"In the off chance we *are* still sleeping, we have to make our way back."

"Back? Back to what?"

"Back to where we started. Back to the lifeboat, then back to the *Limen*."

"And then?"

"Back to the *Promise*."

"Can we?" she said.

"We have to get out of this house. It's like…an arena for our fears. They'll battle us out until we're dead. And I don't mean dead in this reality. I mean *dead* dead. Backtracking, going as far as we can, we might live," Harlan said.

El considered, looked unsure as to what to say next.

"Look, what do people do when confronted with their fears?" Harlan said.

"They generally hide from them."

"Exactly. We can't hide, that's what it expects us to do. That's the problem. We need to go back, press on from where all this started aboard the *Limen*. Hell, we might actually make it to Teegarden or even to Earth."

"I'm not sure I believe that, but anyplace is preferable to this house," El said.

"You want to tell him or shall I?" asked Harlan.

"It doesn't matter. Jaime isn't going to stay here alone, no matter how ridiculous the plan is," El said.

THIRTY-FIVE

Their feet crunched on the gravel path twisting across the lawn. The weirdly underlit trees swayed in some cosmic wind as they made their way back to the lifeboat.

"It's still here," Harlan said. "That's a good sign at least."

Jaime flashed her an annoyed look, but gained the lifeboat first, opened its hatch via the touchscreen. The others followed him through, the hatch closing behind them.

"Welcome back," said Charles. "Was there a problem?"

Harlan unclasped her helmet, removed it. "Oh, there were quite a few problems. Any you mean in particular?"

"Harlan, El, you were only gone for three minutes, twelve seconds," said the AI.

El, who had set her helmet back in the suit locker and had begun to unzip her suit, froze. Jaime turned from the doorway into the cockpit.

"Three minutes? What the fuck?" he said.

"It appears you have brought a new passenger," the AI continued.

"New passenger? If we were only gone for three minutes, how'd you forget Jaime already?"

"I am not acquainted with Jaime. Was he someone you encountered in the structure?"

The three looked at each other in silence, unsure how to proceed.

"I'm Jaime Escondido, colonist on the *Promise*. I was just here, for chrissake."

"I'm sorry, Jaime. I have no record of a Jaime Escondido aboard the *Promise*," Charles said. "I do, however, have a record of a Jaime Escondido aboard the USC *Limen*. Is that you?"

"The *Limen*?" Harlan croaked. "That's not even a real ship."

"Nevertheless," Charles said.

Nevertheless?

"Well, I'm a real person, so fuck you! I'm done with all this shit," Jaime said, stomping past El and Harlan to the lifeboat's main room. El and Harlan watched him go, did nothing to try to stop him.

"Charles, you have records from the USC *Limen*?"

"Yes, Harlan."

"Give me information on the USC *Limen* from your records."

"*Limen* USC 13, launched from Earth on March—"

"Harlan, *Limen* and not *Douglas Limen*?" El said.

"Charles, what is the *Limen*'s full name?"

"The ship's registered name is *Limen* USC 13."

Harlan was shaking her head before the AI stopped speaking.

"That's *not* the name of the ship," she said. "We saw it painted on the hull the first time we approached. And that's not the correct nomenclature. It should be *USC Douglas Limen 13*, not the ship name, USC, and the number."

"Why would the AI have it wrong in its records, then?" El asked.

"I don't know. It's removed the first name and the pretense it was ever a person. I think it's telling us the ship is transitional, liminal."

"We already knew, or at least thought we did."

"Honestly, it makes me feel more confident."

"Why?"

"Because we're going to need to find a ship we saw crushed out of existence. It's our doorway back to the *Promise*."

"But the *Promise* exploded, Harlan. Why is it so important to get back there?"

"Back on the *Promise* was the last measure of reality we had. I don't know what to do now except get back there."

"But I'm seeing reality as a construct of consciousness. Don't you, through all of this? We're drifting through different, warped realities," El said. "We're just as transitional as the *Limen* or that floating space house over there. I'm not convinced we're going to be able to get back to any one reality."

Harlan leaned against the bulkhead, threw her head back, groaned.

"I can't live with that. Look, we're pushing back against...reality, I guess, and so far it's working. This lifeboat had disappeared, and here it is. Jaime disappeared, and now here he is. I killed both of you, and here you are. So, maybe this is a sign it's working. What we're doing."

"Or a sign that it's not working," El said.

"Either we, we stay here at our friendly neighborhood floating space house, or we go back to the *Limen*, *Douglas* or not."

"The devil you—"

"No," Harlan said, legitimately angry. "Don't even go there."

El didn't laugh.

****

Jaime was stretched out on a bunk when Harlan came into the lifeboat's main room. She went to the printer and ordered by rote. A glass of Coke, a cheeseburger, and fries. She tried to make as little sound as possible as she gathered napkins and flatware, sat at one of the galley tables to eat.

"I'm not asleep, so don't worry about waking me," he grumbled.

"Okay, I can chew with impunity," Harlan said, trying to keep her tone light and cheerful.

Jaime raised himself on his elbows. "That smells pretty good, actually."

"Join me for a quick lunch then," Harlan said. "It's on me."

He tried for a grin, but it came off looking grim. He rose slowly, ambled to the printer, came to the table with a plate similar to Harlan's. Sitting, he took a huge bite of his burger, washed it down with whatever was in his glass.

"What the AI said back there..." Harlan began.

"What you really mean is, '*How does it feel to be a non-person?*' right?"

Harlan shifted in her seat, stuffed some fries in to give herself time to think.

"Look, I guess we're headed back to the *Limen*, though I don't understand why you'd expect it to be there. I mean, we did watch it get crushed out of existence," Jaime said, eating slowly.

"I know this is all weird and off-putting and whatnot, but I think we really have a shot at this," she said.

"A shot at what, Harlan? Getting back to the *Promise*? I mean, shit, it was destroyed too, or have you forgotten?"

"No, I haven't forgotten."

"So, then what? We get back just in time to watch it explode? Or go through what we went through when it did explode? Or are we just in some kind of loop here?" Jaime asked.

"I don't fucking know, Jaime. I don't. All I know is we can't stay here, not in whatever offshoot of reality we're in now. We can't. We'll die."

"I thought you said I already did," he said, his tone, his whole demeanor sour. "And even though I'm right here eating with you, the AI agrees I'm not real."

"That's not what that means, Jaime," she sighed.

"Then what does it mean? Let me answer for you. I don't know. So, if you don't know, then maybe I am dead. Maybe that's all there is for us here. Death. Over and over and over. What a joke. What a fucking joke."

He shoved his plate with his barely eaten burger aside, pushed away from the table. Before Harlan could respond, he was back on his bunk, an arm slung over his face effectively ending the conversation.

****

Harlan cleaned her dishes, then drifted back to the cockpit. She found El there, slumped over a console, sound asleep.

The forward monitors showed the enigmatic floating house there to the side of the lifeboat, as blank and silent as before. The sky above still missing its stars. The weird sourceless lighting giving the entire scene a kind of forced drama, a moment of potential violence frozen in a photograph.

"Charles," Harlan whispered, not wanting to wake El. "Do you remember the last coordinates of the *Limen*?"

"Of course, Harlan."

"Let's go...let's go back there, see if we can find it."

Charles didn't argue with her, tell her the *Limen* had exploded, there was nothing left at those coordinates after the *Limen* had winked out.

"Yes, Harlan," he answered. "Speed?"

"Whatever this boat's got," she said. "Open it. Make it quick."

"Yes, Harlan."

She felt the ship move, the vibration of the engines kicking in, rumbling through the deck plates. The flickering light from the plasma engines pulsed over the landscape, flashes of lightning bursting against the faux Victorian façade of the house.

On the monitors, the plastic space house slewed away, slowly at first, then receding fast as the tiny ship pulled from it.

THIRTY-SIX

She woke with a start, getting her bearings slowly. She was still in the cockpit, sprawled in the pilot's seat, her head thrown back against the headrest, feet kicked up onto the console. She lifted her head, and it peeled away from the plastic surface, the skin of her cheek tacky and warm.

Had she dreamt? Was she still dreaming, or was this some new curveball thrown at her? To her side, El was gone, no longer asleep in the co-pilot chair as she had been when Harlan had first entered the cockpit.

She stretched her aching muscles, sore from sleeping in the chair.

"Charles, where are we?"

"We're headed toward the coordinates of the *Limen*. ETA forty-six minutes at current speed."

"Sensors show anything out there?"

"Sensors register nothing at the moment."

Swell.

She stretched again, groaned. Suddenly, she felt she needed a cup of coffee, something strong enough to blow out the brain fog hanging in her head. She got to her feet, looked out the door into the main cabin.

It was dark in there. El and Jaime were probably asleep, so she crept around the corner, not sure what she intended on doing, but sure she was tired of sleeping in that uncomfortable chair. Nor did she want to sleep on a bunk. She was altogether tired of sleeping.

The printer worked up a cup of coffee with extra sugar, and she leaned against the counter, sipped at the hot liquid. She faced into the bunkroom, could see the bunk where Jaime had gone to sleep.

It was empty, the bed remade with military precision as if no one had ever slept on it.

Taking her coffee, Harlan went to the doorway. To the left was the one small shower stall. The door was closed and the "Occupied" icon was lit. Guessing Jaime was inside, she scanned the other bunks for El.

Those, too, were empty, blankets and pillows unrumpled.

Where was El? Cockpit, main room, bunkroom, and shower, that was about it on the lifeboat, except for a small engineering access at the rear and stowage below deck. Why would El be in either of those two places?

Harlan tried to decide what to do next, where to go. It didn't make sense for El to be in stowage or engineering. Maybe Jaime knew.

She went to the shower stall, heard the water running inside. She knocked as gently as she could and still be heard. She didn't want to startle Jaime.

Nothing.

She heard no response or even any change in the spray of the water that might denote someone moving underneath it.

"Jaime?" she said, knocking harder this time. "Hey, do you know where El is?"

No response.

Harlan began to wonder if El and Jaime were in the shower together. Maybe she had missed something, some simmering connection between the two just waiting for some moment alone together to consummate it.

Hesitating, she put her ear to the steel panel of the door, listened. For what? Giggling, feet slipping on the smooth floor, the sound of naked flesh slapping together?

Unexpectedly, a wave of...what? Jealousy?

Jealousy? I don't think so. And of Jaime?

No, that's not it. Another guess?

Suddenly, she flushed, moved away from the door, feeling shame and guilt, as if someone had walked up to her as she eavesdropped.

That's when she heard it, and she had no idea what it was.

It was an odd hissing, clucking sound, like a snake crossed with a chicken. It was low, barely heard over the spray of the shower. But she heard it plainly.

And it sounded menacing.

She scanned the beds again for anything—a telltale lump under a cover or an article of cast-off clothing.

Nothing. And nothing to reveal who it might be in the shower.

"Jaime!" she shouted, with so little forethought that the sound of her voice echoing in the bunkroom made her flinch. "El!"

As the echoes died, the sound of the shower abruptly stopped. There was silence for a moment, just the drip of the shower nozzle and drone of the engines thrumming through the floor.

Then, she heard it again.

The last syllable stuttered out like a child saying an unfamiliar word.

"Jaime?" she asked again, backing from the shower door into the main cabin. "Jaime?"

There was a shudder across the floor. Something had evidently stepped from the shower. Forcefully.

Then another step.

Hiiiiisssssss-cluck-click-click-clickkkkkkk. Hisssss.

Gritting her teeth, Harlan turned and ran the few steps into the cabin, looked around for the needlegun before realizing it had been on another lifeboat, left by Jaime on the crushed *Limen.*

Inside the bunkroom, the shower door whirred open. Harlan couldn't directly see the doorway from where she stood, but she saw a cloud of steam roll out into the bunkroom like a fogbank.

Another step, then another.

She heard water drip to the deck from whatever exited the shower, saw the eddies and swirls of the mist as it moved into the room.

What the shit? And where are Jaime and El?

Why am I always fucking alone when this stuff happens?

Harlan went to the food printer. Looking back and forth from the screen to the door, she swiped through the menu, found Utensils, then Cutlery, then Large Knives. She'd never known this menu existed on a printer, that it would actually print this kind of thing, but she hurriedly keyed in what she wanted.

She felt momentarily relieved as the thing purred to life.

Momentarily, that is, until something stepped from the cloud of steam, stepped into the doorway, filled it with the dark bulk of its unfamiliar shape. It wasn't Jaime and it surely wasn't El.

The thing was massive; not just tall, but broad. Deep-chested with massive arms and thick legs terminating in clawed feet. Its skin was a greenish cast, smooth, metallic. Coils of muscles wrapped its limbs, but also strange gaps, and seams between what looked like plates that slid apart or together as the creature moved.

It looked biological, saurian, but it also looked artificial, mechanical.

The thing ducked its head under the lintel of the door, stepped fully into the room.

A monstrosity, a horror.

Its head was blunt and featureless, as if nature had simply given up at that point. The thing's color faded as it moved up its body, until the nacreous green faded into absolute bone white.

No eyes or ears, just slits for nostrils flaring as the thing breathed. Slits on either side of its stubby head too, these open and dark.

Its mouth, though, was the worst. So bad it might as well have been all mouth. The thing protruded from its face a little, as if it had puckered up to give a big, smacky kiss. But this would not have been a kiss anyone would have wanted.

For inside the ringed muscles of that huge orifice was a series of concentric rings, each smaller than the first, descending down into the thing's gullet. It looked as if they spun all the way down to its gut and perhaps farther. Anything gobbled down would simply be chewed and chewed and chewed.

Harlan wondered, dimly, if its intestines were similarly toothed, and the thing was just a chewer, gnashing and gnashing from lips to anus.

She didn't move, didn't make a sound, not knowing how the creature's senses worked.

The thing eased into the room, its footfalls shaking the deck plates.

From behind her, the printer dinged. Her order was done.

The thing cocked its head in her direction, its nostril flaps snuffling wetly. It raised a hand, wickedly taloned, into the air, fingers flexing as they moved. And its hand moved around the room, palping the air.

It stopped when it pointed at her.

Hissssss...click-CLUCK-CLUCK-CLICKKKK.

"Fuck," breathed Harlan, reaching behind her to open the printer bay, remove the large cleaver she'd ordered. She hefted it, knowing it wasn't really forged metal, that it might not be of much use against a snuffling, clicking thing looking like a cross between a sea lamprey and a human thumb, but it was the best she had.

Her hands closed around the haft of the knife, and she brought it around as she'd been taught in her one day of USC survival fighting tactics course; held by the haft upside down with the blade pointed toward the elbow and out, so when brought up, it was the blade that led as you swiped it out in front of you.

The creature ducked and propelled itself into the room, clicking and clucking and hissing, its biomechanical muscles rippling, armor sheathes sliding into place. Its dumb, horribly blank face swaying, trying to locate its prey.

Suddenly, Harlan felt ridiculously small, her knife hilariously inadequate to the task. She might be able to dash to the cockpit, but it seemed like the thing might reach her before she was able to get inside and close the door.

Then where?

And where the fuck are Jaime and El?

The only other door led to the cramped engineering access, not much more than a catwalk, some consoles and equipment.

She'd have nowhere to go if she chose that way either, but it seemed more likely she'd be able to reach that door and get it shut and locked before it could get to her.

The thing had caught her scent or sound, and it lowered itself closer to the floor, all the while undulating its head and upper body like a snake, the head fascinated on her. Fluid, thick and viscous, dripped from its open mouth, fell to the deck in mucilaginous strands stretching between lips and floor.

It lowered its taloned hands to the floor, now on all fours. Its muscles flexed beneath its translucent skin, preparing to hurtle itself at her.

She feinted left with the knife, and the creature lunged with much more smoothness and celerity than she might have hoped.

Hiiiiisssss! CLICK-CLICK-CLICK-CLUCK!

Harlan thought about throwing the knife at the thing, but she was loath to let it go. Instead, she sprinted to the engineering door. She glanced behind, saw the thing do a double-take, then raise its head and utter a thin, plaintive note, birdlike and high-pitched.

Gaining the door, she slapped at the touchscreen, and it slid open, darkness beyond. Hoping there wasn't another creature waiting for her back here, she slapped the screen on the other side of the door, then keyed in the command for it to lock.

She backed away just as the thing struck the door with the considerable weight of its body, mewling piteously. She heard it snuffling around the doorframe, trying to catch her scent, then raining blows against the metal barrier separating it from its prey.

Harlan backed up a step more, hoped the thin metal of the door would hold.

She heard the scritchy slide of its nails against the steel, swore she saw the door bow inward just the slightest bit as the thing's bulk came against it. She could hear it sniffing and hissing around the doorframe as if searching for the slightest little puff of air carrying her scent, the smallest vibration of her breathing that would tell it she was behind the door.

Harlan turned in the cramped, narrow space, searching for something, anything.

"Charles," she whispered, hoping the AI could hear her, would answer in a hushed voice too. "Can you turn on the lights back here?"

Charles didn't respond, but the lights came on, showing Harlan what little she had to work with. Huge ventilation conduits twisted back toward the engines. The life support processors, waste management and water regeneration systems took most of the room, a perforated metal catwalk between them and a single maintenance console near the door. She could see the slider bars with their reports on various engine functions all seemed normal and completely irrelevant at the moment.

Harlan bit her lip. The thing's kitten-like mewling was deeply disturbing, grating at the frayed edges of her nerves like...well, a kitten.

"Charles, status report. And respond *softly*, please."

"Harlan," he responded in a suitably low voice. "We are on course for the *Limen*'s coordinates. No sensor contact as of yet."

"Do you register either El or Jaime? Where are they on the ship?"

Charles' response made her wince.

"Who?"

"Damn it, Charles, not now. El Haugen, Jaime Escondido."

"There is no one by either name aboard this ship."

Harlan suddenly felt weak. Her knees buckled and she fell onto the cylindrical atmosphere regenerator housing, started to roll down its side.

"No," she whispered. "No, no, no."

The door crumpled in, metal shrieking and clanging. The bulk of the creature filled the frame of the door. Slaver drooled from its circular mouth, and its hissing-clicking turned into a gentle *coo* as it sensed her cowering in the dark.

It stepped into the small room, the metal catwalk bouncing under its weight.

"Charles, vent all the atmosphere," she said, tears squeezing from her closed eyes.

"Harlan," Charles continued. "There is one life sign of indeterminate origin in the main cabin of the spacecraft. Might this be one of the people you're looking for? Harlan? Harlan? Please respond. Plea—"

"Charles! Vent the atmosphere! Vent it! Now!"

Harlan experienced many things simultaneously. The slow, sensual grasp of the thing's clawed hands as they sought her, found her. Their claws sinking into her flesh, her blood rising to meet them. Her blood and its spittle dripping to the deck.

And the air in the room being sucked out, drawing her like another set of hands more closely to the creature, who accepted her with open arms, drew her in to a hideously intimate embrace, kissed her with a mouth filled with teeth.

Teeth, teeth, teeth...

So many teeth.

THIRX#@%^)@

Transition.
  Transition.
  Transition.
  Transition
  Trans—<<*sqwork!*>>

SEVENTEEN B

Harlan awoke, staring into lights so white, so bright, they hurt. She lifted a hand to shield her eyes.

She remembered the thing breaking down the door, finding her, embracing her. The dizzying circle of its teeth as she was drawn to its embrace. The bright white she saw must be the bleached bone dome of its head, circular mandala of a mouth making a hash of her abdomen, her organs.

She was being eaten. She was dying.

She shrieked, strained against its weight, its imagined teeth grinding at her guts.

A cooling hand laid across her forehead, but then the thing hissing and hissing into her ear.

Or...was it someone shushing her gently, stroking her head.

"Where?" She, of course, tried to sit up, only to find she couldn't. Not because her body wouldn't let her, but because she was strapped to a gurney.

No teeth, no teeth.

"Med lab," said El. "Finally."

"Med lab? Where, where?"

"Aboard the *Limen*, silly," El chuckled. "It's okay, we fished you out, got you out. You're safe back on the ship now. Just relax, relax, Harlan."

"What...umm...what happened?" Harlan muttered, then fell back onto the gurney. "Shit. The pod. The blood."

"Yes, but you're safe now. It's fine, it's oka—"

"Back to this shit," Harlan huffed, her eyes closed. "Great."

"Not precisely sure what that means, but okay..."

Harlan strained her arms against the restraints. "Can you go ahead and let me up? I promise I will not convulse. Pinky swear if you require it."

El gave her a strange look, moved to undo the straps.

Harlan sat up, swung her feet over the side of the gurney, rubbing her wrists.

"At least I got back after the bloodbath and not before," she muttered, then waved El's questioning look off. "I gotta sleep a little, gotta relax before I go any further."

"Of course, Harlan," El said. "Do you want anything to help you sleep?"

"Honestly, Doc, I don't think it would do any good," Harlan said, standing and slinging an arm over the smaller woman's shoulders. "I just hope I wake here with no boogeymen this time around."

El helped her to the door.

"You want to put some clothes on before we go?" El asked her.

Harlan realized she was clad only in a pair of panties and a raggedy-ass bra, but she didn't much care. There was no one to see her walk the corridors here except perhaps Jaime and the ghosts of the *Limen.*

She shook her head, put a hand on El's arm to stop her.

"One question before we go, Doc. Is this the *Limen* or the *Douglas Limen?*"

****

Her room was not the same as she'd left it.

When they reached her cabin door, Harlan waved her off. She didn't need help, thanks. What she wanted to tell El was all that blood loss? Yeah, that had been days and days ago, not just a few hours back.

This El wouldn't understand. Would know nothing of the *Limen* squishing in on itself or the floating space house, the bloody dining room or losing Jaime to quicksand wallpaper.

Wherever she was, that hadn't occurred as of yet. Might not occur. Who knew?

Even then, might El understand?

She'd probably would even if she didn't know about all the rest, but Harlan definitely didn't want to have *that* conversation at the moment.

But her cabin...

There was no blood trail on the carpet, no stain on the couch outside the bedroom. It was as if she had never bled here.

Maybe she hadn't.

This she, anyway.

Harlan stumbled to the bedroom, fell onto the bed, and slept like she hadn't slept in a long time.

Which, of course, she hadn't.

****

There is no transition here.

Harlan actually did sleep, and it was a sleep uninterrupted by dreams or other distractions.

****

Harlan woke, showered, dressed as quickly as she could. Finished, she went directly to the bridge. She didn't know when it was exactly, and it didn't matter. Day and night aboard a spacecraft are completely made up, and who knew what sleep patterns El and Jaime were on anyway. She'd bet they were as screwed up as her.

The *Limen*'s bridge was just as she remembered: dark, unmanned, and eerily quiet. So quiet, in fact, the door swooshing shut behind her made her jump.

She moved past most of the consoles to the touchtable. None of the other stuff concerned her, even if it was actual, real information and not just some fictional gobbledygook cooked up by whatever fictional, gobbledygook reality she was in at the moment.

"Charles?" she asked, expecting no response. She was pleasantly surprised this expectation, at least, was met. She stood at the touchtable and scrolled through various screens until she found the exact time stamp their lifeboat initially encountered the *Limen*. Tracing backward, she was able to reconstruct the probable coordinates the *Promise* had been at when it exploded.

She swiped through to navigational, set the new course, checked the engines, and punched in the command. She felt the burst of power thrum through the bridge as the engines came to life, felt the massive ship turning to adjust to the new course.

A clock countdown began.

Twenty-two hours, forty-seven minutes, twenty-three seconds until the coordinates were reached.

Harlan left the bridge hoping there'd be something there when they got there.

Something.

****

She ducked back onto the bridge after she left, went to the touchtable and punched up a colonist/crew roster from the *Promise.* When she'd checked it, she did the same thing for the *Limen.*

One was real, one wasn't.

Neither featured anyone aboard named Jaime Escondido.

Harlan was not in the least surprised.

****

When Jaime walked into the captain's mess, Harlan was twirling a glass of soda on the table, staring off into the distance. She said nothing to him as he strolled to the printer, came over with a cup of coffee.

"May I?" he asked.

She gestured to the seat, said nothing.

"El said you were talking nonsense," he said, sitting. "I asked her how that was any different than before we'd fished you out of the pod."

Harlan smiled, kept twirling her glass. It had made a series of wet, spiral designs on the table. She stared at it, didn't reply.

"Everything that's happened is pretty strange," he said, taking a sip. "Why do I feel like it's about to get even stranger?"

Harlan looked up. "You tell me, Jaime."

He snorted. "Wish I could, but I have no idea."

"Well, maybe start with who you are and where you came from. That'd be a great place to begin."

"We already had that conversation, Harlan, back on the lifeboat."

"Tell me again. What was your role as a colonist? What were you going to be doing on Teegarden? What were you doing when the alarm sirens went off aboard the *Promise,* huh? What the fuck were you doing, *Jaime?*"

She invested his name with as much venom as she could muster.

He recoiled a bit, set his coffee cup onto the table.

"I'm a construction specialist, was going to be in charge of building habitat modules on Teegarden. Came with no one, no family. All by myself. No roots left on Earth, all my family dead. That's me, that's Jaime Escondido," he said, his tone as taut as a snare drum, daring Harlan to poke at anything he said.

Harlan poked.

"You didn't answer my question, Jaime. What the fuck were you doing when the alarms went off?"

He looked from side to side, as if trying to remember something just out of reach, nagging at the edges of his mind.

"I was in the...doing..."

"You were asleep, still in the Hibernation Pod. At least that's what the computer says. Sometimes, at least."

"Sometimes?"

"Yeah, sometimes the computer says there's no record of you on the *Promise*. And right before we came back here, the AI said there was no record of you on the *Limen* either. So who the fuck are you?"

Harlan stood and leaned over the table at him.

"I'm Jaime Escondido, I told you that!" he yelled, standing and leaning into her.

"Then what were you doing on a ship that has no record of you?"

Jaime was breathing hard now, and Harlan noticed two lines of sweat tracking down the sides of his face from his hairline. His forehead was dotted with beats of perspiration.

"I...I... How's it possible the computer has no record of me if I'm standing RIGHT HERE?!"

Spit from his tirade flecked her face, but Harlan stood her ground.

Looking disgusted, Jaime lurched back, growled in frustration, then banged both hands onto the table.

"I'M JAIME ESCONDIDO!"

He spun away, left the room.

"I know, you motherfucker, but what were you doing?" she said to the empty room.

Taking a deep breath, she collapsed back into the chair, chugged the last of her Coke to wet her completely dried-out mouth.

THIRTY-SEVEN

"Who is he?" Harlan asked El. They were in Harlan's quarters, El seated on the small couch, Harlan pacing. "If he's not on the fucking ship roster—*either of them*—then who is?"

"I don't know, Harlan. But does it matter? He's here. He's here *now*, and seems just as real as you or me," El said.

"But he just showed up, just appeared when I was ready to close the lifeboat doors, before the *Promise* exploded."

"I mean, for that matter, so did I, remember?"

Harlan stopped. "Well...yeah...but you're at least on the ship's roster. You *existed* before you appeared in the lifeboat."

El chuckled, put a hand to her forehead, massaged her temples. "Existed. Real. What does that even mean? Have you thought about that, given what's going on? All that's happened since the *Promise* exploded? Are we sleeping? Are we dreaming? Hallucinating? It's like reality is a carnival funhouse. Ever been to one? Old time things, with a hall of mirrors you had to find your way out of. But everything was reflections and reflections of reflections."

"I know you really want to have this metaphysical discussion about things but—"

El shook her head. "No, no, no. This is all metaphysical, and we need to talk about it. You can't just blithely dismiss all that's happened with a wave of your hand and plow ahead, Harlan. This all...it all means something. It has to."

"I'm more concerned with surviving, El. Getting out of this. Whatever *this* is doesn't matter much to me."

"But what if this is what is? What if it's what reality is, and we're just mucking things up being out here where our distorted consciousness can play havoc with space? Then, we can run all we want, we can avoid it or try to deny it, but this is it."

"I can't accept that."

"What I'm saying, Harlan—and listen to me very carefully—it doesn't matter if you accept it. You yourself said the universe is indifferent, it doesn't care. So it follows that it doesn't care if you accept it or not. It *is*. And we have to deal with it."

Harlan stopped pacing. "I'm trying to."

"Then we have to stop running, stop fighting it, stop trying to treat it like a game that can be won or beaten."

"Stay here and die? Is that your recommendation, Dr. Haugen?"

"Harlan, of course not."

"Then what? Because I don't know what else to do. I can't tell what's real and what isn't anymore. And I can't distinguish between *real* and *realer*. I don't think any human can or was meant to. I just know to go forward."

In the ensuing silence, Harlan could hear the processed air puffing into the room, the random ticks of metals or seams in the walls, the deck, the thrum of the faraway engines.

Was that real?

Was any of it real?

Was anything real?

"Don't you feel it, Harlan? Don't you feel how wrong this all feels?"

Harlan sat on the arm of the couch, took El's hand gently.

"I feel this. I feel the couch under my ass. I feel like I need to brush my teeth. I feel all that and a million things more. And now, yeah, I don't know. Am I awake or asleep or dead or what? All I know is right now, right here, wherever here is, I feel *this*."

"Oh, Harlan," El said, placing her other hand over Harlan's, squeezing it. "If you feel *this*, then what does it matter if you're real or not or I'm real or not? Or Jaime? I think it's a fair bet either we're all real or we're all unreal. And if we're all truly unreal, then what *this* is really doesn't matter. We're here. We feel. Isn't that enough? I think it has to be."

Harlan's head drooped. She remembered speaking with the thing that was her father several "realities" ago, what he'd said to the same question.

In the absence of all else, doesn't it have to be?

"But we've still got to get out of here, off this ghost ship."

"But the *Promise* exploded," El said. "Wouldn't we just be going back to our deaths?"

"Maybe not. I mean, we're here back on the *Limen* after we watched it implode."

El patted Harlan's hand. "Jaime's angry."

"Well, that's an understatement," Harlan laughed, looking down at El's hand over hers.

"He's angry about everything, true. Unlike the two of us, though, his concern for all this comes out as anger. He's also angry, I think, about what he doesn't remember. The stuff you've related. He's not real, he's not in the ship's roster, he was sucked into the wallpaper in a floating space house he barely went into. He's afraid on an existential level," El said.

"I get that, I really do. It still doesn't explain why he's here or how he's here," Harlan said.

"And, coming full circle, the same can be said of me. I ask again. Does it matter? Does it really matter?"

Harlan slid her hand from underneath El's, stood.

"I suppose it doesn't. Not really. But it seems like it should. Seems like it does."

El stood from the couch, went to the door.

"On that note, I'm going to head down to the theater and watch a holo. Or maybe a flat. I need to unwind," she said. The door opened, and she moved through it, turned. "Care to join me?"

"Nah," Harlan said. "I've got enough representations of reality to deal with. Don't need another fictional one at the moment."

"See you at dinner?"

Harlan smiled. "Yeah, sure."

****

Harlan drifted back to the bridge. She fought the urge that had built within her during her talk with El. The urge to race through the ship, going into every room, every nook and cranny of the *Limen*. To be in every room, see every thing. To see exactly how much fine-grain detail this ship possessed.

To measure exactly how real it was.

But she realized those measurements would be through her human senses. That analysis through her human brain.

And she wasn't entirely sure either of those things were real or were capable of discerning what was or wasn't.

What would it matter?

She still had an overwhelming urge to get back to the *Promise*, though. Somehow, to her, that made the most sense, seemed to offer the most hope.

Whether that hope was real or not didn't seem all that important to her, a kind of paradox she was unwilling to ponder.

The bridge consoles flashed their information in the dark, bars and charts and flows of data streaming across consoles no one manned, no one saw, no one analyzed or corrected or adjusted. But it all came just the same.

Harlan scanned the data, saw the ship was moving ahead at point-six lightspeed.

"Charles, any hits on the sensors yet?"

"Hello, Harlan. No, there is no sensor hit yet. No sign of the *Promise*."

"Time to reach those coordinates?"

"Twenty hours, seventeen minutes."

"Set an alarm to tell me when we're an hour out, will you?"

"Of course, Harlan. And, Harlan...?"

"Yeah, Charles?"

"I'm sorry I'm not able to help you more."

Harlan had been leaning over a touchtable. At Charles' words, she snapped upright, froze. She recalled the meeting with the chrome-faced, robe-draped being claiming it was a Charles/Trivia amalgam. It had said that to her.

"Who said that? Charles? Why did you say that?"

"I...I'm not sure. The words appeared in my matrix. I spoke them, though they were not my words. But they are my words."

Harlan heard the confusion, the near-anguish in the AI's voice.

"It's okay, Charles. It'll be okay. And it's alright you can't help more. Tell them it's alright."

"I will do that, Harlan."

"And tell them thanks. I think I got it from here."

Charles didn't respond, and Harlan left with a lump in her throat.

THIRTY-EIGHT

She desperately wanted to sleep, but she knew she couldn't. Lately, sleep meant transition, moving to some other space, some other time, some other reality. It was bad enough happening then, worse it was starting to bleed into her waking hours.

She didn't want to eat either, or spend time mooning over a glass of Coke in the mess. Scratch that, what she really didn't want to do was bump into Jaime. Especially not now.

Without being conscious of it, she found she'd drifted to the corridor leading to their cabins. There, just down the hall from her own, was El's. Was she still up? Talking to El usually calmed her, focused her, if not actually comforting her. She was buoyant when Harlan felt weighed down; cautious when she felt manic. There seemed something centered about her, a safe harbor in a storm.

Harlan stopped at her door, put her hand flat against it. She knew El was probably still down in the theater, watching some flat, but she could feel her presence inside there, behind the door. Could she imagine her there, perhaps sleeping, perhaps brushing her hair or reading or thinking about some movie she'd seen or wanted to see?

I should have said yes to her invitation. It would have been relaxing to sit with her there in the dark, maybe eat popcorn, maybe...

Wait, what the shit? Am I...?

Nah...no. No way. Not right now.

She lifted her hand from the door, stepped away, then turned down the corridor and practically fled. She passed the door to her own cabin, hesitated. Go in and laze around, possibly nap until Charles let her know they were close to where the *Promise* had exploded?

No, she didn't feel like sleeping, even though her body desperately needed it. Instead, she decided to walk, just walk the empty passages of this ship, try to clear her head. She set off, past her cabin to what were the cabins of the lower-ranking members of the crew.

This deck of the *Limen* housed cabins for most of the command crew, with NCOs and rank-and-file crew on the lower decks in smaller, sometimes shared cabins. As she moved down the corridor, lights snapped on, showing the next six or ten meters forward.

As she moved deeper into the *Limen*, into areas she doubted anyone had ever been, she thought of what lay next. What would they do if they actually found the *Promise*, whole, unexploded? What questions the crew of that ship would have!

How would they answer them? Was the *Promise* still fated to explode? Would the *Limen* still exist after they disembarked and went aboard the *Promise*?

Jaime.

What would happen to him? Was he listed on the crew manifest on that *Promise*? If not, what would happen to him?

Was he real?

As Harlan walked, lights clacking on as she progressed, she lost track of time, of where she was. If she'd been paying attention, she would have noticed the hallway seemed to go on far too long. That it led farther into the *Limen* than the length of the ship itself, a corridor violating the very space of the ship.

The farther she went, though, the clearer the feeling of violation spread within her, disrupting her line of thought. Violation of a space no one had been in, but paradoxically awaited that violation.

When that mass grew to sufficient size, like a cancer within her, she slowed her pace, stopped. Despite how far she'd come, she was still in the drab ship's corridor with the same bland carpeting, the same uncolored walls, the same blank doors stretching into the distance.

Despite every indication she was onboard the *Limen*, she felt as if she'd left it, was in some other space, some other where.

Down the passage about ten meters, she saw a familiar door.

Gymnasium.

But that room was a deck or two below where she should be, and she'd come in a straight line from the reception area of the ship. How did she end up here?

Cautiously, she walked to it, paused outside.

She felt pressure behind the door. A presence seemed to fill the room beyond, weigh heavily against the walls and doors, like too much water in a balloon threatening to rupture at any moment.

Placing a nervous hand against the solid plane of the door, she felt it vibrate with pressure, as if the molecules of the door were about to fly apart, rupture, releasing whatever was within. For a moment, brief as it was, she could sense the consciousness of each of the atoms of the door, the trillions and trillions of them—even their smallest constituents, the fermions, the bosons, the hadrons—crying out against the stress they were under, struggling to maintain their coherent bonds and mourning their imminent failure, knowing the material they formed, the door, was likely to blow itself to bits.

Harlan didn't want to go inside. She didn't know what was in the room, but she knew it couldn't possibly be good. Just as strongly, she knew she had to go in.

She had died. She had killed. She had walked between dimensions.

What was one more room to her?

She palmed the touchpad, and the door whooshed open.

She immediately smelled the air inside, the funk of the gym, the greasy patina of sweat and adrenaline seeming odd to her because, to Harlan's knowledge, only one person came here.

Jaime.

But this air was different, rank and miasmic as a swamp in high summer. There was an edge to the air, foxed as it were with something dripping of mold and something of a higher note, sweet and foul and mesmeric. Harlan found herself wanting to take lungfuls of it in, but then feeling repulsed with each breath.

Stepping inside, each footfall placed tentatively. Harlan entered the room she understood she had to, was compelled to, though she shook with the atoms inside her—the particles making up Harlan herself—as they screamed at her just as those of the door had.

They *knew* something she only *felt.*

They were warning her.

Back in the far corner of the room, where she'd seen him before, Jaime stood, his back to her, shirt off, curling a small dumbbell. Maybe ten kilos, over and over, his head slightly inclined toward it, sweat dripping from his forehead, his chin, plip-plip-plipping onto the mat.

He seemed to take no notice of her as she approached, but she knew he was aware, knew whatever was in him, whatever wore the skin of Jaime, knew she was coming, knew why she needed to be in this room, what she wanted.

"Hey," he grunted, not turning toward her, not stopping his curls.

In a kind of rapt attention, Harlan stared at his exposed muscles, the lay of them beneath the smoothness of his olive skin, how they flexed and released like ocean waves crashing and ebbing. They moved with a mechanical slickness she found fascinating and attractive.

Until, that is, she thought of the creature she'd encountered in the lifeboat, the thing that came out of the mist of the shower, filled the main cabin with its sharp talons and gleaming, metallic hide and sliding plates of armor. How its rope strands of muscles twisted and stretched under that skin, moving its bulk with a sensual grace.

"Hey," Harlan echoed, finding her mouth dry again, her breathing heavy and labored, as if she'd just complete a run to get there.

"What's up, Harlan? Come to see the fictional character you're sharing a ghost ship with?"

His tone was as tight and coiled as his muscles, carrying with it the same potential, implied release, an explosion of violence Harlan felt as strongly as the door's atomic screaming, the vibrations within herself.

Something was about to give, and give in a big way.

"You're not fictional, Jaime. You're standing right here...flexing, for Christ's sake."

He didn't stop raising and lowering the weight, didn't stop staring at his own bicep, working and unworking.

"I haven't felt real, not since I floated into that lifeboat from the *Promise*. We both wondered where El had come from, didn't we? What we should have been wondering, myself included, is where I came from," he said, sweat tracking down the bridge of his nose.

"There's a lot more going on than that," Harlan said, hoping to deflect the anger she sensed building within him, as if pumping his bicep was inflating some inner reservoir burbling within him. She'd thought the rankness inside the gym was caused by him, oozed from his pores and greased the air. Now, she believed he was taking it in, inflating himself with this horrid atmosphere as surely as if he were breathing it in deeply, sucking it into his lungs.

The thought of that, the odor of those gases, the rancidity of that air entering his body, mingling with his blood and bones and organs, nauseated her.

"What's the matter? Not a gym rat?" he asked, still not looking at her.

"Well, no," she said, gasping. "It's not that."

"Oh, that smell? You don't like it? I don't know what it is, but it's...intoxicating. Isn't it? I'm kinda drawn here. I love it, breathing it in. Clears my head."

"Clears my sinuses for sure," Harlan laughed.

Jaime did not find it humorous. "Why are you here, Harlan? Really?"

"I just wanted to be sure you're okay. I mean, if we actually find the *Promise*, get back there. Make sure you're okay with whatever happens."

He twisted his head slightly, slowly, to bring his eyes into view.

"Okay?" he breathed, still flexing. "I'm not okay right now, Harlan. Why would I be okay when that happens?"

"Look, this is all weird. I get that. I mean, we've all been through some weird shit," Harlan said.

"Fuck that. Weird? I'm not real, Harlan. So how could it be weirder than that?"

"Trust me. It could. And it might still be, but you're here. Now. That's all that matters."

"But I'm fictional."

"Big fucking deal. I told you how we met that guy, the author who claimed he'd written all this. So, El and I, we're fictional too. And yet, here we are. Doing our shit. Trying to get back to some semblance of reality."

"You think reality is the *Promise*?" he said. Now he didn't look away from her, stared with his dark eyes, so dark there seemed no distinction between his cornea and iris, as if they were just one big, fathomless pit. "You think there's any reality there? Why would you think that?"

"Because it's all I've got," she said simply.

"I'm not going to that ship," he answered, just as simply.

"What?"

"You heard me," he said. "I'm not going *there*. I don't exist *there*. Or here. Or anywhere. But like you said, I'm *here*. Now. So this is where I'm staying."

"Jaime, listen to me. You're real. You're just as real as El or me. All of this, what's happened, is screwing with us, our sense of ourselves, of where we belong. But you're real, man. You'll be just as real over there as you are here."

"You don't know, Harlan. You can't promise. I can't remember anything aboard the *Promise*. Have I told you? Nothing from Earth either. No happy memories of family or spouse. Children. *Nothing*. It's like...whoever wrote me didn't flesh me out, just stuck me in a situation and made things move around me. I'm not altogether sure I have any emotions about it all. Nothing. Except one maybe. One single emotion."

"And what's that?" Harlan asked, terribly sure she knew exactly what it was.

"Rage," he breathed, and she could almost see it leave his body, as if the air of the room he'd breathed in had coagulated inside him, gelled into a curdled cloud of absolute anger.

"Jaime, I kn—"

"Nothing. You know nothing, Harlan. You think you do. You think just because you've had these experiences, you're better drawn than the rest of us, you somehow know. You run around like you're the main character in some half-assed book about consciousness and reality, written by an abject idiot, and you think you know.

"Harlan," he said, dropping the dumbbell, whose rebound reverberated in the room and made her flinch. "You don't know shit."

He stood, turned fully to her, and she stepped back. The spring that had been coiled, in the room and inside of Jaime, she felt it preparing to uncoil, and she really didn't want to be there when it did.

She was really going to be there when it did.

Jaime faced her, but even as he did, he froze, stood stock still. He was breathing hard now, sucking that poisoned air in as quickly as he could, taking it in. But he didn't breathe out. He took the air in and kept it there, breathed in more, gulped it greedily.

And he *expanded*.

Harlan watched in horror, rooted to the spot. It wasn't like a balloon, not like the air pushed out against his skin. No, it was like it enlarged every part of him simultaneously, his bones, his organs, his eyes, even his hair.

As Harlan tried to get her feet to move, to take her out of this room and away from him, Jaime expanded, literally doubled, tripled in size. For a moment, it seemed to Harlan the room got smaller, just collapsed in on itself. It was only her perspective of herself within the room, of her relative place within it that kept her senses steady.

"I'm not going to the *Promise*," he said, even his voice filling the room. She could see the thick, envenomed air squeezing between his teeth as he spoke, oozing over his tongue.

"Absolutely," Harlan said. "We're in full agreement there."

"Neither are you," he breathed. "None of us are. I'll see to that. It's the only thing I've got left to do. The only thing that feels like it's not written for me."

"Now wait a minute," Harlan said, suddenly feeling ridiculous trying to calm a fifteen-foot-tall man, shirtless and sweaty, curling and uncurling his fingers now, around either an imaginary dumbbell or an imaginary human neck, in all probability hers. "Calm down, Jaime, really."

"Done talking," he said, then moved toward her. He was so big now he had to stoop, so big his elbows toppled the other equipment, the stationary bike, the treadmill, sent them careening into the walls of the gym.

Something about him muscling past the steel and metal of the equipment seemed to dislodge whatever held her in place. She backed up a few steps, then turned and raced for the door.

Slapping at the touchpad, she tore into the corridor, increased her pace. Behind her—and she couldn't resist looking behind—the gym door finally burst open on a shriek of metal.

Jaime followed, filling the corridor behind her, having to bend down on all fours. He saw her, grunted, then came for her. She was amazed at how fast he was, couldn't believe that something—*someone!*—this size could move that fast. His head scraped the ceiling, and his sides bumped the walls. Doors buckled as he passed and his hands and feet rucked the carpet, peeled it from the deck plates below.

"Harlan!" he shouted. "*Harlan!*"

Nope. Nope. Nope. Nope. Nope.

Harlan buckled down, ran as fast as she ever had as an adult. She felt her legs burning, her thighs, her lungs. But she had to stay away from him, what Jaime had become. What he intended.

She hoped this wasn't the same corridor she'd come down, some endless length of blandness like the looped background of one of those old, animated flats where the cartoon villain chases the cartoon protagonist past endless scenes of boulders, distant mountains, and solitary trees. Where Jaime would chase her and chase her and chase her.

She also hoped she wouldn't find El out here, wandering to the theater or to the mess.

"Harlan," came Charles' voice, stopping her heart. "We have encountered the *Promise*. ETA two minutes."

What? And *Yay!*

And *No!*

That came from Jaime, closing the distance behind her, his cry deafening.

"No!"

THIRTY-NINE

Harlan saw the hallway open ahead, into the reception area at the front of the ship.

Jaime was right on top of her. His head crumpled the lip of the corridor opening to the higher ceiling of this space as he unfurled into the room. Harlan heard the metal twist, spang, and clatter to the deck, electronics and cable spilling from the gouge he'd made, spitting and sparking.

"Charles!" Harlan shouted. "Charles!"

"Yes, Harlan," he said, so calm.

"Hail the *Promise*," she screamed. "Get them online. Tell them...we need to dock with them. Fast, make it fast, Charles! For the love of god, *fast!*"

"I'm not going over there, Harlan," Jaime breathed, standing to his full, ridiculously large height.

"You get no argument from me, Jaime," she said. "I think they'd agree at the moment too."

"I'm not real?" he growled. "No one is then. That's not real. Out there. How can you think it is? What's real is *here*, right now. You said so yourself. I'm not giving that up so you can feel real over *there.*"

"Jaime, stop. Think. We need to get back to our reality. Where normal shit happens, not this. You think you being four meters tall is normal? Is that real?"

"You have no idea how *real* I feel right now, Harlan. No fucking idea."

"If that's the case, I don't want to know."

He came closer, the deck plates jumping as he stepped.

"Why don't you just let me and El go over? You can stay here, have the ship all to yourself."

"You think that's what I want? A reality all alone?"

"Jaime, I don't know what you want. How could I? But this... I mean, what are you planning?"

There was the *sqwork* of the intercom, a burst of static and gibberish.

Then, "Harlan, the *Promise* is hailing us," said Charles.

Harlan replied, "Put it on audio."

The intercom *sqworked* again, then resolved into a voice. An actual human voice.

An actual human voice filled with alarm and concern.

"Unidentified vessel, please immediately identify yourself and your intentions," came the voice. "This is the captain of the Earth ship *USC Promise* enroute to Teegarden b. Our purpose is peaceful colonization. Please respond. Please respond."

"Do you hear that?" asked Harlan. "Jaime, please. They're the first real people we've heard from since this started. Are you really going to deny us this? Deny it for yourself?

"Get out of my way," he said, looming over her.

Harlan found herself back against the door to the bridge.

"Jaime, no," she said, but it sounded weak and ineffective even to her ears, like someone ordering their dog not to poop on the carpet when it was already pooping on the carpet.

Jaime raised a single arm. It was easily four or five times the size of the arm she'd seen curling dumbbells just a few minutes ago. Gleaming with sweat. She saw the muscles jump and bunch as his open hand struck her, flicked her aside like an insect.

Blackness swallowed her before she felt the pain, the impact against the outer wall of the room, slumping to the carpeted deck.

When she snapped into consciousness, though, it all came rushing back. Her side and arm throbbed where he'd struck her, her shoulder and other side where they'd smacked into the bulkhead.

The door to the bridge was now just a tear in the metal skin of the ship, jagged and raw. She heard sounds from within, pounding, crashing, electrical jolts, sizzling.

He was destroying the bridge controls.

Pulling herself up against the wall, she steadied her feet. She felt blood trickle from her nose. Something felt loose and broken in her chest, maybe a rib.

She couldn't let him do this.

Not this.

She staggered toward the bridge, stepped carefully through the ragged metal. Inside, it was a disaster. Consoles were smashed, smoke smelling of ozone and burning plastic filled the air. Charles' voice came through the com, asked repeatedly what was happening, calmly noting the systems that were failing.

Harlan felt the deck buck under her feet as the massive ship lurched quickly enough the dampeners couldn't compensate. The room tilted, and she slid into the navigation console, which flashed various warnings and alarms. She attempted to address them, but then the ship canted again, steeply this time to the other side.

She could see Jaime's form, shrunken to normal size now, shirtless, covered in sweat with streaks of grime, burns across his shoulders, weals like whip marks.

He turned to her, terror bulging his eyes.

But Harlan barely took note of him. She was fixated on what the forward monitors showed.

There, directly ahead, was the *Promise*, stretching out perpendicular to the approach of the *Limen*. The *Promise* seemed to be trying to yaw away from the *Limen*, but they were too close, the *Limen* moving too fast.

They were going to collide.

"Oh, shit," said Harlan, grabbing hold of the touchtable—its screen shattered, its innards destroyed, spewing sparks and tiny flames.

"If I'm not real, you're not real," Jaime said, tears in his eyes. "And they're not real. Then none of this matters anyway."

"Oh, fuck you, Jaime," she breathed.

On the monitors, the *Limen*'s blunt nose buried itself into the *Promise*'s pregnant guppy midsection. The *Limen* shuddered at the impact, tremors rippling out from it. All the metal that made the *Limen* shrieked, ground together.

On the monitors, everything was silent outside. Fires blossomed along the length of the *Promise*, racing forward toward its nose, back to the engines.

"Fuck you, universe," Harlan said. "And while I'm at it, fuck you, John Taff, just for good measure."

She closed her eyes.

The *Limen* whipped around the pivot point of its impact with the *Promise*, slammed parallel into the other ship.

Instantly, there was a concussion of light, and Harlan felt herself pummeled by forces she had no control over, slammed into something, a console maybe, separated from the rest of the bridge, tumbling end over end.

The bulkhead ruptured, and the last thing Harlan felt before she was snuffed out was a powerful hand yanking her out, pulling her into darkness.

FOR%^#@

There *is* transition.
    There is always transition.
    All is transition.
    And so...

ONE B

Blue.

Everything is blue, and Harlan is floating.

But it isn't peaceful, she's being buffeted and thrown around.

Hands.

There are hands on her, grappling with her.

Hands.

But what about the *Limen*...the collision...the explosion?

Jaime?

El?

"Wait, wait, unh...wait!" she cried, but there was some sort of tube or apparatus in her mouth, forcing her tongue flat against her lower palate. She bit down to dislodge it, then spat it out.

"Hold on a fucking second," she yelled, and the hands loosened.

"Are you okay, Ms. Nickerson?" came a voice.

Shadowy figures swam into view. Initially, Harlan had a problem focusing on them, but she blinked several times and they coalesced.

Two men and a woman, all dressed in USC uniforms. They looked stern, professional, concerned.

"I'm... Where am I?"

"Aboard the *USC Promise*. You were showing signs of distress during hibernation, so we pulled you out."

"The *Promise*?" Harlan yelped. "But the *Promise* explodes. The ship is destroyed. I've got to get out of here, back to the lifeboat."

Harlan struggled to free herself, but she was caught in a complex web of tubing and wires, floating in a hibernation pod, blue gel up to her chest. Her movements sloshed the stuff everywhere but did little to gain her any freedom.

"Please, please...I've got to...we've..."

The hands appeared again, on her shoulders, trying to restrain her arms. A pair of warm hands cupped her cheeks.

"Ms. Nickerson, please, calm down, calm down," came the sternest of the male voices. His tone indicated he was already past his tolerance level for Harlan's histrionics. "You were dreaming, that's all.

Just commonplace hibernation dreaming. The *Promise* is still here, it hasn't exploded. It's just—"

"Fuck you, Doctor whoever you are," Harlan shouted. "You have no idea what I've been through. It wasn't a fucking dream. It wasn't."

"Sedate her, get her contained back in the pod," said Doctor Stern Voice. "She's fine."

Harlan writhed in the tank, felt something solid pressed against her neck. Immediately, she felt a warm burst roll through her body, loosening her muscles, tamping down her anxiety and frenzy.

"No," she muttered. "No...idiots. He's going to...crash...*explode.* Again. Ahh...fuck it, I guess...who really cares...anyway."

Each word was spoken softer. Each word more slurred until, by the last few words, only Harlan understood what she was saying.

By then, though, she was the only one who cared anyway.

The only one who cared.

And that was enough...

TWENTY-FOUR C

Harlan slapped back into consciousness, felt hands on her.

Hands. Again.

She struggled against them, batted them away. When she opened her eyes, she saw faces swim before her, foggy and unclear in her just-awakened vision.

"Harlan. Harlan. What's the matter?"

Jaime.

She blinked to clear her eyes as much as her foggy brain. Blinked again.

It was Jaime. Her heart thrummed in her chest, and she kicked herself away from him.

"Harlan, what's wrong?" That was El.

El.

"Nothing..." she stammered, steadying herself. She lay on the foyer floor of the plastic space house. Still wearing her EVA suit, as were the two of them, their helmets placed on the ground near the door.

"Back here," Harlan muttered. "Shit."

"Back here?" Jaime said. "What's that supposed to mean?"

"You wouldn't believe me if I told you, and believe me, I've already told you."

El and Jaime looked confused, but Jaime offered her a hand. Harlan gratefully pulled herself up, took a look around the foyer.

"Recognize the place? Been here before?" Jaime asked.

"Yeah, but this is hardly a homecoming," Harlan said.

"What do you mean, Harlan?" El said, reaching out to touch her hand. "Do you recognize this place?"

"Yeah, this is the house of all our fears," she said. "Every last one of them. And we live here, all of us. Not just us three, but all of us. Humanity. We all live here."

Jaime frowned, but El seemed intrigued. "Is that what this is? This house out here in space?"

"It's a manifestation of that idea, something we can attempt to wrap our brains around. And we could spend an eternity here, going through the rooms, seeing horrible things, being killed in new and interesting ways. You might not believe me, but we've already done some of that."

"As usual, this makes no sense to me," Jaime huffed.

"That's okay, Jaime," Harlan said, putting a hand on his shoulder. "It's what I've come to expect from you. And that's fine, perfectly fine. It's also what's driving this...*mechanism*. It's just a process, a part of the indifferent universe."

As she said this, the floor rocked beneath them, strong enough to send them careening apart, crashing into the walls of the room.

"What the hell was that?" Jaime asked.

Harlan didn't answer, went instead to the half-open front door. Outside, beyond the weirdly lit trees and the hump of the lifeboat in the distance, out where before it had been absolute black, the stars had reappeared, dazzlingly unexpected in the night sky.

And they were moving, whizzing by overhead.

The house was moving, in motion.

Fast.

"We're moving," Harlan said, turning back into the room. "It's taking us somewhere."

"Where?"

"I don't know," she replied.

She knew.

Harlan went out onto the porch, put her hands on the railing, and leaned down to get a better look at the sky over the eaves of the house. It was dizzying to watch them whir by.

"Where could we possibly be going?" El said, coming to stand beside her.

"It doesn't matter, does it?" Harlan said, taking El's hand, raising it to her lips and kissing the back of it gently.

El looked surprised, then she smiled.

In the distance, a line appeared overhead, against the stars. A silver needle in space.

"We care. That's all that matters. Whatever happens, we care."

The line grew more distinct. A bulge in the middle.

The *Promise.*

Whatever light lit the trees shone on the ship, cast its lines in terrible detail as the house careened toward it.

El nodded at Harlan, stared out at the *Promise.*

It seemed, in the last seconds before it slammed into the ship, the house sped up, accelerated.

Mercifully, maybe.

Or in anticipation.

FORX#@%^)@

Transition.
    Transition.
    Transition.
    Transition
    Trans—

FORTY-FIVE

Harlan stared out a window. It was night, and she could make out trees swaying in a cool breeze smelling faintly of citrus, roses. Behind them, the dark humps of distant hills. The stars in the sky were brilliant, unfamiliar.

She stood on a patio, brickwork arranged in a herringbone pattern, light and dark, light and dark. She saw the hem of a sundress flutter around her legs, the fabric smooth and cool. The kind of dress she always liked to wear when she was at her father's house, outside watching him garden.

But he was not here. She knew he was not here, but far, far away.

Nearer though, a small table with an umbrella, four chairs arranged around it. A candle lit a burnt-orange-colored glass container, flickering dim across the table, the bricks.

At her back, a small home squatted, geodesic in shape, no more than about five meters tall. Windows spilled warm, buttery light into the night. Inside, Harlan could see the trappings of the house—comfortable furniture, bookshelves, a fireplace. To one side, a kitchen with all the trappings.

The house and its contents seemed overwhelmingly familiar to her, but somehow as distant as the dark hills. She knew her stuff lay inside, her possessions. She thought of the leather armchair, how it had conformed to the shape of her butt over the years. Thought of the comfort of her bed, her pillows, the blanket keeping her warm, smelling deeply of *her*.

"What did they used to say? Penny for your thoughts?"

Harlan closed her eyes, felt a deep relaxation soothe her muscles, relax her neck and shoulders.

El.

She felt hands come from behind, small, around her midsection, locking together at her belly. The slight buss of a kiss against the nape of her neck. She had to raise herself up on her toes to accomplish that, and the thought brought a slight smile to Harlan's face.

"Just thinking about stuff, that's all," she said, closing her eyes and abandoning herself to the moment.

"Stuff, huh? Sounds deep," El said.

"Oh, it is. I mean, you might be the panpsychist in the family, but I think some fucking deep thoughts," Harlan said.

"Regrets?"

Harlan turned, El's arms still around her waist.

"About?"

"You and me. Here on Teegarden b. Alone."

Harlan closed her eyes, tried to filter out any sarcastic, bullshit replies.

Instead, just, "No. No regrets."

El kissed her lightly on the lips, then a bit more deeply.

"Coming to bed?" she asked.

"Soon."

"Promise?"

Harlan tried not to flinch. "Promise."

She watched El turn and head back into the warm glow of their house, saw the lights go out one by one.

Taking a step or two farther out on the patio, away from the quiet lump of the house, she turned her attention back to the night sky.

Dark and powerful and beautiful.

And entirely indifferent.

As she watched, the stars blinked out, one by one, each fading dot spreading absolute, utter darkness across the sky until there were none left, not one twinkling sun or blazing galaxy or cloudy nebula masking the death of a star.

Nothing.

She felt something familiar. A tickle across her inner thigh, curling down her calf.

Looking now, she saw the meandering line of blood trace her ankle, twist across the open sandals she wore, ultimately to pool on the ground, as dark as the sky above.

She closed her eyes, turned toward the house.

****

Harlan climbed into bed with the sleeping El, curled next to her peacefully. After a moment, their little house went dark too.

Outside, the starless sky gave way to a softly lit ceiling, smooth white and just an inch or two above the roof of the house. The patio and landscaping became plush grey carpeting, the USC logo woven into a repeating pattern, along with the name of the ship.

USC Douglas Limen 13.

Then the ceiling lifted, faded like fog on a warm summer morning.

The house shuddered, blossomed like a crumpled piece of paper, an origami object that hadn't been tightly folded. Became a three-storied structure with grey clapboard and white trim, scalloped shingles, a turret. Tall, narrow, mullioned windows, elaborate cornices, and dormers.

Gothic, dour.

The runnel of blood from Harlan's leg ran across the carpet, sitting atop its fibers as if repelled. It snaked away, across the reception area, past the entrance to the captain's mess, past the lift, down the corridor.

Slowly, it pushed forward, past monitors that were supposed to show space outside, past cabin doors. It turned corners, moving forward as if drawn.

It took time, but eventually it reached the engine room, seeped through the seal of the inner door there, then the outer. Between the bulk of the engines, it plipped, plipped, plipped until it gathered on the deck plates, boiled out into space.

It joined a spiraling, chaotic cloud of blood already there, growing in size as slowly as it had taken to reach the engines and the space beyond...

****

Transition...

AFTERWORD

First of all, let's get this straight. I never intended to put myself into one of my own novels. It came—like most of this novel did—as much of a surprise to me as it probably did for you. I dreamed of the idea first, as I do for many of the things I write, and putting me into the story seemed to fit the nature of the novel. So, I just shrugged and put me in.

That out of the way, let's address the other elephant in the room. The title of this novel. *Plastic Space House*. Let me back up a bit and explain my process for titles. First, I take them very seriously. *Very*. So seriously, in fact, I often come up with the title first and write the story second. Seems backwards, I know, but that's how formative I think story titles are.

But sometimes other variables intercede. For my last collection, *Little Black Spots*, I wrote a short called "Purple Soda Hand." Now, this wasn't the original title for the piece. It was first "No Deposit, No Return," a perfectly adequate title. Would have worked fine. But the deeper I got into the absurdity of the story, the more it called for a title to better align with it. I thought of "Purple Soda Hand," the two most jarring pieces of the story mashed together.

My wife, often my touchstone of sanity, thought it sounded ridiculous. But this, I argued, was exactly what made "Purple Soda Hand" so great. I kept it, and I'm glad I did.

Cue *Plastic Space House*. The story wasn't more than some notes in my journal when I arrived at this title...and for much the same reason I settled on "Purple Soda Hand." Those two thoughts—plastic space and a space house—were central to the story. Again, though, my wife thought (still thinks!) while the reason behind it is was solid, the title is too...well...*out there*.

She wasn't alone. I had a hard time placing this book. I'm not saying it was solely because of the title. The book is hard to characterize. Is it scifi/horror or horror/scifi or something else? I came close with one publisher, but learned they'd want me to change the title. I thought about it, I really did. But in the end, I thought the title just worked, and I didn't want to change it.

One person who did think the title should stick was good old Josh Malerman. As with "Purple Soda Hand," I wrote *Plastic Space House* asking myself many times WWJD—What Would Josh Do? I thought of his work often as I wrote scenes. Are things getting too weird? How about not weird enough? Wrote yourself into a corner, Taff? Great! Now write something totally unexpected to get yourself out.

Not that I wrote like Josh, mind you. That wasn't the goal and is certainly *not* the outcome with *Plastic Space House.* I'm talking process here. I'm talking freeing myself to write outlandish shit, weird, strange things, the more absurd the better—and then veering them off into the realm of horror. I think it works. I'm pretty sure it does here.

I know that sticking with the title was the right call, all the more so because I cannot think, even today, of one, single workable alternate.

Like the title, the rest of the story came forth quite clearly, and mind you, this was written before the Marvel Cinematic Universe's explosion into the Multiverse or *Everything, Everywhere All at Once* was a thing. I just let go of my inner guardrails and sent the car careening down the track.

I wanted to explore consciousness and reality. I wanted to explore humanity's fears and how the one might affect the other two. And certainly, what the outcome of that interaction might be. I adore science fiction, it was one of my first fiction loves as a child. I don't normally write in the genre, but this seemed like the arena to tackle those aforementioned subjects. I hope I've read enough—and watched enough science fiction movies/TV—to make those underpinnings of the story work.

As to the rest, well, I leave it to you to best make sense of.

But keep in mind one thing that drove me while writing this story, more so even than ridding myself of internal limitations. That thing is whether or not reality is real. Or if anything is real at all.

I settled on an answer in *Plastic Space House.* The horror of the story is…

There is no reality.

John F.D. Taff
Southern Illinois, USA
June 2023

ACKNOWLEDGMENTS

Thanks first to everyone—including you!—for reading this weird little book. I always appreciate the fact that someone spends money and time reading anything I've written.

Thanks also to everyone who took the time to read this thing in its infancy. Know that if I didn't take all (or any) of your suggestions, I did think *very* carefully about all of them. I thought a lot about this book while writing it—a lot!—which made me very open to considering readers' takes on characters or scenes or details.

Thanks also to my agent at the time, Mark Falkin, for placing this with editor Scarlett Algee at Trepidatio Publishing. It's been awesome working with her and them on this project. Thanks also goes to Don Noble for the wonderful cover art!

Finally, as always, thanks to my wonderful wife, Deborah, for allowing me to do this.

ABOUT THE AUTHOR

(Photo by Deborah L. Taff)

John F.D. Taff is a World Fantasy Award-nominated and multiple Bram Stoker Award®-nominated author with more than 30 years' in the horror genre, 150-plus short stories and five novels in print. His first collection, *Little Deaths* was named the best horror fiction collection of 2012 by HorrorTalk. Jack Ketchum called his novella collection, *The End in All Beginnings*, "one of the best novella collections I've read," and it was a finalist for a Stoker Award in 2014. A short story from his latest collection *Little Black Spots*, "A Winter's Tale," was a finalist for a Stoker in 2019. Ain't It Cool News called his novel *The Bell Witch* "A compelling and frightening read." His serial novel *The Fearing* released in 2019 to critical and reader acclaim. Robert R. McCammon called it "A powerful and epic trip into the land of feardom!", while Josh Malerman, author of *Bird Box*, said "Taff's best book to date. A modern master at play." The Dark Forces tribute anthology he edited and contributed to, *Dark Stars*, was nominated for a World Fantasy Award in 2023. Look for more of his work in anthologies such as *Orphans of Bliss* and *The Hideous Book of Hidden Horrors*, and *Shadows Over Main Street 3*. Taff lives in the wilds of Illinois with three pugs, two cats, and a long-suffering wife. You can follow him on Twitter @johnfdtaff or visit his much-neglected blog johnfdtaff.com